LAST KNOWN ADDRESS

Theresa Schwegel grew up in Chicago and always believed she would be a crime writer. She studied Communications Media at Loyola University and went on to a screenwriting course at Chapman University in Orange County. Theresa won the Edgar Award for Best First Novel with *Officer Down* and she has written *Probable Cause* and *Person of Interest* since. She lives in Chicago.

PRAISE FOR THERESA SCHWEGEL

'Recounted absorbingly and excitingly in a tale with a dramatic, surprise ending'
Scotsman

'*Person of Interest* quickly escalates into a high-stakes story of risk and suspicion, tole with rich, insightful detail'
New York Times

'A pacey, punchy debut from a thriller writer to watch'
Mail on Sunday

Also by Theresa Schwegel

LAST KNOWN ADDRESS

THERESA SCHWEGEL

Quercus

First published in Great Britain in 2009 by Quercus
This paperback edition published in 2010 by

Quercus
21 Bloomsbury Square
London
WC1A 2NS

A CIP catalogue reference for this book is available
from the British Library

ISBN 978 1 84916 172 5

10 9 8 7 6 5 4 3 2 1

Printed and bound in Great Britain
by CPI Cox and Wyman, Reading, RG1 8EX

For Andy Perostianis,

a fine detective and a true friend

ACKNOWLEDGMENTS

I, too, changed addresses during the writing of this book, and owe thanks to people all over the map for unconditional support, professional guidance, and heavy lifting.

In California, thanks to former Sergeant Ray Fowler, Officer Janine Turner, former Sergeant Jim Simpson, Detective Dave Casarez, Dave Putnam, and Dr. Doug Lyle. Thank you also to Sister Christina Heltsley and my other West-coast sisters: Lori Branson, Heather Harper, Deb Haynes, Marylin Mercado, Sammi Nielsen, Terri Nolan, and Carrie Rogers. Thanks, of course, to my family: Don and Julianne Brawner, and Steve and April Schwegel. And to DJay: it's just not the same without you across the hall.

Elsewhere on the map, I'm so lucky to have Kelley Ragland

and Charlotte Clerk, Kevin Adkins, Dan Judson, Jamie Lavish, and the ever-positive David Hale Smith. When this book
tried to kill me, these people are the reason I survived. Also,
special thanks to Greg Rucka and June Yang, for *you*.

Back in Chicago, thanks are due to Detective Carrie Iser,
Detective David Anderson, Rick Kogan, Ralph Covert, and
Nikki Krohn; to David Johnston, Tony Lagouranis, Bob Da-
vidson, Brian Chambers, and Brian Kaulig; and to Andrew
and Martha Swigart, and Gary and Kathy Nehls.

Finally, for always being there somewhere, I thank my
parents, Don and Joyce. It's great to be home.

LAST KNOWN
ADDRESS

THE COOLEST ONE OF us heard about a new place, a lounge on Damen Avenue, no sign posted, an after-ten happy hour. I don't really want to go, but since this whole thing with Stephen I don't get many invites. I wear a skirt and ribbed tights and knee-high boots because there are ways to show leg, even when winter won't let go of April. I'm single. Leg is important.

Half-hour wait at the door, and well worth it: inside, the select are few. The décor is all royal blue and candlelit; shadows fall on parlor corners where privileged people don't have to whisper when they tell their secrets. We sit in high-backed chairs and marvel at the drink menu, at the unknown bourbons and brandies stirred with ginger syrup or egg whites or house-made bitters.

A singer you'd never hear on the radio grovels and our rockabilly cocktail girl is just so nice; between the two of them we feel a little out of place, here in this outpost for the surviving hip.

After one cocktail, I fit right in. Two, and I'm special.

We talk about the things we always talk about—the three of us and our newish guy pal—and I am interested or indifferent or annoyed, depending on who's doing the talking. I'm not saying much, but I'm not pouting, either. I'm just thinking about how things would be if Stephen were here. About how I'm so much more like myself without him. About how much being like myself sucks.

At some point the coolest one looks at me and wants to know, "What's your problem?" I could tell the truth—that I'm still in love with the guy whose South American temper translated into a restraining order four months ago—but these are the only friends I have left after the breakup. The only ones who think I wasn't to blame. And on top of that, this is the first time she hasn't used the "poor you" tone—the one people use at hospitals and funerals except that with me the compassion feels chilly—probably because, as the judge pointed out, nobody in a case like mine is ever completely innocent. I can't bring up Stephen now—that case is supposed to be closed—so I say that work is my problem, because isn't work everyone's problem?

The coolest one, rightly short on sympathy, says I should quit working for the mayor. I tell her I don't work for the mayor, exactly, but she knows that—she happens to be a lobbyist and so she's got her arguments, and technically, we shouldn't be talking, let alone talking about work. It doesn't matter; the conversation has already gone to vinegar because the other two can't stand the Machine, nor apparently can they tolerate the idiocy of the traffic control cops on Upper Wacker. As if one has to do with the other, or either has to do with me. I spend my days in the pressroom on the losing side of illogical debates like this, so I shut up and try to enjoy the atmosphere and my delicious hundred-plus-proof beverage that I bet Stephen would find much too sweet.

Just inside the next room where more hipsters drink Negronis, their booze-warmed cheeks further flushed by the fireplace, I notice a hollow-eyed Latino looking at me. He's dressed in all black like the barbacks, so I think maybe he works here, which would explain why he's alone and empty faced and near invisible. But he isn't trolling for empty Collins glasses or highballs, and if he's on the clock someone would've chased him from there by now, half hidden behind the fat velvet curtain that stages the room, observing me with black-hole eyes.

He's breaking the rules, looking at me after I've caught him. I know I should be a little creeped, but thanks to booze I take it in stride and flash him an overdone, toothy smile. His black eyes don't change as he takes a step back and disappears, poof, a shadow.

I think, *Oh no you don't,* and get up, the strength of the cocktails hard to catch up with as I cross the room on a mission—and one that's just as quickly aborted when I find him around a corner down a hallway with the girl who is now commanding his attention: she's got him backed up against the wall, arms around his neck, tongue in his mouth. Before I can make myself scarce, a bathroom door opens next to them and a woman strolls out, fresh lipstick; they don't notice as she makes her way past; there's a double meaning to her *excuse me.* The look she gives me lacks solidarity and I think she must wonder just what, exactly, I'm waiting in line for, so I duck into the bathroom, wash my hands. In the mirror I decide I look like a real dumbass.

When I return to my friends, no one asks where I went because they're too busy bitching about Moms, an unaffectionate nickname for a former part of the circle whose brain went to mush after her son was born in June. Moms doesn't come out anymore. I think it's because she found her life's meaning and now lacks the cynicism required to participate in these so-called happy hours. They decide it's because she must be at home relearning the alphabet.

I don't know why they equate Moms's happiness with weakness. I try to imagine her here, her slobbery little reinvented wheel in tow, but I can't. She wouldn't be interested in this bullshit.

The coolest one pities Moms. She's missing out. This is the place to be. Here, all senses indulged, minds rum-clear. The singer takes a break and Tom Waits cuts in on the sound system to assure us *mankind can keep alive thanks to its brilliance.* He's right: We are brilliant. We talk and talk and we know everything—except the fact that tomorrow will be just as stark-white shitty as today.

I finish my third Dark and Stormy and I'm about to order another, but our guy pal announces it's a school night and somehow—these fancy drinks steal time!—we lost an hour. We settle up and tip too much and I follow the others as they float out, heads fizzy, past the long line of hopefuls who are so glad we're leaving. This time, I am, too.

Outside, the coolest one links arms with the newish guy, naturally. He tells his story and then she tells the real one when they head off to the Blue Line together because the train doesn't run past her place, last time I checked. I should have known. Not that I care; I just should have known. The remaining one asks if I want to share a cab west and I say no thanks and *hasta noche* because, lucky me, my apartment is less than a dozen blocks away. Yes, it's cold, but spring is just around the corner, and yes, it's late, but it's only getting later while we stand around talking about it.

I walk Damen Avenue south, trying to right the alcohol in my step. Tomorrow morning I'll probably still taste spiced rum in the back of my throat while I watch my boss climb our office walls, her Xanax and Wellbutrin no match for the latest political blitz. We'll be waiting for an alderman—the mayor's most vocal opponent, of course—to officially gripe about a recent property tax incentive program. The alderman will have a legitimate point, but my job is to dispute it, so I'll spin his statement out of context and into a sound bite while my boss writes the City Hall response. Then, while we wait for our work to hit the newsfeed and find out whether the media decides a Hollywooder did something worse, or Obama something better, or that their readers/viewers/subscribers aren't interested in more allegations against the mayor, she'll ask me therapy-grade personal questions, the answers to which I will also have to spin, because last time I opened my mouth—about Stephen—she was "contractually obligated" to involve the cops. I can't imagine she'd report a hangover, but at this point I wouldn't trust her with my dry cleaning.

I cut over on Potomac through the Jose Diego school grounds to get to my street. Most of the new three-flats on this block sit half finished, vacant, and off the market, since their sellers gave up chasing prices into the tank. I've been keeping my eye on a brand-new condo development just south of here, but I don't really want to move again so soon. Right now I rent a little place on the cusp of Humboldt Park where it's even cheaper because the housing bust slowed all expansion west, stalling the neighborhood vibe at sketchy. I don't mind sketchy. It's where people with real city legs live.

Funny that I'm thinking about city legs just as I trip and wind up facedown on the sidewalk. I don't think I can be all that drunk so I roll over and sit up to convince myself.

I fell pretty hard: skinned my knee—ripped a hole right through my tights, damn it; landed on my shoulder and my elbow, both of which will bruise and hurt like hell tomorrow; and I scraped the shit out of my arm trying to protect my face.

The damage, though, as assessed, is concealable: long sleeves, my new pants suit. For once I appreciate the thankless weather in this city—it'll keep my skin covered until Memorial Day at least. Some story this would be to hide from the boss. If she were privy to any of tonight's activities, however blameless, she'd march me straight over to the Board of Ethics. *You went where with a lobbyist? She's a friend, is she?* Good-bye employment. Nice to know you, health insurance. All over a stupid crack in the sidewalk.

I'm about to get up as a car turns down the street and the headlights angle off the back hatch of a parked SUV a few cars away, and this would all be totally normal if there wasn't some guy who's standing there, hanging out behind the SUV. Immediately I decide I am either stupid and clumsy and embarrassed, or just being paranoid. After that I decide I could be all of those things except paranoid, if he's following me.

I get up, not exactly graceful, and the car drives on, so I lose the light but I don't lose the bad feeling about the guy.

I just rewrote the *Chicago Safety Manual for Women*, where it advises addressing unknown men directly, so I say, "Stephen?" because he did follow me that one time. I know it's wishful thinking, I haven't seen Stephen in months, and he is a stranger to me. Anyway, he wouldn't come at me like this—this man who is now maybe ten feet away and closing like he's going to tackle me.

Which he does. And I'm back on the ground, his hands over my mouth and my face, my head against the pavement.

He says something—I think he says "Bite me"—and he doesn't sound like Stephen, but I don't sound like me, either, when I shout "Stephen!" again, for help, or reason, and my voice is muted against his leather gloves.

I can't see his face because we're between streetlights and beneath trees; he is a shadow, his eyes black holes, just like the man who watched me at the bar. And I am that dumbass I saw in the lounge's bathroom mirror.

I can't let this happen.

I wrestle and push and I use up all my strength too quick while he just holds me there, arms locked, strong. I breathe hard between the slits of his leather fingers and I know I have to fight for details now, I have to memorize them: his striped shirt, dark coat. I don't remember this shirt or coat and I can't remember what the man at the bar was wearing. Just black.

I twist sideways and for a second I think I can get away, but then I realize he let me go just enough to get around me, behind me, his forearm against my throat, a better grip. Then he pulls me up and I hang there, headlocked, breath gone, my boots hardly touching the ground. I dig my finger-nails into his arms but my nails are bitten to the quick and the sleeves of his coat are canvas-sturdy—I might as well claw wood. I can't get air and I'm afraid he'll crush my throat and my brain skips like it's going to short out; there's no time left to think. My head thrashes, my legs scissor-kick, and every part of me takes up the fight until the tip of my boot catches the pavement. I throw him off balance: we both stumble forward, feet tangled, onto the grass—the near-frozen, still-wet grass that's just a little softer than the pavement. He lands on top of me and I hear something snap and we're both hurt, now, I hope.

I get up, a reflex, to escape—I can get to the street at least, get into the light. I'm crawling fast across the cold, sharp grass when I start to cough. I can't stop. My lungs can't catch up. I keep going, hands and knees, coughing, sucking air. Coughing, sucking air.

Then I hear him. Behind me. Laughing? Is he laughing? He sounds both surprised and certain, like he can never get over how amusing this is.

"Stephen?" I ask, not because it makes sense, but because it would be okay. If it were Stephen, at least I would know what I did to deserve this.

Then he's at me again, his hands over my mouth and my face, his strength holding steady; and this time, for me, fear sets in differently: I freeze up. I let him smother me. I taste the musty residue on his gloves, same as bile. I hear traffic and wind and my boot heels kicking the sidewalk in faraway waves.

As he is choking me I think he says "bite me" again, like a dare. I won't dare. I look up, I look for his black-hole eyes, but until this moment I've never seen such black.

1

SLOANE PEARSON DOUBLE-PARKS THE unmarked on Damen Avenue, buttons up her slicker, and skips between fat drops to the three-flat's doorstep. Plastic flags on the OPEN HOUSE sign spring yellow and wild against the gloom. She rings the buzzer but doesn't wait to go inside.

She counts each step up the long, straight flight. Fifteen to the first landing: three more than the stairs at Eddie's, though these aren't as steep. She's winded when she reaches the top floor, more so when she sees Scott Zwick leaning against the penthouse doorframe, casual, like they've already met.

"Hi. Miss Pearson? Thanks for coming." Zwick offers his hand, a shake she can find little agenda behind, even though she knows that's the point.

"I was in the neighborhood," she says, playing it just as cool. She leaves out the part about being in the neighborhood because a concerned parent reported a registered sex offender parked outside Peabody Elementary.

Zwick wipes his feet on the welcome mat and she follows suit, her heavy black boots making her feel bigger than she is; clunky. Especially compared to this guy, smooth as they come: at once dressed up and down in frayed boutique-pocket jeans, a silk-screen designer shirt with stripes so faint they're a suggestion, and the softest leather shoes—probably Italian, if Italian's in this season.

"Miserable out there, isn't it?" he says, not so it's a question, so she doesn't answer. It's unlikely they'd have the same definition of the word, anyway; he probably doesn't have too much that makes him feel bad. An unlucky weekend in Vegas, maybe. A head cold. The Bears draft picks.

"Come on in," Zwick says like it's his place. "Check it out."

When Sloane steps inside, she catches the fresh scent of cut grass, heady from the rain. At first she thinks it must be a Realtor's staging trick, but when Zwick leads the way, she realizes it's his cologne.

They round the foyer corner and the penthouse opens up like a gift: high ceilings, lots of light and space, and warm, sleek lines. It's pleasantly, impersonally furnished and maid-clean, like a model or a hotel room. Reminds Sloane of so many of the places she has called home.

"Can you tell me why this place came back on the market?"

she asks, since she'd had her eye on the address just before it sold a few months back, its low-low price suggesting a steal. At the time, she'd been too chicken to steal it.

"Fell out of escrow," Zwick says, bringing the lights up a little in the living-slash-dining room.

"Something you should be telling me? Code violations? Damages?"

"Nothing like that. Buyer's loan app was fraudulent." He motions her over to the dining table set for a fiesta of four, where he's got one mango-orange plate moved aside for paperwork. He traps a contact form on a clipboard and hands her a pen. "Formality," he says, same way he said "fraudulent."

Sloane takes the clipboard and fills in the required blanks, feeling Zwick over her shoulder, a casual supervisor. She writes her real name and resists the urge to transpose the last four digits of her phone number, as she has before. Authority. Always gets her.

"Are you working with another Realtor?" Zwick asks. They all ask this question; he manages to make it sound like an afterthought. She wonders if he already knows her answer will be as canned as cream corn.

"I'm not working with anyone." Which is true. But she couldn't strip away the gummy sweetness that coats a lie so she says, "I'm just seeing what's out there. I've been waiting, you know. Watching the market."

"Haven't we all," Zwick says, nothing sweet about it. He smiles, drawing lines at the corners of his eyes: conclusions.

He glances at her contact form long enough to read it twice, check whether she filled out anything more than the required fields. He asks, "Do you currently own a home?"

"No," she says. "I'm staying with a friend. In the West Loop. A loft." She looks down at her stupid boots and feels huge, inelegant. Full of it.

"My ex and I used to live in a loft," he says. "Twenty-four hundred square feet and not a single one of them private. If I learned one thing from that place? Space is nice. Walls are better."

"Walls would be good." She takes a listing flyer from the table. "Space would be good, too." She studies the page like a warrant: no need to comprehend a single word, the facts already so clear. A friend, she said. Admitted. But not to Eddie. Not yet.

"You need a place of your own," Zwick says, and when Sloane looks up at him, those lines around his eyes, those conclusions, fade just enough to be possibilities instead.

She manages a nod and checks the fine print on the listing—not that she needs to: she'd snagged a copy from the flyer box yesterday and memorized the details before ditching it in the trash outside the station. The place looks exactly like the photos—better—and the price doesn't look too bad, either.

"Why don't you go ahead," he says, "take a look around? If it's space you want, you don't need my song and dance."

Sloane's had so many sales pitches from eager Realtors these past few weeks she wonders if her bullshit detector has blown a gasket, because Zwick doesn't even register. No song, no dance? The way he cares and doesn't care: she wants to hold it against him. She really wants to hold something against him.

"Thanks," she says, pulling away from his smile. *Just seeing what's out there*, she had said. Scott Zwick suddenly part of it. Has she lost her mind?

The thrill chases her through the kitchen so she doesn't stop to look, though the room is one of the main reasons she's interested: the island layout with acres of countertop, the four-door, side-by-side Sub-Zero, the dual-fuel, six-top range. She could feed a gourmet army.

Down the hall, the first bedroom is a page from a furniture catalogue, all color-coordinated and strategically cluttered. The corkboard calendar just looks like it should be scheduled with important things to do.

The master bedroom, at the end of the hall, is an advertisement for the best dreams: everything some grade of soft and shade of white. The California King is too big for the room. *As it should be,* she thinks, its feather pillows perfectly good excuses for naps.

The master bath is just as impressive, though distinctly warmer than the bedroom; makes Sloane break a sweat. The room is sizeable, anchored by a Jacuzzi tub and six-way spray shower; above the tub, a large window frames a perfect picture of the treetops and the clearing sky. It's art, the way the light comes in, and at night she's sure the city skyline burns, distant candles. She imagines herself here, part of the picture: a long soak, the room still, her skin pink and heat-swollen.

Imagines, and wipes sweat beads from her upper lip, knowing her face will soon go splotchy, and that art is never practical, and that the room is too humid to be properly ventilated.

Sloane steps into the dry tub, her boots fixed against the nonslip rubber strips. The emerald green, inch-by-inch tiles that run up the wall sparkle, and the smell of bleach is caustic. The grout between tiles has thinned, the caulk at the fixtures peeled, probably from a wire brush and too much elbow grease. It wouldn't take a crime scene team to call mold a suspect here.

She reaches up, feels along the window: the wood frame is brand-new—no rot—but fixed so it can't be opened. Sloane's helped install enough of these windows to know they're good for aesthetics, and for security, and for the pocketbook; in a room with regular condensation, they're also good for growing fungus.

She gets out of the tub and switches on the exhaust fan positioned above the toilet on the opposite wall. The motor kicks on and sounds just fine, so she drops the toilet lid and climbs up to check the register. The airflow is weak, so she guesses there's a problem with the vent: miscalculated capacity, maybe, or a faulty roof trap.

Her cell buzzes, so she steps down and looks at the display even though she's certain it's her partner calling about being late, which is why she isn't running on time, either, and why she sends his excuses to voice mail. She can't tell Heavy where she is, anyway; he's not the type of guy you want to enlist to weigh options. Ask him to come in on an arrest and he'll want to work the case all over again, cover his bases. Hell, ask him to pick a lunch spot and you won't eat until four. Sloane knows it's better she tell him about this when all is said and done. If all is said and done.

She looks again at the listing sheet: the ink has smudged on her hand now, and transposed the price. No matter which way it reads, it's a deal. Last week, when it came back on the market, she'd assumed the worst—a structural issue or some other problem discovered during inspection. The property *did* look too good on paper. Then yesterday, after a long shift that was only longer because she didn't want to go back to Eddie's, she called Zwick. Told herself she had to come, just to find out what was wrong with it. She had hoped for something else she couldn't fix. She had hoped she wouldn't have to be the deal-breaker.

Her cell buzzes again, Heavy again, another reality check. If he calls twice it means he'll call a third time, and a fourth, so—

"Heavy," she answers.

"Where are you?" he asks, always so polite no matter how he means it.

"I'll be there in ten," she tells him, though it'll take at least twenty to get to the station from here.

"Don't bother," he says. "Meet me at 553 North Leavitt.

We've got another one. Sounds a lot like the Meyer-Davis case. Same game, same winner."

Sloane's sweat goes cold. "Aren't you waiting on Meyer-Davis now?"

"She called and cancelled. I guess this is a busy time of year for accountants. She says she can't talk to us again until after the fifteenth."

"We're not doing taxes, Heavy. We can't afford to file an extension."

"We can't afford to lose her, either. Come on, Sloane. It's only a few days."

Sloane figures there's no point in spending those days arguing. "You said 553 North Leavitt, right?"

"I'll see you there."

Sloane hangs up, finds Scott Zwick: he's feet-up on the couch in the front room, no worries, *mi casa es su casa,* all that. "What do you think?"

"Thank you," she announces, "but I have a situation—I have to get to work."

Zwick moves toward the door so she can't get by without a handshake, at least. "Before you go I should tell you the sellers are very motivated," he says, a side step in line with hers.

"Now the song and dance?"

"Yeah, okay, you got me. But situations like this? They're all in the timing. I'm not sure I told you this, but the seller's wife is having twins in July. I mean, you can imagine they're thinking in terms of trimesters. Tick-tock."

"Tick-tock," Sloane repeats, no heart in it, because starting a family is one thing she can't imagine at all. She moves past him, her boots falling flat across the hardwood and she is again too big, too much for this.

"Please," Zwick says, staying with her, "take my card. If you are interested in this place, I know we can make a good deal. If not . . ." He leaves the statement there for her to pick up.

At the door she says, "I don't need a Realtor."

"I don't want to be your Realtor." Zwick smiles, the lines at his eyes sneaking toward those possibilities again.

Sloane thinks of Claire Meyer-Davis. And the new girl. Their possibilities all risks now. From now on.

"I'm sorry. I can't afford it."

2

THE VICTIM'S ADDRESS IS a duplex along a residential stretch of Leavitt in Ukrainian Village. It's a quiet block, a little too far south to be good-quiet; even though the sun's out now, it isn't fooling anybody.

Sloane pulls up behind a blue-and-white and finds Mark Buchanan and Rob Stagliano outside the place, a couple of beat coppers she could take or leave—as in take Buchanan, leave Stagliano. Stag's one of the morons who's made a sport out of messing with Sloane's ponytail. She's been in Area Five a total of three months, and for a whole team of guys like him, it's already well into the regular season.

Buchanan she knows from when she was in Twenty—and

not very well: a good thing. She can appreciate a guy who does the job and makes a name for himself that way.

Right now, he's making a name for himself, all right: he's standing outside the victim's home, one cheek fat with tobacco, his attention fixed on Stag's blabbering as the two of them take turns spitting brown streams of gunk into a short row of pansies. The flowers are having enough trouble as it is in a tight spot between the vic's attempt at a yard and the neighbor's trashcans, and these two aren't doing them any favors. Chicago's finest, merciless in the fight for reputation.

When Sloane approaches, Stag's saying, "Every speed-balling motherfucker on the block is ratting on this brother they call Belushi. Bad package, whatever." He spits, pansies. "I think he's smart, he's outta here, he's on the first Amtrak back to Little Rock. But no: last week? *He* finds *me*. Wants to know who's talking. Wants to make *me* a deal," Stag juking his hands, "so now I'm what? I'm the sheriff of Dopeville?"

That's about right, Sloane wants to say, but it's too obvious, so she asks Buchanan, and only Buchanan, "Where's Heavy?"

"Miss East Pearson," Stag greets her, a stupid nickname one of his teammates thought of when she showed up to the station in what he considered a Gold Coast–caliber suit. It was a nice suit until she wore it to the morgue. Couldn't get the smell off. Hasn't worn it since.

"Heavy?" Sloane's eyes on Buchanan.

"You're the first one here," he tells her.

"You were the first one here," she tells him back. She removes her sunglasses, cases the place. Looks like a remodel instead of a teardown, the building's shell still old gray brick. Security's probably no more than a door lock, deadbolt maybe, and the ground-floor windows might as well be invitations. She says, "I take it you've secured the scene?"

"This isn't the scene." Buchanan shifts his stance, hooks a finger in his cheek, clears out the tobacco, and pitches it in the grass, real official-like. "Vic came home last night, cleaned up, called us this morning."

"Do we have a scene?"

"We have a stretch of three vacants on the 2300 block of West Erie. She doesn't know which one."

"Close to home, anyway. I'll shoot over there. Did you bag her clothes?"

"They're in the squad."

Sloane makes a point of stepping around Buchanan's left-over chew to look in the front window. The sun is too far past noon to pitch any light inside, so instead she sees her reflection, and Stag's, and he's checking out her ass. She ignores him, asks Buchanan, "So where'd they take her, Saint Mary's?"

"She's inside."

"She's still here? Come on, guys, you know if you don't stay with her, keep her in the moment, you're only giving her time for second thoughts."

"She said she had to use the bathroom."

"What did you want us to do?" Stag asks. "Wipe her ass?"

"Don't worry, Stagliano. No one will ever confuse you

with someone who cares." Sloane can't blame the guys' reluctance, really; in these cases it's best for everyone to stay
out of the personal stuff, let the vic remain the *whom* of *who
did what to*. Still, there's no cause for waiting around.
"Where's med transport?"

"She doesn't want an ambulance. We're waiting on an
advocate."

"Shit," Sloane says, because she's never met a crisis advocate who likes her. She doesn't intend the feeling to be mutual,
but it usually shakes out that way. The cold-eyed bleeding
hearts: big sisters in the victims' club. And Sloane is so fortunate, they think; justice her only concern.

"Shit," from Stag, less an echo than a gripe, probably because his Belushi story will never make it off the back burner
now.

"Buchanan," Sloane says, "what do we know?"

"Vic starts downtown last night, meets a date for drinks.
It gets late, he's no Romeo, she hops a cab. She gets dropped
at another bar, the corner of Chicago and California, to meet
a friend. Vic's too late: the friend already bailed. So she
drinks a double-self-pity on the rocks, decides to hoof it
home."

"Great," Sloane says, because he hasn't even mentioned
the crime and the trail is already long and forked. "Do we
know names? The date? The friend?"

"Yes," Buchanan says, "but I didn't put them in the report. Figured that'd just jam you up. Especially since the
victim doesn't believe she knows her attacker."

"The victim doesn't know what she's talking about," Stag says. "A stranger doesn't do this."

"The vic says she doesn't know him."

"The vic is an idiot."

"Excuse me," Sloane cuts in, "why have I been called here? To referee you two?" She gets on her cell, dialing Heavy, asking Buchanan, "Why didn't we meet at the hospital?"

Buchanan pulls a folded manila envelope sealed with red evidence tape from his back pocket, offers it to Sloane. "Because of this."

On one side of the envelope, Buchanan's name and the RD number are signed across the seal. On the other side, a white sticker labeled EVIDENCE reads: 16MM CLEAR PLASTIC BUTTON, 4-HOLED, HAIRLINE CRACK. 1 PIECE BLUE THREAD, ATTACHED, APPROX 40MM. "The suspect's?" she asks, hanging up on Heavy's voicemail.

"Vic managed to snag it from his shirt. Hid it in her mouth. Thinks she broke a tooth."

"Let me see your report—and bring the clothes."

Buchanan nods and makes for the blue-and-white.

"I'll tell ya," Stag says, "the vic's a piece of ass, but I don't think you're gonna hang a case on her. You ask me, closed-captioning might be too much at once."

Sloane turns to him direct, the first time, says, "I don't care if she's a fucking stump. I didn't ask you."

Stag spits the rest of his chew at her feet and it hits her boots and she can't help it, she laughs: this thick-skulled mook, his insults fit for a playground. She hates these god-damned boots anyway.

"What's so funny?" A voice from behind them; and between Stag's stern-as-shit lip and the girl's tone, defeated, Sloane knows the vic has come outside, and has heard enough to get the gist.

And Sloane, some ally, doesn't even know the girl's name. She gives Stag a custom-tailored scowl and then goes face-to-game-face with the vic when she turns, hand leading, to introduce herself. "I'm Detective Pearson," she says, at the same time slipping the evidence bag to Stag, behind her. So inappropriate and another point goes, however unintentionally, to her asshole co-worker.

Sloane makes brief eye contact with the vic then focuses low, submitting. "Thank you for calling us."

By the look of the young woman's neck, blood vessels in bloom, it's clear someone's choked her. Just like Claire Meyer-Davis. Sloane's eyes dance, nonthreatening, around the girl's face, managing to squeak details: early twenties, five-five, a hundred pounds, blond with help, eyes blue, swollen. Her lips are split at both corners, and nothing says "rape" like the way they're pursed, trembling, still waiting for an answer.

"I'm sorry," Sloane says, casual and sincere. "Officer Stagliano and I were just speaking about another case." Not so sincere.

The vic asks, "What did he mean about the closed-captioning?"

Sloane would defer to Stag—he's obviously the one pinched

and rightly so, suggesting this girl is too simple to keep up with subtitles—but Sloane's got to keep this thing flowing, keep the vic—*What is her name?*—calm, strap the poor passenger in for the rest of this awful fucking ride.

"He meant we've got to do everything possible for you to understand that the more you can help us, the more we can help you."

"But I'm not deaf," the vic says. She folds her arms, and then crosses one leg over the other, her body language the first to cease communication.

Stag steps back, out of the line of questioning, so Sloane has to look straight into the vic's puffed-up, cried-out eyes; she owes her that much. And her heart breaks just a little for the girl, for all the girls, because Stag is the deplorable reality.

But then the vic's face sparks, sudden: hope. She says to Sloane, "I know you."

Sloane pieces her features together and yes, she is familiar— *What the hell is her name?*—she doesn't like being caught off guard like this, losing even the slightest grip of her handle on the situation.

Nobody's supposed to know her; she's new to Area Five, and she doesn't have casual friends or old friends or at least the kind of friend who would be a victim. How is this girl familiar?

Sloane shouldn't be but she's relieved when Buchanan returns, too oblivious to hang back and steer clear of intruding or overwhelming. "Detective?"

"I do know you," the vic tells Sloane again. "You came to one of my open houses. On Roscoe? Or was it the new construction on West Armitage?"

"You must be mistaken," Sloane says, though she isn't, and with context, now, Sloane knows her name: this is Holly Dutcher, the Realtor who did not see her at an open house on Roscoe or Armitage but did in fact show her 2022 North Wolcott, in Bucktown. It was a factory-turned-loft that sat between expressways and was far too industrial with far too many windows for people to see inside and the parking sucked and Sloane didn't like it at all.

"It was you," Holly insists, not buying anything Sloane's selling now, not after the BS about Stag. "I tried to call you—I had another unit in your price point I thought you'd really like."

"It wasn't me," Sloane says, finality to it. Then she turns to the beat cops to offer an even smile and to Stag, a couple extra-long blinks that agree, *Yes: this woman is an idiot*. "Buchanan," she says, "the report?" She snags the case file from him and gives it a once-over, and since Buchanan's handwriting is for shit she goes over it again, hoping her show of indifference is just enough to keep this little slipup from getting legs. She swore she'd never date a cop again but she is, she's with Eddie Nowicki. Even though he's in Twenty-four it wouldn't be hard for him to find out from someone who talked to someone who talked to Buchanan or Stag that things aren't going so well. That things haven't been going well for some time.

The report soon feels like a prop—she never relies on a

beat copper's narrative, anyway—and there's only so long her authority can trump the truth. She can't stand around, waiting for the crisis advocate, shooting down small talk that'll invariably be about real estate. She's got to split, Holly in tow, before the guys get curious.

She closes the file and tucks it under her arm, easy as the morning paper. Says, "I don't want to lose ground here, so I'll take Ms. . . . Ms. Dutcher?"—a visual check with Holly, who half-nods, the seed of self-doubt sprouting quick—"I'll take Ms. Dutcher to the hospital. Buchanan, you guys please wait here and instruct Heavy to go tape off the scene. Then ask him and the advocate to meet us at Saint Mary's, and you take the evidence to Homan Square." She gives Buchanan the tasks and again ignores Stag, because he'd see right through her, right to the guilt, if she enlisted him now.

"Okay." She starts to say a good-bye, but—

"Pearson?" Stag asks, "you making a move?"

She knows exactly what he means, about Eddie; he must have sensed the pull in her voice. Or else he already figured things with Eddie wouldn't ever go well. Either way, she can't let him win this one.

"I'd have to be an idiot," she says, hoping he picks up on the way she emphasizes "idiot"—same way she says, "Ms. Dutcher? You ready?"

"I guess so." Holly's response uneasy, and irrelevant.

"That's my car," Sloane directs, "the gray one behind the squad." She lets Holly lead, squeezing between two parallel-parked cars toward the unmarked.

"Pearson," Stag calls out, "was that denial or agreement?"

"Please," she tells Holly, who's practically tiptoeing around the unmarked, "sit in front with me." She puts Holly in the car and rounds the trunk, thinking she might go back over there, tell Stag what she said was the truth, make the point, but then she looks down, sees the leftover tobacco on her boots.

"Hey Stagliano," she says. "You know of any nurseries around here?"

"What, for babies?"

"No, officer. A Kmart or a Wal-Mart or some place with a garden section."

"Yeah, why?"

"I'm thinking you should take a ride over there and buy Ms. Dutcher some new pansies. Or, I guess you can just stand there, fill in."

"Yeah, fuck you, Pearson."

Fuck you? That's the best he's got? She waves, fingertips, slips on her sunglasses, and gets into the car. Match point.

Sloane checks her mirrors, starts the engine, turns the corner, and heads west. Her passenger sits quietly, even as she turns north on Oakley, a quick detour by the vacants. She makes the turn on Erie and says nothing; not until she feels the silence hangs at her discretion. Up on the left, she sees the stretch of buildings Buchanan must've been talking about.

She takes her foot off the gas, says, "Holly, you're right. It was me. I looked at your property. In Bucktown. The one on Wolcott—"

"I knew it."

"—and in a few minutes I'm going to have to ask you to hold your thoughts until we get to the hospital, check you in, and get everything on record. Okay?"

"Okay?" The way she asks her answer reminds Sloane of a child. She will begin young, naïve, and through this become so old, so fast.

"It's best that way, and easier for you, to have a single statement. For court. For your own sanity. But first I want you to take a look out the window, at these properties here, and tell me if you recognize the place where you were attacked last night." A shitty thing to do, yes, but the case is nowhere without a somewhere.

"Oh my god," Holly says, instant panic, "I don't know. I told those cops I don't know, I was just walking and—he grabbed me and—I couldn't breathe and—" her cries come heaving, dry, hard for her to say, "he made me fight him."

Sloane rolls to a stop, nice and easy. "Okay," she says, "it's okay. You remembered the street and that's great. Now I just need for you to look at those buildings and tell me if you remember anything about them."

Holly cries a while longer; she can't do it. Can't even get the breath to sit up and look. Sloane would like to park, walk the area, poke around. But she can't without Holly, the somewhere might as well be nowhere. "It's okay," Sloane says again, "I just wanted to give it a try, while your memory is fresh. I'll come back later and take a look. Holly?"

Finally, "Yeah."

"Before we go, I need to ask you one other thing." Sloane gives her another moment to wipe her face, to find her breath; though the question will be simple, and Holly's response should be equally so, the real answer will mean so much more: her reaction the truth, and the yes or no that goes or doesn't go with it, the tell-all for trust. For courage. Conviction. And this case.

"Holly. Do you know who he is?"

Her reaction: defensive. Her answer, not one. "No?"

"No as in n-o? Or as in k-n-o-w? Because that's much more like a yes."

"You think I know who raped me?" Defensive again, and in the worst way. If she thinks Sloane is judging her, the state's attorney might as well work from home.

"Listen," Sloane says. "I know this is hard. I'm just going to say something, off the record, no frills. Is that okay?"

Eventually she says, "I think so."

"That's the thing. From this point on, nobody is going to care what you think. Even if you're right. Because the truth is, there are any number of ways a woman can get fucked in this town. And what happened to you, last night? That might not have been the worst of them."

Right away, a shock switch. "What?"

"People are going to ask you a hundred questions twice that many times and that's just going to be today. And they're not asking because they care. They're asking because you're making some serious claims that will affect careers, reputations, futures. And nobody involved in this case—no matter what they say—will care about you more than they care about themselves. Believe me: I'm one of them. But I'm also the only one who will find the man who did this to you, and if that's what you want, we need to make a deal: you be straight with me, I'll be straight with you, and fuck everybody else. That's how you'll fight this, and that's how you'll win."

Holly looks down at her hands. "I don't know who raped me." She picks at her self-applied nail polish, the tips worn and chipped, one torn, probably part of her useless fight.

Sloane extends her fingers against the steering wheel; her polish is already gone. "We have to go now," she says, light on the gas toward Damen. "We'll save the rest for the record."

It isn't until after they pass the last of the vacants that Holly sits back, looks out the window.

And it's some time after that when she asks, "Why didn't you want those cops to know you're looking for a place to live?"

"Same reason I'm taking your case," Sloane says, "so they won't fuck it up. Trust me, they are not the only ones who will try."

3

SLOANE GETS HOLLY CHECKED in ahead of the noncritical patients and stations her in the waiting room next to a black kid who's using his oversized Cavaliers jersey as a tent, the number 23 up over his 'fro, probably hiding his crack headache from the lights. Today the room is rounded out by the local hypochondriac who's developed a convincing cough, a guy with a bled-through bandage on one arm and a bug-eyed woman on the other, and a handful of patients whose less apparent ailments will no doubt also hurt their wallets. Holly looks nervous, and her face goes puppy dog when Sloane gets up to leave, but she won't have to wait long; rape vics always cut to the front of the line. Besides, she'll have better luck blending in without Sloane there, her star drawing the wrong kind of attention.

Sloane goes outside, paces an empty stretch of sidewalk. She hangs up on Heavy's voicemail a few times—where the hell is he?—and then calls Sue Burkhart, Area Five's evidence coordinator. She gets Sue's voicemail, too, and bookends a message about the incoming forensic evidence with promises to buy some peanuts and whatever else from her daughter Madison's postcookie Girl Scout sale, because it's smarter for Sloane to keep Sue in her corner than it is to play grab-ass with the guys at the lab. And anyway, Sloane's dad loves peanuts.

Her next call goes to the watch commander's desk. "Guzman," she says, "I'm at Saint Mary's. I can't get Burkhart. I need an evidence tech."

"*Siempre necesita algo,*" he says. "You want to know what I need? Furlough." Guzman hangs up, which is fine, because he always bitches but he also always gets it done.

As Sloane paces back to the emergency entrance, a doctor comes out a side exit and looks twice. He's got to be on the intern end of MD: skin pale and clear as a comic-book character's, lids weighing on his eyes, hair like he just woke up. He's younger, maybe, but in no way shy of handsome.

"Hello," he says on approach, probably because Sloane's flat-out staring at him, and his voice is smooth and confident and finished with an incredible smile, same as the one on the photo badge clipped to his lab coat. Underneath, it reads ED-WARD MANZKO, RESIDENT.

"Hello," she says, only after he passes by, her own voice small. She wonders if anybody still calls him Eddie.

Sloane keeps on toward the hospital and she doesn't look over her shoulder because it would be just to see if Edward the doctor is doing the same.

She finds a spot by the emergency entrance, watches the paramedics smoke cigarettes. *Killing time,* she thinks, feels her hands curled to fists.

Fifteen minutes later while Sloane's wondering who, exactly, decided patience is a virtue, Jacquie "CQ" Jones comes through the automatic doors.

Sloane picked St. Mary's because she knows this is Jacquie's shift; everyone knows the four-foot-tall, factory-built, Jamaican charge nurse. Those few who know she spells her name with a *cq* and that she's most proud of her purple hair extensions and her one-year-old granddaughter, in that order, also know she's more likely to work with a cop than oh, say, 99 percent of the staff at this hospital. She just takes a little finesse.

"CQ, how's Iniesha?"

"A little angel. I thank God every day."

"She walking yet?"

CQ has a picture waiting in her scrub pocket: it's Iniesha, a wild-curled baby stuffed into a ridiculous yellow lace Easter dress and trapped on an oversized rabbit's lap, the moment captured midmeltdown, crocodile tears coloring her cheeks the same deep pink as the bunny's permanent smile. CQ says, "Girl can't help but step on hearts."

"I see she's got your cheerful disposition."

"Ain't nobody gonna snow her." CQ tucks the photo away, her smile with it. "Sloane, you know you can't snow me, so don't tell me you're hanging around because I'm so good lookin'."

Sloane evens her stance, makes it so CQ has to look up. She says, "We had another one like Holly. Last week."

"I don't know nothin' about that. Only thing I know is Miss Dutcher's physical condition, and that's not something I should be telling you."

"The other girl," Sloane says anyway, "she wasn't as strong. Didn't put up much of a fight. Doesn't want to now, either."

"You think Miss Dutcher does?"

"I think she's got it in her. If her story matches her marks. What do you think?"

CQ arches an eyebrow. "No-ahh, no way," she says like she shouldn't have to. "How come all you five-oh come to me? I'm here for my patient. Not your investigation."

"CQ, if your patient's story isn't straight, I'll be playing hangman with the state's attorney instead of getting the guy who did this on the gallows. And come next week, here we'll be: another patient, another investigation, same conversation."

A medic strolls by, the smell of his last cigarette a stale interruption. Jacquie CQ inhales deep. *Once a smoker, always,* Sloane thinks. The urge brain-wired, unreasonable.

"We're talking about a predator," Sloane says. "He's not

going to wake up one day and be okay with a wife and two point two."

"You're sure it's serial?"

"You want to wait for another vic to prove it?"

CQ twirls one of her purple-brown curls. She's done exams like this a thousand times; a thousand and one shouldn't be any different. Or should it? Holly's chart will read clinical, but its accuracy will actually depend on any number of subjective forces: Does the doc trust CQ? Does she respect him? Is one of them working on an empty stomach or the other on no sleep? Has the doc just saved a life and CQ just lost one? Can they hustle through this before the ambulance arrives from the crash on Armitage? What about the thirteen-year-old Spanish Cobra with the knife wound in his abdomen—was he sent to ICU? Wait, which room did they put that rape vic in again? In chaos like this, details get lost. And from there, so do cases.

As far as Sloane's concerned, CQ's role amidst it all is simple: she can help, or not. She can help this victim, this one-thousand-and-oneth time, by keeping Sloane close. Or not.

Sloane asks, "Who's going to do the kit?"

"I can try for Dr. Raupp."

Raupp: a so-so doctor and a way-out eccentric, but also a hell of an advocate for the CPD. Ever since he inherited his parents' mammoth house that sits on what's now one of the worst blocks on the West Side, he's been throwing lavish parties for—and money at—the Fraternal Order of Police. In return, the cops in Fifteen patrol his block all the time, stop in for coffee occasionally, and never say anything about the dozen black-tied mannequins that lounge in his great room, forever poised to party. Last fall, Sloane and Eddie went to one of his FOP fund-raisers. He called it "Funtopia." Toward the end of the evening, Sloane got stuck talking to Raupp at the player piano. He insisted she meet Demetri, the tux-and-tailed dummy that sat at the keys; he said they'd been lucky he was able to take the night off from his regular gig at Jilly's. The way Raupp spoke was just serious enough for Sloane to feel compelled to offer a compliment. "I love this song," she'd said to the mannequin.

Later, Eddie joked, "Who's that dummy you were flirting with?" Sloane shushed him. She liked Raupp, and thought maybe he kept the dolls because he wanted someone to talk to who'd never need saving. She could understand that.

"You want Raupp," CQ says, "it's going to be a little while. Why don't you take off, let me call you when we get somewhere?"

"Right," Sloane says, "and then something gets screwed up or overlooked and the kit goes one way and the vic goes another and the case goes straight into the toilet."

"Girl, I let you stick around and I'm gonna get a reputation."

Another of the medics passes by and Sloane steps back, gives him space. He ditches his cigarette on his way inside, his cough raw and thoughtless.

CQ watches after him, mouth heavy, that unreasonable

urge to smoke returning when what's left of the cigarette rolls toward her and stops just shy of her feet.

Sloane says, "Doing the right thing isn't ever all that fun." It isn't hard for her to sound blue about it.

Smoke drifts up from the butt; CQ looks down, says to it, "Noo-ah."

"Jacquie, you know why I'm here. You saw what this guy did to Holly. He wants to fight. That means I have to. The thing is? I'm the one who's got rules. Trust me, the first chance I get, I'm gone. I'm at the scene. But right now I've got an advocate and a tech on the way, and you know better than anybody where a boat with six captains winds up. I need Holly's story straight, and I need you to help me keep it that way."

CQ steps up, stamps out the butt. "This isn't going to be cake. She doesn't remember much."

Sloane says, "She hasn't talked to me yet."

SLOANE WAITS JUST OUTSIDE Holly's room while Jacquie CQ readies the rape kit for Dr. Raupp. When CQ is finished, she cracks the door so Sloane can go in, be a hero.

"Hi," Sloane says to the women from the doorway, a warm smile just for Holly. "Mind if I have a minute?" Not so warm to CQ.

"Can't stop you," CQ says, a thin layer of fake-nice over the flip response. If the state police's big white med kit and all its official etceteras didn't intimidate Holly, this little exchange should do the trick—the illusion being that CQ is insensitive, which makes Sloane the obvious choice for Holly's gut-spilling.

Sloane walks in like she's twice CQ's size. The boots help. "You're right, Nurse Jones, you can't stop me."

"We're doing an exam here, Detective. Not an interrogation."

"Nobody's guilty here," Sloane reassures Holly, who's got her gown on backward, the ties in front. She regathers the thin cotton at her breasts and lap though there's not enough material to cover herself completely. Nice of CQ to leave her this way: good and uncomfortable.

"Where's her advocate?" CQ asks, peeling off her latex gloves.

"You know I'm the biggest supporter she'll get."

CQ docks Holly's chart in the file holder at the door, grumbles something under her breath.

"I'm sorry, what did you say?"

"Nothing that'd help you sleep at night." She looks Sloane up and down, head back, like she's swallowing vomit.

Sloane checks with Holly—*Can you believe this woman?*—but Holly looks like she hasn't taken a breath in some time. Sloane decides the act worked. Too well.

"I'll be brief," Sloane says to CQ, yielding.

"I'll be surprised." CQ makes herself scarce just before either one of them cracks a smile.

As soon as the door closes, Sloane lifts Holly's chart, tosses it on the desk next to the exam table, and says, "Holly. I'm sorry. Unbelievable." She rolls the doctor's stool out of the way and goes through the cabinets, making a show of her search though she knows exactly where the gowns are stored. Yes, it's completely manipulative, but she wasn't lying when she warned Holly about the way things would be. Everybody fucking with her. Sloane has to think this isn't so bad. She has to think so.

When she gets to the gowns, she shakes one out and hands it to Holly, her approach somewhere between military and motherly.

Holly says, "Thank you."

"Of course." Sloane rolls the stool back to the desk and cranks the seat as low as it will go, positioning herself as a nonthreat. She opens the chart, no big deal, and confirms that CQ came through: checked the right boxes, skimped the narrative. Not much there to read, but Holly doesn't know that. She doesn't know Sloane's just waiting for her to get straight with the second gown and utter some eventual, audible sign of relief.

Eventually comes. Nothing comes. Then the silence is tricky. So this might as well come next: Sloane pivots, looks up, direct, and says, "Holly, I've got to talk to you. About the rape."

Holly clutches the second gown to her collarbone, a blanket. "I already told you."

"I need you to tell me again. In your own words. Without my interruptions, and before we're interrupted. From the beginning."

"From the beginning," Holly repeats, the relief strange in

her voice, remembering how it was, just before. Then her face clouds, eyes first; the rest of the memory a storm, imminent.

Sloane hates this: watching Holly, like all the others, go back to that first moment, when luck is out and instinct is late and there's no such thing as impossible anymore, because it's happening. And it's worse.

"It's okay." Sloane closes the chart and puts it out of reach, out of play. She shows Holly her empty hands and promises, "This is just for me."

Holly lifts one leg, then the other, away from the exam table; its paper sticks to her skin, damp with sweat. This is no place for her to get comfortable; a room this characterless can only take on the prevailing mood of those inside. Holly is anxious. Shifty. She shifts; the paper tears under her hundred-and-nothing pounds.

Sloane eyes the clock over the door while she mentally rewords her reassurances, but Holly gets her restless drift and says—

"He came from behind me. His arm around my throat? He covered my mouth, my nose—he was wearing leather gloves. I couldn't breathe."

Sloane registers that familiar thrill: having made a connection to Claire Meyer-Davis, and to the suspect, she glimpses the chase. She's dying to get to the details, to turn them over and pick them apart and help Holly remember things just right; she wants to know if Holly knows things Claire does, about the suspect being Hispanic, maybe a maintenance worker, and about his Chevy Impala. Then there's the recovered button—a new link—and there must be more, but she can't shape the story without knowing all its angles. She nods, leaves it at that.

Holly says, "I tried, you know. To turn around, to get his hands away—" She coughs, the memory catching there. "He was dragging me across the grass, away from the street? I was trying to plant my feet or stop him somehow and then I reached back and got ahold of his shirt and I just grabbed on, trying to get his skin, too? To hurt him, or throw him off, I don't know. That's how I got the button, I caught my nail on it—" She shows Sloane her ring finger, the torn nail. "But I wasn't stopping anything. I was just making him more . . . aggressive? He kept saying, 'Fight me. Fight me.' But I just . . ." Her gaze falls away with the rest of the sentence. "I felt like I was underwater. Like he was holding me below the surface. Then, for some reason, I thought that if I didn't fight, he would let me go. He would realize what he was doing and just let me go. And I felt so calm. It was the only answer. So I gave up." She looks down at her gowns now, flimsy covers. "It was stupid. He just kept choking me."

Sloane says, "What you did, Holly, it wasn't stupid. Not at all." Because a victim has to feel like she tried not to be one. She has to believe she did something.

Holly says, "I didn't fight him."

Sloane rolls the stool toward the exam table and sits on her hands, roughly mimicking Holly's position to offset this new proximity. She says, "You are now."

Holly's face steels. "I am now."

"Keep going."

"It gets fuzzy," she says. "When I realized we were in the building he was holding me down on the hardwood, by my neck." She lowers her gown, shows her bruises. "I was face-down and he . . . was already inside me."

It's all Sloane can do to maintain eye contact; she feels like some kind of voyeur, persuading Holly to be so utterly and indecently exposed.

"I thought I should act like I was still unconscious," she says, "so he would leave me alone when he was through? But then I realized I still had the button. I don't know how I held on to it. I was so scared, I thought I'd drop it, or he'd find it, so I raised both my arms and put it in my mouth and then right away I made like I was trying to pry his hands away." She raises her arms to demonstrate, flinches, and stops short. "He loved that. He wanted me to resist. He started in again, 'Fight me, fight me' . . . I thought my spine would break, the way he pinned my neck and pulled me back and just kept going. He pushed me across the hardwood. I thought he was going to kill me, but I just bit down and cried through it—"

A quick knock at the door sends Holly nearly out of her skin, and when Dr. Finkleman lumbers into the room, Sloane wishes she had her .22 and a reason. From the hallway, CQ mouths the first syllable of *sorry* before he elbows the door shut. Every muscle in Sloane's neck turns to rope and her jaw goes so tight she could crush her own teeth.

"Hello," Finkleman says to Holly, one hand across the

never-trimmed hair matted to his forehead, the other going for her chart. "I'm Dr. Mike."

Holly must speak Sloane's body language because she pulls the second gown up to her neck and looks like she's got less than nothing to say.

Dr. Mike is what Finkelman likes to be called, and the bullshit starts there. His bedside manner is about as authentic as SWEET'N LOW. His favorite catchphrase is "be patient"—a clever play on words, if he meant to be clever. His smile is the same, certain kind that politicians wear after reelections and gamblers can't help after risky bets—a smile for the compromised. In a place like this, where most everyone is compromised, Dr. Mike's smile means even a terminal patient might be okay.

Unless, of course, the patient happens to be a prostitute named Kitten, and Dr. Mike wears that smile all the while he's telling her to get the fuck out of his ER. And unless, of course, the detective on her case happens to be Sloane, and when she shows up to interview Dr. Mike, she gets the same smile, and a much different story: He didn't tell Kitten to leave; what he said was that he didn't think a full rape kit was necessary because Kitten fucks men for crack, and he'd rather fuck her himself than make the taxpayers pay for her medical care—and thereby her habit.

"Detective," Finkelman says, closing Holly's chart. That smile. "Will you excuse us?" He moves his tray of instruments around to the exam table in an arc so wide that Sloane has to roll her stool back toward the wall. Then he stands in front of Sloane, his back to her, and says, "I can assure you, detective, I'll be doing the full kit. You are free to go."

Sloane could kick Finkelman, his bucket-ass in her face, his big feet stepping in front of her and all over everything she started. She doesn't know what happened to Raupp or how the hell Finkelman wound up in here, but she's pretty sure it has something to do with the complaint she filed for his negligence during Kitten's case. He shouldn't care, since Commander Wojciechowski killed the complaint on account of some off-the-books house calls. Finkelman shouldn't have taken it personally, either. Regardless of his being an asshole, Sloane would've lobbied for the full rape kit—always does— and she doesn't do it to appease the victim or right the record or keep the doctors in check, not even for the long-shot DNA database match. Getting a full rape kit is for the state's attorney. Period.

"Dr. Mike," Sloane says, the name sharp from her lips, "I think Holly would prefer it if I stay."

Finkelman pulls on an exam glove, *snap,* a no. "Miss Dutcher, your privacy is my responsibility," he says, like Sloane suggested national airtime. "This is a very personal procedure, and in my experience, much easier to get through without distractions." The other glove, *snap.*

Sloane says, "Holly, you can get through this however you want—and it's your right to have someone present, whether it's a family member, or a friend, or me. I can call someone "

Finkelman turns around to eye-fuck Sloane and behind him, Holly is terrified.

"Please stay," Holly says.

"Absolutely," Sloane says.

"Have a seat," Finkelman says, though stripped of its saccharine coating the order would sound a lot more like *Go to hell*.

"I don't have anyone else close by," Holly explains to Finkelman.

Sloane resumes her seat on the stool and, just as soon as nobody's looking, sticks her tongue out at the jackass doctor.

Finkelman repeats CQ's initial exam, adding notes to the chart; Sloane takes notes, too, and she's encouraged, since all Holly's answers match the version she gave to Officer Buchanan, and to CQ.

Once finished with the repeat initial, Finkelman takes the plastic off all the remaining instruments and receptacles that go with the kit. He puts the stirrups in place and says, "Okay, Miss Dutcher, I'll need you to lie back." The way he says this is all sugar, and Sloane hates him for it.

Sloane knows this part of the exam is invasive, and all-out terrible, so she puts her head down and tunes out, scribbling notes about her possibilities. She makes two lists: one for Claire Meyer-Davis, the other for Holly. With all the similarities, even the state's attorney might admit one guy is responsible—

"Ow, God—" Holly says and Finkelman says—

"I'm sorry, I know it's uncomfortable," but immediately glances over at Sloane, so she knows he meant it for her.

Motherfucker.

Sloane's on her feet at Holly's side and she's asking, "Are you okay?" at the same time it occurs to her that *she* is responsible for this. Because she fought for Kitten, because she filed the complaint, and because she stayed in the room today.

"I'm okay," Holly says, though she looks worried by Sloane's sudden panic.

"Good. That's good," is all Sloane can think to say. She can't say she believes Finkelman would actually hurt a patient to make a point, because in doing so she's hurting the patient worse. She can't say she knows the doctor's ruthless-pissed because she fought him on Kitten, and called him out, and saw through his Dr. Wonderful bit from the first handshake, because then who's the victim? Sloane can't say anything because she can't prove anything and Finkelman fucking knows it, sitting there, commander-certified, board-licensed to have his hands on Holly.

"Is there something wrong, Detective?" Finkelman asks, a dare.

"I was just thinking," she says, and not to Finkelman, "I need to make sure things are rolling on my partner's end. Okay if I go, Holly? Catch up with you later?"

"Yes?" Holly says, no less worried.

"May I finish now?" from Finkelman. Sloane can feel that fucking smile.

"You've got my number," she says to Holly, hating herself because it's clear that Dr. Mike had it all along.

4

SLOANE TIES HER HAIR back on her way up the steps to Area Five's detectives' offices. The whole thing with Dr. Mike set her off, so when she walks by the "Amazing" Mumford, one of the property crimes' dicks and a heavy hitter on Stag's ponytail team, she's thinking, *Go ahead, go for it, I dare you.* But Mumford doesn't even look up from his desk; apparently he's actually working. Usually, she'd be happy about that.

Lieutenant Guzman's standing around the main office like a manager at an electronics store who's anal about the hardware, his customers a bunch of idiots. Doesn't help that all the reports are filed and managed online now, and that most of the guys at the computers type one-fingered. The whiteboard on the wall that used to be the case clearinghouse is now a blank slate, save for one corner where a red-markered stick figure relieves himself, his eyes X's. Last time Sloane saw the little red man, he was chugging a bottle of beer. Guzman obviously hasn't seen what he's up to now.

The rest of the property crimes detectives busy themselves in that mid-afternoon way, bullshitting each other, ties loose, biding time on robbery and theft cases while they wait for the shift change. Nobody wants to catch assignments after lunchtime anymore—not since the city cut overtime. Breaks up the natural flow. Makes so much of the work seem futile.

In the middle of the room, dubbed the Demilitarized Zone after a fight between Mumford and a since-gone SVU detective forced Guzman to put demarcation tape on the floor, three homicide dicks are holding some kind of pow-wow. They stand, palms curbed around a desk of paperwork, faces screwy, like someone turned their map upside down. Sloane doesn't particularly like any of them; they aren't pony-tail guys, but tail is certainly a topic of many of their conversations. On the evolutionary scale it goes Marchetti, then Olsen, then Warwick, who's about one hair away from gorilla.

Next to the detectives, two of the three interview rooms are occupied, which means the guys must be waiting on the state's attorney, who will eventually appear from one or the other room with a perfectly good reason why they've got no case.

"Pearson," Guzman says like there's more after it, but as Sloane gets into the room she sees Heavy hunched over at a desk in the corner of the DMZ. She waves the lieutenant off and ignores the rest of the guys' unnecessary attention; they each have their own way of acknowledging her, but she wouldn't call any of those ways professional.

"What the hell?" Sloane says when she discovers Heavy sitting there drawing mustaches on a six-pack of men's booking photos. "Why haven't you answered my calls?"

"What calls?" Heavy's laugh hangs awkward, same way his suit fits today. He's been a little thin lately—not so that anyone would question the nickname—but there's something going on. Something he's not saying. What he says is, "I figured you could handle things at the hospital."

"Did you figure Finkelman would be there to exam-fuck my victim?"

"Wait a minute, Sloane. Finkelman might be an asshole, but he's not a monster."

"How would you know? Looks like you've been sitting here playing Chester Gould all afternoon."

"Dick Tracy didn't solve a single crime without him." He hands her a clean copy of the six-pack. "Look at this: I went through CHRIS and I-CLEAR and found a whole slough of Hispanic offenders in the area who happen to drive mid-'90s light-colored Chevy Impalas."

Unlike Sloane, Heavy has no game face, so she can tell he's only playing at workday like the rest of the guys.

"You're killing time," she says, so frustrated he's another one of just about everybody.

"No I'm not." Heavy gets up, points a bloated finger at his

photos. "I have leads here," he says, his quiet voice dispro-
portionate to his stance.

"Heavy," she says, "Meyer-Davis never said anything
about a mustache."

"I made clean copies."

"What are you even doing here? You were supposed to go
to the scene."

"Sloane, I can't shut down the entire 2300 block of West
Erie without the vic's confirmation."

"That's why I was trying to call you. I drove her past."

"She confirmed?"

"Not exactly."

"You're going to build a case on 'not exactly?'"

"At least I have evidence. You're building a case on the
make of a person and the model of a car."

"Do you think your evidence will be back from the lab by
the time our suspect is old enough to need a prescription for
erectile dysfunction? Tell me what else you'd like to do, when
we can't do anything."

Sloane knows he's right. Even if they put a rush on the
lab, it'll be a good two months before they get anything back.
Unless . . .

"We leak it."

Heavy huffs his slack cheeks, looks up to Area Five's
polystyrene-tiled heavens. "You are out of your ever-loving
mind. All a press release is going to do this early is scare off
our suspect—or worse—serve as exhibit A when we're clipped
for racial profiling."

"It's better than waiting. Better than nothing."

"Sloane, we have to take care of these women. We don't have a case at all if we don't have victims. Meyer-Davis doesn't want to talk to us. Dutcher will probably run and hide after what happened at the hospital." He uses his shirtsleeve to wipe his upper lip even though the room is always set at sixty-eight. "And no," he says, "I don't want to know what happened at the hospital."

Sloane considers the photographs: six Hispanic guys who couldn't be mistaken for one another in a blackout. "So this is your plan? To file this bullshit six-pack and tell Guzman that if he needs us, we'll be out cruising for white Chevy Impalas?"

"You're not listening," Heavy says, and takes the copy back. "Forget the suspect. We don't have a suspect. Not without victims." He wipes his forehead this time, his shirt soaked through. "I don't claim to understand women," he says, "but if there's one thing I've realized about the lot of you, lovely or not, it's that your other X chromosome must be the one with all the compassion. You might not step up for yourself, darlin', but if someone else needs you? Consider it done. So this is my plan: we show the vics these photos. We tell them he's still out there. Tell them there are other victims. That there will be more. And that we need them . . . to help each other?" The question mark that curls the end of his sentence goes with a sudden smile and Sloane realizes it's directed at someone behind her so she turns around to see who his theatrics are for.

Of course they're for Brendan Everman. Everyone's favorite state's attorney has just come out of the third interview room, and now Sloane knows why the homicide guys were stressing: Everman is the be to anybody's wanna, professionally and, oh yes, otherwise. He's tall and just as cut as his suit, but not so that anyone could say he spends time getting that way. He's the rare kind of good-looking that comes without cosmetic dentistry or high-end accessories. He's on top of the game, but not because he had connections or makes them. And, he's got conviction, strong as faith. Women love him; men can't hate him. There isn't a jury out there who won't yea when he yeas, or nay when he nays.

Today Everman looks no more knockable, standing there, everyone else acting like he's telling them what they should have known.

But Sloane doesn't know, so she leans back and *pssts* to Heavy. "What'd I miss?"

"That Nunez girl. The one shot crossing the street for the *elotes* cart in Humboldt Park."

Sloane knows who he means: a nine-year-old killed in gang crossfire, the mother and a few others in the neighborhood brave enough to call out a couple of Insane Dragons and an apartment full of Black Souls; it was a top local news story, as long as those last.

Heavy says, "Marchetti got the shooter," just as Everman returns to door number three and Sloane catches a look at a kid she won't ever forget: "Nigeria." He's a member of the

Black Souls nicknamed for his home country; if his reputation is anything like the place, it must be awful.

Marchetti and company resume their powwow while Everman hangs in the doorway, Nigeria looking up at him, through him. Sloane knows that nonlook, since she got real familiar with Nigeria when she worked the Keyshon "Kickstand" Davis/Zookie Truman murders last year. She was still in Area Three. At the time of his arrest, Nigeria was the Black Souls' newest trustee, so he had plenty of people backing him.

But Sloane had Zookie Truman. She had him, this thirteen-year-old wanna-be banger who was going to testify at the Kickstand trial. Zookie was going to say that he saw Nigeria X-out poor Kickstand simply because Nigeria found out his new girl knew firsthand how Kickstand got the name. So Nigeria went after him, Zookie said, "Shot him up, let him bleed to death." Sloane suspected Zookie remembered things that way because he blamed Nigeria for his older brother Miah's twenty-five-to-life, but Zookie insisted, "Nigeria was the shooter." At least that's what Zookie swore the night before some beat cops from Fifteen found him dead on an Austin doorstep. He was shot in the guts and he had a black and white bandana stuffed into his mouth, much like the one hanging out of Nigeria's low-slung Hilfigers today. The jury believed Nigeria's shitbag attorney when he opined that Zookie was a Raiders fan. Nigeria was in the clink when Zookie was hit, so then, as good as sprung.

So, Sloane was in trouble. Because if the gang dicks ever had a line on Nigeria, she cut it with Zookie: after he was killed, Nigeria switched up all his top guys, got rid of anybody worth a dime. All the dicks in Three blamed Sloane—said she was emotional about the young banger. Truth was, she did like Zookie, but that was because she thought he could make the case, and her career, too. At the time, she had no idea she'd be responsible for the boy's murder; then again, she had no idea Nigeria had arms so long they'd reached into the department. Problem was, she couldn't prove it. Only thing she could do was take the transfer.

"They actually got Nigeria?" Sloane asks Heavy. "For the Nunez girl?"

She doesn't hear Heavy's answer, because right then Everman brings Nigeria out of the interview room, and Marchetti steps up to undo his cuffs.

The room softly deflates.

Nigeria rubs his wrists, follows Marchetti toward the exit just as easily as he could slip through a crack. Sloane wishes she couldn't believe it.

She would ask who's behind door number two but it doesn't matter; whoever it is must be taking the murder rap. No doubt Marchetti and his boys will be on their way out for beers just as soon as they finish the paperwork.

And, Sloane decides, as soon as she is finished with them.

"Marchetti," she says, and loud enough for all the ears on the other side of the DMZ to perk up. "You going to let Everman slam-dunk this one?" Olsen and Warwick look at each other. Marchetti looks down at his shoes.

Sloane starts across the room and Heavy says, "Pearson,"

a warning for everyone else; both Olsen and Warwick take heed and back off.

Marchetti stands his ground and he says, real reasonably, "Pearson, Humboldt Park is a disaster. The neighborhood needs someone to blame and we need to get one of these guys off the street. Everman says the case is a lock with the kid's confession."

"What kid?" Sloane asks on her way to see for herself: through the second room's window there's a kid, maybe ten years old, looking at the plate of fried chicken in front of him like they've served him his dead parakeet. "This kid?" She wonders how much longer he'll feel like one.

Marchetti steps up beside her and he doesn't say anything. Pretty soon, watching the kid, Sloane decides there's no use in picking a fight; making Marchetti the bad guy isn't much different from convicting a ten-year-old. There's something sad about Marchetti; like maybe someone squashed his confidence when he was younger. When he was this kid's age. When he didn't know any better. Makes Sloane want to like him. Still, "You're killing him, you know that."

"Pearson." Said by Lieutenant Guzman this time. He's standing on the edge of the demarcation tape. On the fighting side. "This is not your problem."

"If that kid in there shot Nunez," Sloane says, "Nigeria gave him the order."

"Not your case." Guzman crosses his arms, armor.

"I know Nigeria," she says. "I should be in on this. I should talk to Everman."

"My office?" A demand more than a request.

The leftover property crimes dicks aren't even pretending to work anymore; Mumford and the rest are just slack-jawed behind Guzman, watching this play out: watching Sloane's face flush, her chest rise and fall fast with her breath. She can't concede. It's what they all expect. It's what they really want to see.

She says, "Lieutenant, I'm trying to help."

From the stairwell, a group of patrollers' pent-up, after-shift laughter comes in advance of their arrival.

"Detective Pearson," Guzman says, and he's looking at Heavy even though he's talking to Sloane, "just do your job."

The stairwell patrollers reach the landing, Stag leading the charge into the room. "I says come on, Belushi. You can't tell me 'no coke.'" Three of his four followers laugh, most of them obligatorily. The fourth is Buchanan; when he gets a handle on the potential situation they've walked into, he elbows the copper next to him, who passes the message up the chain.

"Hey," Stag says to the room, and then to Sloane, "What's up, Real Estate?" He obviously didn't get the elbow.

Guzman turns around, probably to put the hush on Stag, but Mumford and the other dicks scatter from him like pigeons: They're off to the file cabinets and the coat rack and the exit and just like that, quitting time commences.

"Pearson," Guzman says.

Sloane feels like she's been fishhooked out of the sudden rush "Yeah," she says, exactly halfway between polite and defiant.

Guzman's answer, in a single nod, says, *You know better, and don't make me doubt it.*

Sloane's return nod? Halfway between *absolutely* and *fuck you.*

She tucks her tail and goes back to Heavy's work station, thinking she owes him a good-bye.

Heavy asks, "What's Stag talking about, 'real estate?'"

"What's he ever talking about?" Sloane knows she sounds defensive but she should be, after Guzman's scolding, right?

"Don't worry," Heavy says, the mustached photos pinched in his fattish fingers. "We're on top of this. Tomorrow I'll call Meyer-Davis, and you can work on Dutcher."

"Tomorrow," she says, a throwaway. "Tomorrow Guzman's going to tell us that all we have to keep this case open is a Mexican with a hard-on. And then he'll close it."

"You're right, darlin'," Heavy says. "Forget it."

Sloane thinks he's being sarcastic. She can never tell.

She says good-bye, and she knows he won't say anything when she takes a copy of the six-pack before she heads out.

Stag bats her fucking ponytail when she goes.

SLOANE MAKES THE DRIVE home without any music. After a day like this, she'd usually crank some crap eighties rock like Whitesnake or Kingdom Come; she'd sing all the lyrics she'd memorized as a kid when she thought she was so grown up.

Or else she'd play something mellow. Calexico—her current favorite—or the Eagles, her dad's. Sing along with those, too, sometimes.

This evening she drives without any of it, and she takes the long way.

When she gets to Eddie's place downtown, the place that he calls theirs, she finds a parking spot right around the corner, and lucky, too, since he only has one garage spot and parking's been a pain since the two new condo buildings opened up just north on Kingsbury.

Sloane parallel parks and she isn't careful because she hates her hand-me-down Honda Pilot. It'd be fine if she had tools or a dog or kids to haul around, but she feels pretty ridiculous these days; the SUV, gas prices. She gets out, hates that the sun's up near seven o'clock, too, and that the days just keep getting longer. She considers stopping at Caribou for a latte, since there's so much more of this day. Then she sees the line inside, a bunch of after-workers jonesing for precocktail espressos, so she skips it, zips her coat, and decides to walk through Erie Park. She should move her legs. The cold air will wake her up. And it's a nice, quiet patch of city-manicured grass.

She also can usually see what Eddie's doing on the twelfth floor. Even though she probably already knows.

By the angle of the building and the layout of the condo, Eddie's unit is in plain sight. It faces west, though, so he's pulled the shades, probably to see his fifty-two-inch HDTV. She still can't understand why he pays for the view when he never looks out at it. He says it's human nature to get so comfortable with your surroundings that they become near invisible. It's certainly Eddie's nature, though the television debunks the theory.

If routine serves, Eddie's in there, feet up, drinking a
Miller Lite, watching whatever isn't news. He's not waiting
for her, and it won't matter if she comes home with food, or
wanting food, or ready to cook dinner; he'll be equally happy
with Giordano's delivery, or a trip through the drive-thru, or
with the harissa-rubbed halibut with couscous and mint jelly,
Sloane's latest specialty. It's all great. All fuel.

Sloane calls him on her cell, waits through the rings it
takes for him to get up, get the phone from its charger, check
the ID, answer. "Hey baby," he says, which bothers her because she's sure he's called all his previous girlfriends the
same old standard.

"Hi, E. You home?" She calls him E. She never calls him
Eddie.

"Of course." He's distracted; she can tell.

"What're you watching?" Trying to sound like she cares,
or doesn't. She's not sure it matters.

"The opener, remember?"

Of course. The Cubs and the Rockies. He couldn't get
tickets.

"Did you eat?"

"Nah." If Eddie isn't starving, he could care less where his
next meal is coming from. "Jee-zuss!" he yells, into the phone,
though he must mean it for whoever's batting on TV.

From across Erie Park, Sloane finds his windows again;
the sun glares just so, making them bright orange, on fire.

Sloane says, "I have a lead." It's not a complete lie. She

knows that. She just doesn't know why she can't bring herself to go up there.

"I'll order Reza's," Eddie says, his attention no less divided. "Kabobs?"

"Okay," Sloane says. She wishes he would say something else before she says, "See you later," because she knows he'll be asleep when she finally returns.

Worse, she's counting on it.

5

SLOANE ZIPS OUT ON Chicago Avenue toward Garfield Park, one of those neighborhoods the downtowners call "bad." Sloane knows too many people who share the opinion, and they're always people who know someone who "knows."

Like the woman from her dad's girlfriend Carolyn's "Loop lunch bunch" who took the 65 bus west by accident one time and survived to tell about it. Block by block, she said, the buildings deteriorate, the sidewalks crumble, and the people? They just hang around, addicted or welfaring or worse. The empty storefronts aren't that way for nothing, she tells them: business gets done in the alleys, and crime right there on the streets, probably. And there's no Whole Foods. No PJ Clarke's.

She was afraid to get off the bus, she said, but didn't dare venture past California Avenue. The bunch was aghast she went that far. Carolyn spent that lunch picking at her roasted quail and fretting over Sloane's transfer from her cush job in Area Three—*Wrigleyville!*—to what the brave bus rider called a sprawling, dirty, land mine of an area. She didn't even make it past Ukrainian Village. No matter: Carolyn was beside herself when she returned from the Union League Club that day and so asked Sloane's dad, "Is your daughter insane?"

Insane, no. Hypocritical, maybe, since she could never live where she works and no less than a half hour ago she considered standing in line for a delicious brand-name five-dollar coffee.

Still, she feels more like herself out here, a few miles from the one called Magnificent. Apart from the urban mountains that will forever scrape the Loop's sky, the city's remaining foundation is laid here. Generations of families still speak Polish or Ukrainian or Spanish at home and go to church every day. Men work in one of the factories or at a machine shop in what's left of the Industrial Corridor; women raise their children and cook every meal—for the kids, and their grandparents, and cousins, and anyone else who stops in, hungry or not.

And this is where Sloane works. Where the old ways fight, knives to the new; where tight-knit communities hang together by old threads. It's when those threads come loose—when they give way to change and the neighborhoods' fabrics are refashioned—that holes are made. Those holes become the whys of crime, and they're another reason Sloane took the transfer.

Sloane gets to the 2300 block of West Erie in time for the last few minutes of daylight. The north side of the residential street is lined by FDR-era single-family homes, the term "single family" true as far as it has nothing to do with the actual number of relatives under one roof. On the other side, down toward Western Avenue, Sloane finds the vacants set between some eco-modern townhomes and the car dealer on the corner. The three buildings are shells, each one at a similar stage of nondevelopment, stunted by the economy. Still, their stoic gray structures are far more sophisticated than the old yellow-brick homes across the street that'll probably be the next to go, when the market turns.

In front of the westernmost vacant, a developer's billboard announces IMMEDIATE OCCUPANCY URBAN LUXURY CONDO-MINIUMS, and Sloane wonders what, besides "urban," is true; the building behind the sign has no glass in the windows, and through them she can see that the place has been gutted, probably left exactly the way it was when the builders, advertised as Panther Construction, got the stop-work order. Thankfully, it doesn't look like they'll be starting up here again anytime soon; Heavy lost the scene evidence in the Meyer-Davis case because the contractors at the West Town property she identified were there the very next morning, the thinset mortar long-dried, ready for the granite flooring.

Sloane pulls forward, parks the Pilot in front of the car dealer, gears up, and gets out.

Her first pass along Erie is a broad sweep. She snaps photos of each of the vacant buildings, then the surrounding homes, trees, and streetlights, each in relation to the scene. She imagines where Holly walked, where she was attacked. Reshoots it all in sequence.

There isn't much by way of grass in front of the vacants, but there is a neighbor's yard adjacent to the east building. It's full of stone statues and plastic gnomes and weeds; Holly didn't say anything about lawn ornaments, but Sloane wouldn't expect her to remember. She takes photos.

On her return pass, Sloane snaps pics of everything that isn't growing out of the ground. She wishes she could bag it all, take it with her, but she can't exactly show up at work tomorrow with evidence she wasn't supposed to be collecting. "Do your job," Guzman said, and this afternoon that meant *Shut the fuck up and go home.* So, she'll do it by the book and get a team here tomorrow. Right now, she'll just take these pictures, and hope they'll serve Holly's memory.

She stops outside the building and takes a photo of the developer's sign so she'll remember the specifics, then she pulls on gloves and tries the front door on the vacant unit next to the yard; it swings open on fat, old hinges and chases dust inside. She sweeps a flashlight along the perimeter and finds the rain that came down earlier also came in through the side windows and pooled at the lowest part of the floor, which happens to be the entire right side of the room. There are scuff marks and streaks of dust just inside the door, but the water has come in and taken everything else to the pool. Sloane belts the light, edges her way around the entry marks, and resumes snapping photos.

She shoots the floor first, then the room, the windows. She looks at everything through the camera's display so the flash doesn't skew her vision, not that there's much to see. She's losing the last of the daylight, and the water is murky from the dust and whatever else. She scrolls through the photos and realizes the flash has reflected off the water's surface, rendering the images about as useful as a film through a microwave. Goddamn rain. It's always something.

After another unsuccessful try at the photos without the flash, she decides that by sticking around, she's only leaving her own evidence. For now, she's got to skate.

On the way back to the Pilot her stomach growls, and she realizes it's been a long day. She would've had something this afternoon, if not for the stop at St. Mary's, and Finkelman isn't even to blame for that one; food is never on the same list with hospital. Ever.

There is a great little place right around here—a *jibarito* joint with the best fried-plantain sandwiches—just up California Avenue, so she makes the drive, puts an order in for one steak and one chicken.

Twenty minutes later she's already gone back south, parked. She loses the suit coat, the Kevlar, and the utility belt; she swaps her boots for a pair of square-toed heels, an ankle holster, and her .22. Then she gets her slim, camel-colored leather coat from the backseat, tucks her camera and Heavy's six-pack in one of its pockets, and grabs the sandwiches. If Holly's at home, Sloane hopes she likes plantains.

6

"I DON'T REMEMBER," HOLLY says, yet again. She was home all right, home and making one hell of an attempt to get unconscious. When Sloane knocked, Holly was barely able to answer the door, let alone form a sentence any more coherent than *Heyo, duhtetiv.* Sloane convinced her to eat part of the chicken *jibarito,* but it wasn't enough to soak up the near bottle of merlot she'd already used to wash down the painkillers Finkelman gave her.

"The color of the cab?" Sloane asks, sitting back in the other slender dining room chair, the legs wobbling, its design much like all the other furniture in here: modern looking, but slight and cheaply made. Reminds Sloane of the bedroom set she threw away when she put her things in storage.

The furniture didn't hold up so well. Same as her last relationship.

Sloane sits forward, says again, "The color of the cab. The company?"

Holly looks out her only front window, to black. The potent alcohol-and-Valium cocktail hasn't helped her make much sense, but it's certainly loosened her up: she's been as candid with Sloane as a college roommate just home from the pub. On the plus side, Holly's allowed Sloane to take notes. The minus: she's got a story for everything but the rape. Ask her anything about that night and she goes blank.

This whole time Sloane has been kind, and receptive. Conversational, even. And okay, yes, when Holly went to the bathroom, a little bit sly: she dumped the glass of wine Holly poured for her—along with the remainder of the bottle—in the sink. All of this has been for Holly's well-being, of course, and with the hope that Holly's narrative will also eventually work its way to the assault.

So far, though, Sloane's only been logging backstory: she now knows all the ins and outs of Match.com—mostly the outs—including Holly's blind date before the rape. If her description of Marc Denoon is even remotely accurate, the Match.com mismatch couldn't have attacked her, even if he was as tall and athletic as he claimed in his Web profile. Sloane will check him out, no doubt, and he won't be hard to find: Holly said he checked the "lives with roommates" box on the Web site questionnaire and, after a second beer and the buzzed assumption that Holly was interested, divulged that his roommates happen to be good old mom and pop.

In the strained family business department, Sloane's also got the scoop on Holly's complicated relationship with her older, wiser, financially stacked sister, Amanda. Always ahead of the curve, Amanda got into real estate right in front of the housing boom. When Holly was let go from her loan-processing position at Allied Mortgage, Amanda brought her on at Dutcher and Grey and, no doubt, gave her the shit leads. After six months Holly's sold a total of one property, and that was to her friend's cousin, who found the townhome himself.

"Anything you can tell me," Sloane says, calling Holly back into the room from her far-off, black stare. "The color of the vehicle. The route. The fare. The driver's name."

"Who remembers anything about a cab ride?" Said sleepy, not snotty.

"You have any coffee?" Sloane asks, figuring right about now, Holly's going to need something to keep her up, or to finish her off.

"I don't," she says, rising from the table, unsteady as she takes on the hostess role. "Did you get enough to eat? Do you want some more wine?" She tosses the last of the *arroz con grandules* in the takeout bag and Sloane is sorry to see it go. She's a little more sorry when Holly disappears into the kitchen and comes back with another cheap merlot.

"Let me help you," Sloane says, and because she will not leave without a good reason for showing up in the first place, she uncorks the wine, clears the dishes from the table, and spends the next fifteen minutes learning about an overly-involved conflict between Holly's insurance company and the broken dishwasher.

Cut to the two of them: side by side, Holly half-ass washing, Sloane re-rinsing, drying, reasking, "Holly, do you remember anything about the cab ride? Even a weird vibe? Sometimes I get that myself, you know? Like something's not right. Did you feel that way?"

"No," Holly says, draining the sink. "The driver talked fast and drove fast and took me where I wanted to go."

"The driver spoke to you? Do you remember what he said?"

"No. He was . . . I don't know. Black? Arab? He was on the phone the whole time. Talking in some other language. Jamaican, South African, I don't know."

Obviously not, Sloane thinks, since both those guys would be speaking English. Sloane makes a mental note to play down the cab ride, at least until she can figure out how to make sure Holly's ignorance will be judged separately from her innocence.

Sloane stows the silverware and asks, "Mind if we sit?" everything dry now but her hands. "I can't stay much longer." Sloane risks mentioning departure, as it could be Holly's easy segue to the front door, but then Holly pours them both some more merlot, and she's not going anywhere.

Once back at the table, and Sloane back at her notes, she says, "Okay. Cabbie takes you to the Continental."

"Yes. Well, to Rockstar Dogs first."

Sloane reroutes the direct line she drew from *Paramount Room* to *The Continental* and writes in *Rockstar,* resisting the urge to tear out the page and start over. If Holly changes her story one more time, Sloane's notes are going to look like they were going drink for drink, and Sloane doesn't even drink wine. Never red. Except in rare cases. Like this one. "Okay," she says, patient as ever. "Cabbie stops, waits while you get a hotdog?"

"No," Holly says. "I was still in the cab when my friend Jason texted me and asked me to meet him, so I said to forget it."

Sloane crosses out *Rockstar,* reroutes her line of questioning. "Forget the cab. You're at the Continental. To meet Jason. Who is . . . ?"

"Just a friend. I know him from U of I. He found me here after graduation—he was working at a florist, and saw my name on a delivery, isn't that crazy?"

Sloane scrawls a thick black question mark next to *Jason*? Writes *crazy.* "What's Jason's last name?"

"Delgado."

Sloane takes down the name, an addendum: *Hispanic?*

"I knew I had to go when I got his text," Holly says, "because he only drinks at the Continental if he's already obliterated. He loves to cause trouble when he's drunk."

"What kind of trouble?" Sloane glimpsing the chase again.

"You know what I mean. He's a flirt. He loves to dance. Girls, guys, whatever."

"And the other night? Did you dance with Jason?"

"He wasn't there. Drew told me Nate showed up and made him go home."

Sloane takes the new names down and asks, "Who is Nate?"

"Nate Savage. Jason's boyfriend? Nate changed his name though—his last name. I don't know what it used to be. I guess he had to because he already had a wife and kid and a medical practice out in the suburbs. Geneva, I think. The practice is why he changed it. People out there were pissed. But that was forever ago. Jason's been living with him for like, two years."

Sloane strikes lines through *Jason Delgado* and *Nate Savage*. "What about Drew?"

"Drew Hickenlooper. One of the bartenders I know." Holly grins, blue-tinged teeth; there's obviously a crush there, an unspoken reason she was high-tailing it to the bar. "Drew said it was pretty drama, when Nate showed up. I guess Jason was well into the Grey Goose, but it was Nate who made a scene. He always takes the Golden Globe."

"Tell me about the bar," Sloane says, circles *Drew,* lassos it to *The Continental*. "Crowded?"

"No. It was early."

"You said it was midnight."

"Early for the Continental."

"Did you talk to anyone other than Drew?"

"Just the tamale guy."

"Claudio?" Sloane knows the roving salesman, having pulled him over well past 2:00 A.M. on his scenester-bar route to confiscate a midnight-shift snack from his trunk.

"No," Holly says. "The fake guy. His tamales are shitty, right? So I only ate one and gave the rest to Drew."

Funny, Sloane thinks, she's had Julio's tamales and likes them better, but the debate is part of the guys' success, so she knows Holly is telling the truth. "Did you speak to anyone else, apart from Drew and Julio?"

"No. I just ate and took off."

"Why didn't you call a cab?"

"For sure I wanted to, but cabs are tough to find down there. And it's not like I haven't ever walked from there."

"Was anyone outside the bar, when you left?"

"I don't remember."

Sloane asks, "From Chicago Avenue, do you remember which street you took to get to Erie?"

"No."

"At some point you cut over to Erie, do you remember anything about that? Did you hear anyone, or get an idea anyone was around on the street? Hanging out on a porch, walking a dog, anything like that."

"I don't remember. I was just walking, and then, there he was . . ."

Holly goes for her merlot and Sloane, her camel leather coat. She retrieves her camera, scrolls to a long shot of all three vacants, hands the camera to Holly, and says, "You do remember these."

Holly looks at the picture, goes blank. "I don't."

"I believe this is where you were attacked," Sloane says, "and I can't search it legally until you confirm that fact."

"I really don't know."

Sloane watches Holly take a sip of wine and picks up her own glass, to share the aim, but the wine smells corked and when it hits her tongue she's sure the taste will stay with her for days. She thinks about showing Holly Heavy's six-pack of suspects, but fears the images will linger, sour and indefinite. So instead, she drinks the wine, puts her camera and notes aside, and says, "You know, this reminds me of a case I worked last year. A cabbie who was robbing passengers." Holly doesn't need to know the guy was also killing his rides, a quick shot in the head and an unceremonious drop-off on a random Lincoln Park corner. Sloane says, "Seven thousand cabs in this city and it takes us three weeks and two more robberies to get a description—and that's only because one of our victims was an off-duty cop who recognized the driver." And jumped out of the cab while it was still moving, thereby shooting himself in the leg, but Holly doesn't need to know that, either. "What does the copper remember?" Sloane asks.

No idea from Holly.

"Purple," Sloane says. "That's it; that's all a trained police officer, our only witness, could give us: he says the taxi's purple. Can I ask you, Holly: have you ever seen a purple cab?"

"I don't think so. No?"

"It's okay—I hadn't, either. I thought our witness must have been colorblind or nuts or at the very least, pressed into remembering something. But guess what? There are almost five hundred of those cabs. Licensed and operating. On these very streets."

Color Holly surprised.

"We caught the guy a day later," Sloane tells her. "You think it's because we found out his taxi was purple?"

Holly's answer is a no-brainer, and expected, and wrong. "Yes."

Sloane's response is planned. "It was maroon. The real reason we caught him? We believed our witness." That, and every cop in Twenty was out to get the bastard for trying to snuff out one of theirs, but no need to go on and on.

Holly clearly isn't getting the point; she squints at Sloane like she would the sun, her center of gravity now lost somewhere between the wine and the Valium.

"I'll believe you, Holly," Sloane says, since the point is beside itself. "Whatever you tell me. Because even something you think doesn't matter could be the thing that changes your case. Like the purple cab."

"It's just that I," she says, hands through her hair, brushing it away from her face, "I can't remember things in order."

"The order doesn't matter." Sloane says. "You could have a hundred-piece puzzle missing ninety-nine of its pieces; it's that one piece we're looking for."

Holly ties her hair in a knot. "I don't know where to start."

Yes, you do, Sloane thinks, victims always know it. It's the moment where life goes from normal to not. Like when they told Sloane's mother her tumor was malignant and inoperable. She wanted to go back; they all did.

Sloane says, "Tell it to me backwards." She's used this instruction in a number of homicide interrogations, to poke holes, but she's never used it this way. Not to find out the truth.

"From the end?" Holly asks, a spark there somewhere.

"Yes. From the moment you were attacked. What happened right before that?"

Holly pushes her wine glass away and props her elbows on the thin wood table, her eyes set on a space in front of her. She zones for a moment; then she looks at Sloane and says, "I was just walking. I had my phone out? I was texting Drew to say thanks for the drinks."

Sloane picks up her pen, turns to a new page in her notebook. "And before that."

YOU GET OUT OF work late. You always get out of work late, but that's because you're new, and you want to make a good impression. That, and you have to stay on top of things, because you'll never get your own accounts if you can't manage the current campaigns, let alone fine-tune the diplomacy required to navigate office politics.

Case in point: the creative executive calls your boss—who's basically the executive executive—"Aldous" behind his back. You haven't yet figured out how the nickname fits; as far as you can tell, he takes full advantage of this brave and bright and new and improved world. You've traced its origin to the boss's refusal to take on a nonprofit drug-awareness client, or because he's a registered Republican.

Either way, you would never call the man you work for anything without a Mr. in front of it. Even if it could score you points.

You're doing just fine, anyway; the boss seems to like you. He also has a bachelor's in art; at your interview, he declared your portfolio "Koonsian" and hired you on the spot. Since then, his complaints have been few and far between. Completely nitpicky, but few and far between.

You're near certain the CE likes you, too. In fact, he's already given you a side project: You're charged with scouting global Internet sites and compiling ad trends. You've already assembled quite a catalogue for this in your off-hours, and just today when the CE flipped through a couple of the couple hundred Web page reprints, he nicknamed you "JPEG."

By the time you get out of work, as late as it is, the rest of the Loop might as well be extinct. Monroe Street is empty. Your company's building, once strictly office space, stands lifeless save for a few winks of light left on some fifty floors up: little specs of hope for the residential reskinning project. You can't imagine actually living down here, in one of these luxury high-rises; a doorman and a lake view and an indoor pool. Of course you say you can't imagine, but right now you're still wrapping your head around the fact that you have your own place up north. Your own kitchen and bathroom and bedroom and all your stuff right where you want it: *home*.

Trash trapped in the building's curved corridor whips six ways at once, so you aren't completely surprised by the epic wind blowing around the corner from Wabash. It's probably the reason nobody's outside Miller's Pub, the usual place for a smoke break. You don't smoke, though you're starting to think it'd be a smart career move. It seems like all your new co-workers get a lot of work done in bars, and within fifteen feet of them. The CE smokes Parliaments.

It's okay. You're new. You'll get there. You're getting there.

You hold on to your hood as you cross under the El at Wabash, toward the Palmer House. There was never wind like this where you grew up; when you were young, the rolling farmland in southern Illinois saw its share of tornados, but those you saw coming. The tricky wind here steals your breath and, if you aren't careful, whatever else it wants—your umbrella or work papers—and always your hairstyle, if not your hat. You quickly learned the windblown look doesn't fly in the boardroom, so you now keep an emergency stash in your cubicle drawer: a wide-toothed comb, set of clips, cover-up, neutral lip gloss. For the weather and the wind and for your first professional position.

Professional. That's you! You know your parents are proud, even if they'd hoped you would find a job closer to home after graduating from Mac Murray. Your dad thought St. Louis, maybe. But Chicago, you said, it's the town for advertising. It's the second town for advertising, he corrected you, since New York City is the first. New York is too big, and too big a move, said Mom, even for you. Even for someone as smart as you. What about St. Louis?

You are sure this was the right choice, no matter their reservations. No matter the wind.

You keep moving, against Mother Nature's wishes, your bag worn safely cross-shoulder. A few more blocks to the Blue Line station and then you can take off all this weight; you can sit and crank your iPod and take a half-hour break from your to-do list, from yourself. Let your classical playlist reconstitute your brain: Vivaldi and Haydn and Bach restoring order after the barrage of buzzwords that'll keep you awake, along with the half dozen client profiles your boss asked you to mentally file, tonight. *Attention. Appeal. Impression.* Pianissimo. Adagio. Legato. You won't get to bed before midnight.

At the corner, you wonder if State Street looks this dreary all year: old storefronts, their signs as out of date as the stuff in the windows. Really, who shops at Rainbow Fashion? You decide you appreciate their truth in advertising, though: what you see is all you get. Up the way, Macy's displays its wares in twenty different windows with an attitude to befit Oak Street, but the brands are no better or different than whatever you'd find at any other big-box department store. You pay attention to these things because growing up, you only learned about advertising from TV commercials before dinner and during after-school shifts behind the counter at the Bushnell Drugstore, where you'd read *Teen*, next *Seventeen*, then *Cosmopolitan* between customers.

Now? All the advertising you can handle. All the time. And your job—your *profession*—is to find a more effective way to appeal to the masses. Well, right now your job is actually to make sure the boss has—and has looked at—the CE's pitch packages. But when it's your turn? Just take a block-long walk on State Street. It's going to be easy.

Before you go downstairs to the train, you ready your iPod: buds in your ears, playlist set and paused. That's because riding the El is similar to work: You have to act like you're doing your own thing, yet remain aware of what everyone else is up to. You turn your grandmother's wedding ring around.

A quick swipe of your transit card and you're through the turnstile. You skip steps and just—just—catch the northbound out to O'Hare. You feel kind of awkward for hustling when there's hardly anybody in the car, and those hardly anybodies look at you like you just brought a bad smell on board: a black guy with a fast-food bag, greasy at the bottom, which he retwists closed up top; a white guy who's untwisting the cord to his iPod. And in the far corner, a mother with her child: his head held to her chest, arms around him, rocking. At first he appears too old to be coddled that way, dapper in his school uniform, his oxford-clad feet tapping, staccato. But then he wiggles from her embrace and you see what she'd been covering: his black skin burned pink and white, set thick like the palms of his hands; fat streaks of smooth, old scarring on his face, forever unnatural, melted wax. Then he looks over. Even if his scars were invisible, you could tell by his endless black eyes that he's already seen too much.

You can imagine that whatever happened to him will never seem too far away.

You take a seat as a Hispanic guy gets on board, last minute, and sits on the opposite side of the car, other side of the doors. He puts his duffel bag between his legs, pulls his gray ball cap low on his forehead. He zips his coat over a work-shirt with a name patch, *JORGE*. He catches you watching him, so you hug your bag, turn on your iPod, half-close your eyes, and listen to Dvorak's Cello Concerto in B. You mean to mind your own business, and it should be easy; you became accustomed to this commute within days, your body learning the train's gait, its stop-and-go. But tonight your curiosity keeps you present. Aware. Thinking.

Your boss and the CE recently got into it over the efficacy of in-transit advertising. Your boss says it doesn't work, that the messages are lost to distraction. The CE says nonsense: The messages *are* the distraction. You wish you'd had an opinion.

You do a quick scan of the billboards running in repeat above the windows: easy banking, online courses, cable news. A transit map. An HPV awareness campaign. You close your eyes, a test. What do you remember?

A guy in a suit. Green lettering. A bank. Was it North-shore Community?

A girl, graduation cap, laptop. Too generic. Can't brand it.

Stop: The train pulls into North and Clybourn, the white

guy gets off. *Go:* The train jerks forward, righting itself on the rails.

You close your eyes again. Where were you? The bank, the school . . . then another guy, another suit. CNN? CNBC? You don't have cable. Forget it.

Next, the El map. That one you know.

Finally an everyman—wait, no—an everywoman? Short hair. Natural. Serious. Sick. Was it HIV or HPV?

You open your eyes, check the ads, score a two out of five. Either you're distracted, or the messages are ineffective.

Stop, go.

You try again. This time you sneak a look around the car. Close your eyes. Think. Remember: the black man, sitting, same side as you. It's a Wendy's bag he's guarding, wound up tight at the top. He wears a black nylon jogging suit: White Sox. White shoes. Whites of his eyes caught in the window's reflection. You knew when he was looking at you.

On the other side: that schoolboy. His oxfords, feet tapping. Navy pants. Uniform. Skin burned so badly. Eyes seeing through everything. Saw through you.

Stop, go.

The boy's mother: her young face turned down. Outgrown clothes. Grown-out cornrows. No way to keep people from staring at her son. Exhausting for her to stare back. And she's so, so sorry.

And Jorge, the Hispanic man who came in behind you: plain gray ball cap, striped work shirt. Thin black duffel bag, big enough for a change of clothes, though it's doubtful he's going anywhere past O'Hare. He's got to be on his way to work. Or home. *Home,* you think, and feel the smile on your lips.

You open your eyes, check your score. You call it four for four because Jorge is gone. You decide in-transit advertising would work just fine if the messages were as memorable as the passengers.

The concerto's third movement is just beginning when you reach your stop. You go.

It's ten o'clock when you get down to California Avenue, and the usual homeless guys are hanging around outside the station. By now they've stopped asking you for money, and simply say their hellos.

You walk south, toward home, and decide the wind isn't so bad up here; if you think about it, nothing's so bad up here. Might not be as white and sparkly as it is downtown, but you're starting to prefer a little diversity. You don't really understand why Logan Square still gets a bad rap, or why your co-workers call you a social pioneer—though you guess that's nicer than the CE's comment about you doing important fieldwork for the Herdez account. When you told your parents, and your dad did some recon, they acted like you were planning to live in public housing.

Your landlord didn't say anything when you brought your parents to see the place and told them they were in Bucktown. Technically they *were* in Bucktown, when you took them there for lunch.

Your landlord picked up on the parent situation quick and

was savvy enough to talk up the unit's proximity to the
Fourteenth District's police station. He didn't mention the
Fourteenth's ongoing preoccupation with stolen catalytic
converters, even though he rolled up in his clamorous, cat-
less Toyota.

The landlord also took one look at your mother, busy
working her rosary, and told her that the woman upstairs is a
sister. At this point you're pretty sure she's someone's sister,
though you're not sure she'd appreciate your Polish landlord's inappropriate reference to the color of her skin.

It's okay. You like your neighbor. And you like your landlord.

When you get to McLean you cross over California and
you're amazed by your timing: the concerto's final violin solo
section is swept up by the rest of the orchestra just as you pass
the empty lot that neighbors your building. You can't wait to
get inside, take off these uncomfortable heels, heat up the rest
of the pizza you ordered from Lucky Vito's late last night, and
get back to work. You are, after all, a professional.

You reach down into your cross-shouldered bag for the
house keys.

You anticipate the warmth of home, as the concerto's fi-
nale crescendos: cello and strings, B Major, triumphant.

Then you feel cold leather hands around your throat. The
buds are ripped from your ears. The shock steals your breath,
nothing at all like the wind.

You grip your keys so tight you're sure you've broken skin

and when you let them go, they hardly fall because you're on the ground, clawing at the concrete, your nails ripped right to skin as you're dragged away—away from home.

You can't understand what comes next, or why you think of St. Louis.

7

SLOANE HATES TO SLEEP. Since she's been with Eddie, she's tried to take advantage of his company: to curl up next to him and doze off while he watches ESPN or late-night talk. But most nights, no matter how exhausted she is, her restless mind won't let her off the hook: she frets and fights, her easiest dreams riddled with fear and confrontation.

Even in the natural process of waking, her guard is the first up; that's why her eyes are not yet open this morning before she's out of bed and answering her cell phone, first ring.

"Pearson," she says, pulling on her pants as she takes in the room: cool white daylight behind the blinds; digital clock trying for 5:00 A.M., and Eddie, sound asleep on his side of the queen-sized, a corpse.

"Pearson," she says again, at the same time she's aware enough to figure out the connection's dropped. She returns the blankets Eddie kicked off in his sleep while she checks the phone's display. It reads UNKNOWN but it has to be someone from the station, this time of day. Sloane curses the call, and the high-rise metal-framed building, and also the fact that Eddie's phone always works just fine and nobody from Twenty-four ever tries to get his ass out of bed.

Then Sloane curses again, because the disruption didn't trip a single wire in Eddie's system and she knows he wouldn't wake up if she beat the phone against his thick-framed head.

She finds one of his Hanes undershirts on the floor, smells the pits, pulls it on. She stops by the kitchen to start the coffeemaker manually, set up when she got home a few hours ago for an automatic 6:00 A.M. start. Then she takes her phone to the westernmost corner of the unit, by the big screen, because sometimes she gets reception there.

She's actually a little juiced, thinking the call could be an overnight lead, or—as bad as it sounds—another vic. Last night Holly gave her some good leads, but when it comes to prosecuting the suspect, the more victims, the potentially merrier.

Sloane checks the phone reception from the corner, then tries a higher angle, and another, based on the theory the phone works like a TV antenna. When six or eight different angles don't pan out, she shakes the damn thing; grease might not do the trick, but at least it's a little satisfying.

Shaking gets bars, and a voicemail alert.

While she waits on the message, Sloane opens the western-facing slat of blinds. No one is in the park below; the river sits curved around it, indifferent as ever; the first wave of traffic barely swells on the Ohio Street Bridge. Though the sky is still figuring out its game plan, Sloane would bet on a nice day.

Until she hears Carolyn's voice. "Sloane honey. It's your father. We're at the hospital." A pause. Too long a pause. "I'll . . . I'll call back."

Sloane doesn't know how much time passes before she finds herself, dead phone still at her ear, forehead flush against the floor-to-ceiling window, looking down. Way down.

But she does know that right then, every single thing she has ever been, or tried to be, is gone.

Sloane doesn't remember how she gets to the Pilot, or what streets she took to wind up driving south on 90/94. She didn't wake Eddie, didn't even leave a note; she just got in and drove, automatic.

She calls her dad's phone. Then Carolyn's. Back and forth. Again and again. A recording stating her call "has been forwarded" every time.

Fucking bitch, Carolyn, Sloane thinks. *What fucking hospital?* Sloane will find it and it will be too late and it won't be Carolyn's fault for not telling her where to go. Nothing is ever Carolyn's fault; she's a victim of circumstance. First time they met, Carolyn had just received a parking ticket—because of a poorly marked sign and bad weather and a surly officer and crime must be down, if the police have time to pick on her—pretty soon Sloane took the blame, just to shut her up. Carolyn will have plenty of people to blame this time, of course, starting with Sloane's dad.

Again, automatic: Sloane steps on the gas. Cuts off some traffic in the middle lane past Cermak.

Calls dispatch. Identifies herself; pulls some strings, figures out that James Pearson was taken from 4822 South Ellis Avenue—Carolyn's house—to University of Chicago Hospital. Nine-one-one for chest pains. 11:30 last night.

Fucking Carolyn. Why did she wait so long to call? Sloane's own chest feels hot, carbonated.

Automatic: Dials Area Five. Gets put through to Guzman's voicemail. Says she won't be in today. Says, "Family emergency."

Gets off at 56th Street. Takes a left, right, left, right, left, left, hits construction. Turns around. Leaves the Pilot on Cottage Grove, hazard lights.

Inside: flashes her star. Finds out James Pearson is in D Corridor. ICU.

Has trouble swallowing.

Goes to the corridor. Looks at every door tag. James Pearson is not there.

Does not freak out. Talks to the charge nurse. Finds out James Pearson has been moved: O Corridor. Other side of the hospital. Noncritical.

She swallows, angry now. Storms over to O, finds Carolyn

in the waiting room, filing her nails. Resists the urge to confront her. Moves on.

Finds the door tagged JAMES PEARSON. Doesn't hesitate.
Sees him: tubes, blood, gown, monitors, sweat, machines—

"Hi, Sloane." His voice is weak, his smile groggy.

Realizes calling him James Pearson doesn't distance her
at all anymore.

Says, "Dad," and finally loses it.

For a while she sits with him on the bed, head on his
shoulder, watching his chest rise and fall through her tears.
More than once he says, "Deputy." The same way he'd say,
"Don't cry." She doesn't say anything, because there have
been so many hospitals, and so many words, and not one of
them changed a thing.

Pretty soon after that Carolyn is there saying, "Deputy
honey," but it sounds more like "It's about time." And, "I've
been trying to call you. I called her, Jim."

He must feel Sloane go stiff because, for one, he's the only
one who calls her Deputy and two, no one calls him Jim. He
takes Sloane's hand, says, "It's okay, Dep. I'm fine." Knowing
Sloane is not. Letting go when she pulls away.

And knowing he's stuck there, tubes etcetera, when she
asks, "Excuse us, Dad?"

Sloane doesn't have to make sure Carolyn is following her
to the waiting room because she hears her just a step behind,
yammering on about something. Sloane tunes out most everything. Not *Jim*.

Just inside the waiting room there's a bank of couches and

Carolyn sits. Sloane doesn't. She doesn't quite know how to enter this discussion since her father's girlfriend is already well into her side of it.

". . . the doctor doesn't think it was a heart attack. Of course now Jim says it was just indigestion . . . very expensive indigestion . . ." Carolyn's eyes bounce and blink, like a doll's. Everything else about her is put together, though, and tasteful: specks of diamonds in her ears, a touch of makeup, a clutch purse, same blue as her heels. Same blue as her eyes. Even though it's only 6:00 A.M. and she's been here since midnight.

Sloane stands there wearing yesterday's pants and Eddie's T-shirt. She's pretty sure her shoes are a pair. She has no idea how her dad can love them both.

"I cooked a beef roast," Carolyn says, "with creamed spinach. Jim always jokes that I should serve cracked Lipitor in the pepper grinder . . ."

Sloane wants to jump at her, ask, *Then why the fuck do you cook it in the first place? If you know it's bad for him. If you know he's got a bad heart.* But it comes out like this: "Why didn't you call me right away?" She can't believe how nice she sounds.

Carolyn looks up at her, says, "Your dad didn't want you to worry." Her eyes fixed now, the truth.

God damn it, Sloane thinks, wanting to hate this woman, especially because she is telling the truth.

"He told me he would be okay and he asked me not to call you. I'm sorry, Sloane, but I wasn't going to start an argument. Those were his wishes." Carolyn has the perfect amount of difficulty saying this.

But then it's too easy: the way she sits back, crosses her legs, her petite pantsuit still wrinkle-free. She says, "You know what? Jim's okay. That's what's important."

It's that last *Jim* that's the capper.

"You don't know what's important," Sloane says, pacing now. "You've been with my dad for what, a year? You should have called me."

"I did call you," she says, so calm and so fucking reasonable.

"Six hours later."

"They were running tests. I wanted to have answers for you."

"The only answer you've given me so far is creamed spinach."

"The doctor still hasn't said why they're keeping him," Carolyn says, and Sloane expects her to get up or raise her voice or get pissed, but no, she stays even. She says, "I did call you, yes. I tried leaving messages. Reception is a problem here. Don't think I'm making excuses: I knew you'd be mad, but I also knew you'd understand. I love him, too, Sloane. I'd like for us to help each other."

"I don't need your help."

If Carolyn is hurt, she doesn't show it. Instead she moves over a little, presumably so Sloane can sit, calm down, whatever.

"I don't want to sit," Sloane says at just the same moment some kid, some six-year-old kid with no apparent supervisor, climbs up on the couch. He's dressed in helicopter pajamas and green rain boots and he uses his coat for a blanket; the space Carolyn made is his bed. He pays no mind to Sloane, just squeezes his eyes shut.

Sloane remembers being that kid. Used to the place. A regular.

His presence snaps the rest of the people here into Sloane's focus: over there, someone's mother. There, a worried wife. And someone's brother or father or friend, hands wringing. Across the way, a family of three is huddled; the fourth has been admitted. Others, too, all helpless, suspended in the gray-green antiseptic room, the white noise, the never-ending ridiculous narrative on television; the only other distraction the one window that overlooks the plain black parking lot four floors below.

And all these people are watching Sloane's shitty reaction to finding out the very news they hope for: that their loved one is okay.

Sloane says, "I'll go talk to the doctor."

THE CHARGE NURSE IN the O Corridor is Esmeralda, a thin, fresh-faced blonde at the top of her shift who took over the floor for what she calls a floater—an off-schedule resident on the last leg of his thirty-hour stretch. Unfortunately, she says, the sleep-deprived resident floated out of there right after accidentally deleting the entire corridor's updated online patient charts. This, says Esmeralda, means she has just been put in charge of a dyspeptic circus.

When Sloane asks about James Pearson, Esmeralda assumes a narrow hip-handed stance, checks her whiteboard, diagnoses him stable, and says that when her staff is stable also, she'll follow up.

Sloane would press the issue, but minutes before, while she stood waiting at the nurses' station, she had watched a hulky doctor try to Don-Juan his way into special treatment for an incoming patient. Esmeralda gave him the same floater story, and she didn't take a single one of his compliments. Sloane can't argue when the game is played straight. She thanks Esmeralda and gets out of the way.

Back in her dad's room, Sloane is unnerved by the fact that he's asleep; she hopes they've got him on Demerol or Seconal, something like that, to knock him out. Otherwise he'd stay awake, wouldn't he? Knowing Sloane is here? He told her he was okay. He wouldn't lie.

She tiptoes behind the bed and pulls his chart. His medications are listed, and these she knows: Lipitor, Vasotec, Lasix, potassium, nitroglycerin. Tests were ordered, and these are familiar, too: angiogram, electrocardiogram, cardiac catheterization. Some results are pending, others noted—and numbered, and coded, and charted: these might as well be written in Chinese.

Sloane is rereading the parts she understands when her dad coughs, and lickety split his chart is replaced, Sloane's face going for blank, a not-so-innocent kid caught. But then he falls silent again, and she rounds the bed, and finds her dad: out of it, his face spiritless, his thin skin freckled and old.

The sight of him steals her last nerve. How dare she spy on what's left of his privacy.

IN THE WAITING ROOM, Carolyn is half sleeping and half watching television, probably because the volume is cranked up so high, there isn't a person in O who can't hear it. The bass rumbles the bottom of the squawk box, and the commercials are all advertisements for blown speakers.

Sloane sits next to Carolyn. The boy in his helicopter pajamas has gone, hopefully home. Most of the others are gone, too, off to be visitors instead of worriers, or maybe down to the cafeteria for an egg sandwich, some juice.

Sloane's stomach catches up to that thought, and then turns. She hasn't eaten yet, and won't; not here, where ammonia and burned coffee and lilies are just as potent to the nose as urine and blood and shit, and none of them are any match for death, the smell of rot that is instinctually awful because it is inevitable.

Some doctor on TV is explaining men's hair transplants, and Sloane pulls her coat over her shoulders and shuts her eyes tight, like the kid who curled up here earlier. As sleep quickly tugs at her senses she wonders what guy is going to listen to his wife when she suggests he watch the really informative *Oprah* episode she TiVo'ed. Ridiculous.

Pretty soon Sloane's thoughts get mixed up; the TV audience sounds like they're in the waiting room, too, and one of the guests laughs like Ed McMahon. *A-hou-hou-hou!* She drifts, thoughts scattering, fleeting.

Then jerks awake, reaware, though confused now by how readily she can fall asleep here, all lights and noise and action. Same as when she was a kid.

Back then, when it was just Sloane and her dad, he'd tuck her in, a dark room; she'd lie there, breathing shallow, listening for Johnny Carson's or her dad's laugh, and for the new noises in whatever place they'd leased. She could always name the sounds of a home settling into its foundation: wood swelling from rising temps, beams compensating, pressured supports shifting. Like the giant plates under the earth. Natural. Necessary.

What was not natural or necessary was to lie there and be terrified that she'd still be awake when her dad fell asleep. He'd turn off the *Tonight Show* and then it would just be Sloane, trying so hard to stay awake in the quiet, afraid she'd miss something. Knowing that she already had.

Then they'd move. Every year, it seemed, she'd have a new place to get used to, and for that, a legitimate reason to stay up a little later. Maybe fall asleep on the couch, her dad at the other end, the TV turned down low, his laugh tempered. The two of them, there.

Ed McMahon laughing.

The house settling.

The audience laughing.

The two of them, never settling.

Her dad, laughing.

Sloane trying so hard: to settle; to fall asleep; to laugh, too.

A-hou-hou-hou!

THANKS, TOM. WE'LL GET to that nasty weather pattern in just a moment, but first: another overnight shooting in Humboldt Park leaves one dead. . . .

A-hou-hou-hou!

Despite the call to action from residents after the murder of young Elena Nunez, gang wars continue.

Thousands of microincisions are made in the bald scalp and the individual follicles are implanted . . .

And in Rogers Park, police this morning are investigating an attempted sexual assault . . .

Each follicular unit contains one to three hairs . . .

. . . Hispanic man of medium height, black hair . . .

You really can't tell the difference!

. . . left after she fought him off . . .

A-hou-hou-hou!

"Miss Pearson?"

"Yes—" Sloane says, her eyes opening to Esmeralda, and Carolyn behind her. Both trying on smiles.

"I just spoke with Dr. Lin. It seems your father needs to stay on his medication. Come with me?"

8

SLOANE DRIVES TO THE drug store on South Halsted by her dad's apartment to update his medications. She fills prescriptions for Coreg and Imdur, and refills Lipitor, Vasotec, and Lasix. She also picks up a bottle of aspirin, as Dr. Lin advised; a bottle of Excedrin; and a bottle of water.

Those last two are for her. Sloane's headache sits firm over her left eye. Esmeralda was helpful to a point, and stubborn from there on. Sure, Sloane asked a lot of questions, and when Esmeralda's answers weren't good enough, she had to get pushy. And yeah, when Esmeralda pushed back, her charge-nurse diplomacy easy to mistake for some inflated sense of authority, Sloane played trump, her star. It was the last thing she wanted to do, since it set them at odds for the duration, but at least it got her on the phone with Dr. Lin direct.

Sloane asked the doctor for the good news first. There wasn't much of it. Lin said the test results did not indicate that her dad suffered a heart attack, but that the one he had last year caused significant damage to his heart.

"So?"

"So now, he suffers from what's called peri-infarction angina."

"In English?"

"Basically, that means he has multivessel coronary disease."

"Surgery?"

"No. We can't bypass. Won't transplant."

"Why not?"

"When he arrived in the ER, his ejection fraction was down to 20 percent."

"What does that mean?"

"It's a measure of how much blood is passed through the heart with each beat. The number was simply too low."

"How do you fix that?"

"We don't. The muscle and vessels have been under extended stress for so long that at this point, the damage has been done. We can only compensate with medication, and apparently, he hasn't been diligent about taking his medication. He needs to take all of it. As prescribed. Consistently."

"He will now."

Back in the room, Esmeralda told them James would have

to stay overnight, to make sure his medications are correct and all systems are still go in the morning.

Out in the hallway, Sloane stood by when Esmeralda pulled Carolyn aside to reiterate the importance of James's medications, and also his diet, from now on.

At the elevator corridor, Sloane told Carolyn to lay off the cream sauce and, in so many words, to lay off, period. Said she'd handle it.

Now, in the drug store's Home Medical aisle, Sloane spends a good fifteen minutes shopping for a pill dispenser. She had no idea there'd be such a selection. She compares the various models based on simplicity, categorization, and capacity. She decides on a weekly organizer, and that she'll check in on her dad at least that often, to make sure he's got everything straight.

She's feeling pretty upbeat until she gets to her dad's apartment, where there's at least a week's worth of the *Sun-Times* piled up outside the door. She knew he'd been spending a lot of time with Carolyn, but she didn't think he had entirely abandoned his home.

It drives Sloane mad, this whole thing with Carolyn. Her dad has had other girlfriends, of course, but ever since this one came along, he's completely dummied up. And his business might as well be circling the drain, since he'd rather do odd jobs around Carolyn's overdone Hyde Park home than pick up the phone and bid on a paying project. *Funny,* Sloane thinks, since it all started when Carolyn hired him to renovate her bathroom.

Inside the apartment, it's cold; Sloane is glad she had a V-neck sweater in the backseat of the Pilot. More evidence of her dad's absence: enough mail stuck through the slot to signal an extended vacation; the fridge keeping nothing cold but moldy leftovers and bottled beer; the plant in the window brown-tinged, its soil dry and cracked; and the air, sitting stagnant, as sweet and stale as one of his cigars.

He won't be smoking those anymore.

One consolation, if only for its familiarity, is that the clutter remains: books, blueprints, paint chips, paint cans; drill bits, floor plans, saw blades, sawdust; dust. All of it ordered according to her dad's compulsive craftsmanship.

Sloane still knows the order. Cleaning was always her job.

She finds a garbage bag and makes the rounds in the kitchen and living room: She tosses the newspapers, the junk circulars, the spoiled food from the fridge, and a pair of soft, long-eyed potatoes left on the counter. The cigar stash fits nicely into the two empty spaces in the twelver of Bud, and she puts that by the door; she'll take it with her, for Eddie.

She moves the rest of the mail to the table, bills on top. Then, she puts books where they go and the tools where they go and the drill bits with the drill, etcetera, until all that's left out of order is the dust. She finds an old rag and the end of a bottle of Windex; not what she'd use all-purpose, but good enough for a quick wipedown.

There will be nothing quick about tackling the bathroom. It's hairy. The shower is brown underfoot, after so many post-job-site washes. There are three used-to-be bars of soap, all of them thinned out, stuck like caulk to the tub ledge. No soap at the sink: just dried-up toothpaste, more stubble. There's no way to clean in here, let alone get clean. No possible way. Best Sloane can do is to empty the wastebasket, collect the expired medication, and start a mental list: *Clorox. Comet. A scrub brush. Toilet paper. Bar soap. Help . . .*

The bedroom smells faintly of something cooked down in oil: an onion-slash-garlic-slash-pepper combination that after a few days just smells like oil and something else. An acceptable funk. Well, maybe not acceptable. Not familiar, either, since the only thing her dad ever cooked was Thursday night steak and eggs. Every Thursday of Sloane's young life they ate steak and eggs, just the two of them. They called it "Thursday Night Club." Even when she got her star and started midnights, they had a standing date: before her shift, they'd get together, steak and eggs.

Every Thursday night until the heart attack a little over a year ago.

Then things changed, namely, Sloane's insistence on her dad's healthier diet. He was right: The Club wasn't the same with Egg Beaters.

The covers on the bed are pulled up over the pillows. Given the condition of the rest of the place, Sloane's sure the sheets underneath haven't been washed since just after the last time she asked if they had been. She pulls the once-white cases off the pillows and balls up the pin-striped top sheet. It doesn't match the fitted sheet below from a plaid flannel set.

She kicks a day's heap of clothes out of the way, pulling

the tucked sheet out around the base of the mattress. The mismatched bedding isn't the only reason Sloane can't imagine Carolyn sleeping here. The woman would have a heart attack herself, this mess.

Or, she would overlook it. She would wind up caught in the moment, the passion, the rolling around. That must be how she got her peach-colored, high-waisted panties stuck between the sheets, down there where her feet were when she first tucked in. She was probably clothed when she got into bed, a nightgown, maybe, playing coy. Lord knows how she felt going home, all unwashed and pantiless in the morning.

Sloane nixes the laundry idea and decides Carolyn was on to something when she said they should help each other, because there is no way in hell Sloane is going to wash the woman's underwear.

She returns to the kitchen, moves the mail out of the way, and sits down to fill the pillbox, labeling the time tabs as she goes. She tries to stay focused: this pill at nine, that one at noon. The side effects for some of these drugs don't sound much better than the conditions they treat: chest pain, disorientation, fainting, fever, lightheadedness, nausea, severe dizziness, shortness of breath . . .

Sloane starts to feel a little lightheaded herself. It's probably from the caffeine in the Excedrin, making her jittery. She should eat, except that her appetite isn't much, being here alone.

She knows this is all part of the general progression of things, and that the emotions that come along with it are normal amidst the shift from parent caring for child to child caring for parent.

But what's really bothering her is a different shift: this one from parent and child caring for each other to the child caring too much about the parent and his vacuous girlfriend's relationship.

She tells herself she wasn't snooping. The guilt still hangs on, like her headache.

She takes a piece of junk mail addressed in fake swirly computer-handwriting to *Mr. James Pearson* and uses the back of the envelope to start a list.

Comet. Clorox. Scrub brush. Things her dad needs. That's why she's here. She wasn't snooping, and she certainly wasn't looking for Carolyn's panties.

Paper towels, toilet paper, toilet bowl cleaner. All things her dad needs. Why she's here. To help him.

Oatmeal. Tuna fish. Leafy greens. Walnuts. All things she remembers from the list Esmeralda gave Carolyn, though she knows her dad won't eat any of it. How many vegetables has Sloane dumped from his dinner plate over the years? Everything but the potatoes.

Cauliflower. Asparagus. Almonds. As she writes these things, she can see the ambivalent look on her dad's face; there's no one on earth who could get him to eat anything but the nuts. She's got to be kidding. Kidding herself, anyway.

She remembers Esmeralda telling Carolyn to focus on low-fat meals, so she turns over the envelope and tries to think of more subtle diet changes her dad might not mind:

Light ranch instead of regular. Reduced-fat cheddar. Diet Coke. Whole wheat bread. Brown rice. Rice milk. Her dad makes that face again. Rice milk? Right. She knows. He wouldn't be caught dead.

Then the reality reads plain, right there through the Capital One envelope's cellophane window: *Mr. James Pearson.*

In black and white, he is going to die.

He is just a man, after all; just another man with a low-low APR credit card offer and a weak heart they can't fix.

Looking at it, black and white, Sloane sees around herself: she sees that it's ridiculous to get bent about Carolyn and her peach briefs and her big fat dinners. Sees how silly it is to use her cop brain to snoop. To be pushy. To look for a culprit. Sees the futility in trying to make this a case when she should be making sure her dad has health insurance.

And knows that the problem is Mr. James Pearson. The man with the weak heart. His own culprit.

But looking at it, without the black and white? His heart is the only one Sloane's ever counted on. No good way around that.

Of course it's happening like this, she thinks, leaving everything in the apartment as is.

Leaving.

Because her dad always told her he could fix anything. *Anything,* he said, *but a broken heart.*

She puts on her duty belt and goes to work. She doesn't know what else to do.

9

SLOANE PLANS TO GET in and out of the station as fast as she can since Guzman is at lunch, Heavy is out on a domestic, and the half dozen dicks that are on the floor drop whatever they're doing as soon as they get a whiff of her.

The Amazing Mumford starts. "Look at Pearson, all hot and fashionably late. What, you have a spa appointment this morning?"

Sloane ties her hair and ignores him; she's so bored with the innuendos.

"I'll bet she got a wax," another detective says; doesn't matter which one.

She crosses the DMZ, knowing better than to entertain the guys' bullshit when they'll happily entertain each other, though she could say plenty about Mumford's muppet eye-brows.

"You know those Brazilian waxes?" another dick says. "Makes 'em look like little girls?"

"Don't tell me your wife tried that, Swoop." Mumford again. "You can't skin a moldy peach, can you?" Hardly amazing.

Sloane wonders if she should be miffed by the conversation, but it's so terribly unoriginal, it's not worth the energy. Smarter to tune the boys out, just like she does the televised sports announcers who provide running commentary at Eddie's: the big-suited, bigger mouthed men who yell at the camera and at each other as if they're actually in the game, their own glory days benched.

It's hot up here today, but she imagines where the conversation would go if she took off her sweater. She'd probably be the immediate champion of the Area Five wet T-shirt contest without a single drop of water. In the interest of keeping comments to a minimum, she decides to sweat.

She logs in to her computer, ready for some legwork. She starts by updating Holly's case on I-CLEAR via E-track, and then searching the databases for new assault cases: anything reported since she left yesterday. There are no hits.

Next, she runs the names of Holly's acquaintances: Jason Delgado, Nate/Nathan Savage, Drew/Andrew Hickenlooper, Marc/Marcus Denoon. No hits there, either, even after she spells Marc/Marcus with a *k* and runs Nate Savage statewide, and as an alias. She has to exhaust every exhausted possibility. Legwork. The Job.

She Googles "tamale guy, Chicago" to find Claudio and Julio's last names. She clicks through to a *Chi-Town Daily News* article, gets their names and calculates their ages, and runs them through CODIS, too. She's glad when neither of them hit, since she likes them and they're some of the best bar eyes and ears from here to the Hideout. She makes a note to follow up with Julio, assuming Holly got her tamales right.

After hitting and missing all Holly's angles, Sloane switches gears and checks the Meyer-Davis file for progress, to see if Heavy got to her this morning, before his domestic. Since Sloane can't seem to be in the same place as her partner lately, the online report will have to do.

It doesn't do much. The file indicates a change this morning, which is promising, but when Sloane scrolls through, it seems all that's been updated is the time. The rest is background Sloane already knows. She reads it anyway, hoping something will come into focus through the new, though narrow, lens Holly provided last night.

On page one she skips through the narrative: Claire Meyer-Davis used to live South Side, has since moved Near West; she used to work for H&R Block at 50 East Monroe, and now works for an H&R Block at 56 West Madison. After hours most nights she's at the East Bank Club or the West Town Tavern, the latter being the place where she'd been throwing back Stellas and beer cheese with a co-worker,

Rebecca Pleasant, just prior to the assault. *Note: victim re-fuses Det.'s request to contact Pleasant.*

Posttavern, Meyer-Davis took the train one stop south to Grand/Milwaukee and walked, as always, toward her home on Hubbard Street. When she turned south from Grand onto . . .

Page two, narrative: . . . Sangamon, she noticed a man she thought was a maintenance worker as he was Hispanic and dressed in a light-colored striped work shirt with a name patch. She did not see the name on the patch or remember any other details about the man.

A half block down Sangamon the victim was attacked from behind and pulled into a vacant house, held facedown, and sexually assaulted. She never saw the man's face and she didn't so much as squirm when he asked her to fight him. When he was finished, he suffocated her until she was un-conscious. Or at least he thought she was unconscious. He didn't know about all the Vinyasa flow yoga she'd been tak-ing at East Bank in order to reduce stress, or how good she'd become at controlling her breath. So she held on—she called it *wakefulness*—and waited for him to leave; then crawled to the window, and saw him drive off . . .

Page three: . . . in a light-colored Chevy Impala. She did not see the man get into the car.

After that, Claire Meyer-Davis went home and decided to meditate over the whole thing for a few days.

Sloane rereads the part about the attack, but there isn't

anything specific enough to jot down, take with her. Writing the narrative light is supposed to be a good thing, so when victims are asked the same question sixty-two ways, they have a limited number of inked details to memorize. It's so screwed, Sloane thinks, that a sexual predator can walk because the victim says he grabbed her with one hand in the report, and the other on the stand.

Meyer-Davis will probably never take the stand. Thanks to her delay in reporting the assault, the builders covered her attacker's tracks at the development on Sangamon and there was never any scene evidence in the case. And, because Meyer-Davis reported the assault before it was a known serial, the rape kit didn't get a rush—not that anyone expected solid physical evidence after so many days, so many showers, and liberally applied essential oils. "For healing," Meyer-Davis explained. Sloane thought about explaining, in nicer terms of course, that the oovy-groovy bit would be about as easy to sell to the SA as a hundred-dollar box of shit, but Heavy wouldn't let her. She didn't argue; she didn't figure Meyer-Davis would ever see court.

Now that it's serial, though, Heavy might be able to get somewhere: With luck, Meyer-Davis's kit results might get moved up and the DNA results will come through in a few months. At that point he'll have to refind Meyer-Davis and reconvince her to press charges. Given her current reluctance, and Heavy's soft approach, getting her to rally is, at best, a long shot.

Sloane exits the file; right now, rally or not, it looks like all that Sloane can prove Claire Meyer-Davis has in common with Holly Dutcher is a night she'd like to forget.

Sloane quick-checks the evidence status in her case before she logs off. Nothing's been processed. She should go find Sue Burkhart, butter her bread with a check for the Girl Scouts, remind her about the rush. But Sloane's itching to get out on the street, to work, to maybe talk to Holly again now that she's slept off the pills and booze. To get a better story, backward or forward.

Something's still tugging at her, though, keeping her at the desk. Something she overlooked. Or didn't give herself the chance to look at. She returns to Holly's online file, her own notes. She hates the fact that most of what she got from Holly last night simply proves that Stagliano's take was correct: Holly's not that bright. She might be an easy one to keep, but she'll be a tough one to keep from getting quickly lanced by Everman, or whichever SA jumps on the case for a swift shutdown.

Sloane circles "Marc Denoon" again. He's certainly the strongest possibility. The whole Match.com connection bothers her a little, too—Holly pitched the site as a place to meet two kinds of people: liars and cheaters. Sloane makes a note to stop by Denoon's parents' place up in Sauganash. Won't they be thrilled.

She hits the Google tab again, a trick Heavy taught her to get an outside line on the city. She can hear Heavy saying, like he always does, *just for shits and Googles!* Incredible: He hasn't told a decent joke since they met. Then again, she appreciates that; she'll take his cheese over all the other coppers' dirty laundry and toilet mouths any day.

When Google comes up Sloane types "recent assaults Chicago." Top of the list, a headline: ROGERS PARK: MAN SOUGHT IN ATTEMPTED SEXUAL ASSAULT :: SUN-TIMES :: NEWS.

Of course: what had been tugging at Sloane was the subconscious replay of the TV clip she heard when she was half asleep in the hospital waiting room. She double-clicks the story.

The article is as thin as what little she remembers: an unknown suspect, said to be Hispanic, medium height. Attacked an unnamed woman at an unnamed location at 8:00 P.M. last night. Nobody in custody. Last line says "Area Three detectives are investigating." They always say that when detectives have no comment.

The staff writer is Kurt Lutz; Sloane puts a call in to him at the paper, says she's an Area Five detective, leaves her number. She'll get more from him than she will from the Area Three dicks; she's got kind of a rep up there, on account of Zookie Truman.

She wonders how the story hit the AP; she doesn't think the Area Three guys would go out to the press with a one-on-one. Could have been some presstitute hanging around when the cops caught the case. Or, the vic might've gone to the paper instead of the police. *It's parasitic,* Sloane thinks, the way the media works these days: civilians so connected, the news a twenty-four-hour reality show.

Since the show must go on, news is made—by the bad guys, of course. In lieu of bad guys, there are the ones who can't catch them: the overworked, undertrained, corrupt, and stupid police, caught on camera, vilified for ratings. The people eat this up, and Channel Two gets a breaking story before the detective gets the damn assignment. It's no wonder cops get a bad rap these days.

"So, Pearson," says a voice from behind her. It's Mumford. "Are you smooth, down there? The boys and me, we have a bet going."

It's no wonder, the bad rap, Sloane thinks, the raw urge to turn around and knee Mumford in the balls tamped by her rational brain, still reeling. That, and the fact that physically hurting him would only satisfy her temporarily. If she's ever going to get Mumford, she's going to get him for good.

"You know, Mumford," she says, and leaves it there.

"Yeah?"

Sloane logs off her computer, gets up, and tucks the files into her bag. Then she takes her hair down as she turns toward him, avoiding eye contact right up until she says, "Being an asshole probably ruins your chances of ever finding out."

She walks past him, and by the look on the other dicks' faces, Mumford doesn't up his bet.

10

SLOANE TAKES GRAND AVENUE toward Holly's place. On AM 780, they're saying traffic sucks, which is no surprise at 4:00 P.M. They're also saying it might snow. That shouldn't be a surprise, either; the weather always plays games in April.

As she drives by Smith Park she spots an unmarked pulled up on a sidewalk next to the fieldhouse. She's already past the building by the time she wonders whether the other copper is crawling or parked—as in patrolling, or doing a whole lot of nothing—though the fact that he's there at all probably means he's on twink-watch. She and Heavy chased a group of teenaged boys out of Humboldt Park last week, so now the surrounding parks are potential problems: whenever there's any kind of john/johnny roundup, the kids disperse. They aren't ever hard to find, of course: the johns just take a different route, through a different park, a secret eye out for a quick, cheap fuck—a pit stop before going home to the missus.

It isn't hard for the police to find the kids, either; it's just that there are only so many cops. And so many more bad guys: bangers, burglars, petty thieves, parolees; drug runners, pimps, con men, mob men, crack dealers, kingpins, killers—serial rapists.

Makes chasing a kid seem like a parent's job.

It was tough for Sloane last week, arresting one of the twinks in Humboldt. Fifteen years old, and a tough fifteen: foul mouth, permanent scowl, but gorgeous, slender and soft-haired; the child still there, however feral, in his cold-weathered cheeks.

When Sloane found him he was wet-kneed and wild, mad at her for busting things up, disrupting the flow of considerable cash to his pocket. What was worse —what was so much worse than being called every kind of whore by the kid as he wrestled with his cuffs—was watching the men who trolled past, while he fought. They were fearless, driving slow, gaping at the kid and at Sloane, too: tonight's wet dream.

The very worst part? Sloane knew that when the kid was processed and kicked back to the street, he'd be taking a ride with one of those men. Same scowl, though his adolescent complaints would be silenced for a very grown-up twenty-dollar job.

Last week's park sweep was totally different from Sloane's experience in Twenty, where all the tricks were consenting adults, their chance encounters and one-night stands keeping each other entertained and out of circulation. And, if they weren't consenting, well, they were about to be rightly fucked by the law.

Sloane waits to turn left on Western Avenue, the fat gray sky in front of her. *Snow would be good,* she thinks; a few inches tonight would chase people inside for days. Sure, there'd be an increase in domestics—relatives and unhappy couples finding themselves all cooped up and incompatible— but beat cops would handle those cases, at the start. And Sloane would use this time for some added up-front work on Holly's case; she'd certainly get to the domestics, statistically destined to repeat, before the weather turned again.

She floors it, turning hard through the intersection, and for a second she thinks it's a second too late when an oncoming car slips around a stopped bus and nearly T-bones the Pilot.

She keeps on, her nerves stunned and reset—like they've been defibrillated. City driving is like that. You hesitate, you lose.

Timing, she thinks. It makes her wonder how Heavy's handling his end of the case. If he is. It drives her nuts, his ass-dragging. Every cop she's ever met, from street to superintendent, knows that the one reason they lose leads, suspects, arrests, and cases is the same reason everybody loses, eventually: time. Time changes everything and everyone, whether it's a split-second left turn, or a yearlong shot at a relationship.

At 4:15, Sloane parks the Pilot a block south of Holly's. She leaves everything in the car but her keys; no need for the vic to know any more than she needs to about her detective friend.

Sloane walks up the street, hands in her pockets, the brisk wind noticeably cold. She didn't call ahead; claiming she just happened to be in the neighborhood for an impromptu wellness check would wind up *being* the wellness check, and cancel any reason to stop by. Besides, stopping by, asking the same things over again, is the point.

Not calling also prevents the chance of Sloane getting Holly's voice mail and having to choose between leaving an open-ended message or hanging up, both choices leaving the ball right in the middle of the court. There are only so many times Sloane can give Holly options before she opts out.

Unfortunately, not calling also means Sloane has no idea whether Holly is actually home, so when she gets to the building and all the lights are out, she's disappointed, but so it goes. She knocks once. There's no answer. She leaves it at that; she's got a few other things she can do before it gets too late to explain to Guzman why she was working off-duty.

Minutes later and blocks over, Sloane parks on California Avenue across from the Continental. It's a corner tavern on the nicest edge of East Garfield Park; the area used to be pretty bad until the real estate boom chased gangsters west, and the following bust turned it into a ghost town. Now a bunch of stalled developments sit waiting, from here to Division Street, for the next boom. Last month, Sloane looked at one of the unfinished buildings a few blocks north of here. She thought the units were well built, the pricing reasonable, the move-in add-ons a nice touch. Then she checked the block's gang stats and knew she'd be on duty 24/7.

Sloane chews a random half stick of Wrigley's Spearmint she finds in her purse while she looks for her mascara and lipstick, figuring she should get decent for Drew Hickenlooper. Then she checks herself in the Pilot's rearview, decides makeup isn't going to cut it. She hasn't changed clothes, and after a day like today, she'd have a better chance blending in behind bars at Twenty-sixth and Cal.

Anyway, the .22 is the only thing she really needs to get with Drew, no matter what kind of girl he's into. She straps on her ankle holster and unties her hair and hopes this isn't another waste of time.

Just inside the Continental's door she hesitates: *Oh Jesus,* she thinks, if that's Drew behind the bar she wishes she had her star and her .38: he's a good six-four, covered in black tats, neck to knuckles. Black trucker cap, black-on-black clothes; pale skin, a red beard long enough to nickname. He's lining up shot glasses along the rail, his face fixed with all-around distrust, like every time someone comes in they're testing him. Again.

He looks over, Aryan-blue eyes. Says, "ID."

The pissy way he says it makes Sloane want to spit her gum on the floor and turn around and walk out. There's not a single other body in the place and he could well be the reason.

He could also be Drew. Since the attitude she's getting doesn't promise a long-term relationship, she walks up to the bar and cuts to it. "You Drew?"

His response is a cracked-tooth smile. "I said ID."

She isn't sure if that's a yes or a no, but she's the first one to respect rules, so she hands him her license. He pinches it between his fingers and walks around the near end of the bar, back toward the entrance.

"Where are you going?" she asks, thinking by his aggro stride, he's pegged her as a cop, and is on his way to escort her out the front door.

Instead he inserts the ID into a compact scanner.

"What's that?" she asks, though she knows.

"Insurance," he says, over his shoulder.

"A copy?" She tries to sound impressed, act like a spectator, as she gets a closer look at the model: it's a Z22, pretty common.

When the scanner reads Sloane's license and kicks it back, the guy hands it over and returns to his place behind the bar. Apparently he'll let that be his answer.

Sloane knows places that serve booze can do this with IDs—even back in ninety-seven, when she worked a Near West Side beat in Twelve, she collared more than one kid after local club bouncers chased off underagers who chickened out as soon as they realized their fake IDs were going to be copied. Sloane still can't believe a private business can legally keep a record of a clean civilian ID, but the fact that it's also legal for her, as a city employee, to enter a licensed business and search for the place's cocktail onions if she wanted to, seems equally intrusive.

She hasn't seen a scanner in a long time and figures it's a precaution for the bar, or a deterrent for the shadier side of the neighborhood. Either way, she'll be taking copies of whatever the machine kept last night.

After she warms up to Drew. Assuming this is Drew, and that Drew has any interest in helping her, since his customers aren't going to be too regular if they're attacked leaving the place.

Sloane takes the best seat at the bar; a guitar and drums speed metallic over the bar's speakers, and she can hardly hear him when he speaks.

"What can I get you." A statement.

"Coke, please."

"You lost?"

"Just thirsty."

He does a one-eighty to where the Collins glasses are set up, takes one: ice, Coke.

"Thanks," she says.

This time he's just shy of one-eighty as he makes for the back bar's iPod and occupies himself with his music library.

Sloane takes her Coke and decides it's enough to be here, for now. She'd like to take off her coat, get comfortable, but she's still wearing Eddie's pit-stained T-shirt; for a minute she thinks it might be the perfect attire for this place. She leaves her coat on, anyway, and spins in the red naugehydecovered stool to case the place. The theme is a hybrid, for sure, though she's not sure what's crossed with what. A second-hand shop and a soft-porn movie set? A furniture showroom's 50 percent-off sale and a bourbon ad? It's coated with cool—but not the nostalgic kind, or because of the local color. It's credit-line cool, like someone walked in with a high-limit AmEx and decorated it in a day.

The music is another story, and it has just become faster, and angrier, and really fucking loud.

Sloane spins back around, finds the bartender underneath the flat-screen TV where skateboarders are negotiating a half-pipe. He stands there, arms crossed, head moving in a U with the skaters, like there are no speed-metal drums or a singer's beast-roar doing his best to bust eardrums. Is he deaf? Stupid?

Or trying to chase her.

Sloane had hoped, Drew or not—and prick or not—that she wouldn't have to press this guy; that he'd tell her if he remembered anything out of the ordinary last night. A patron he didn't recognize, or one who gave him a bad vibe. What the guy drank. Who he talked to, how he paid. Who he left with.

Nope. Instead she gets Hatebreed. She gets a song called "Destroy Everything," a guy screaming: "Even an empty threat/deserves a response you won't soon forget," a lyric that might not be decipherable, had a person no hardcore exposure. She still can't find a way to thank Eddie for that.

"Drew," she says, about four times, and she's pissed now, enough so that by the time she says it loud enough for him to turn around, she's got her star in his face.

"Drew isn't here," he says.

"I don't give a shit." Sloane angles her star at the scanner. "I want the pictures from that machine."

11

SLOANE SITS IN THE Pilot across the street from the Continental with the scanned IDs and dinner from Feed, the joint next door. She ordered a half chicken, some black-eyed peas, and fries for takeout. She thought she was hungry.

The chicken's okay, but admittedly she lost her appetite while she was waiting for the meal. When Eddie called. She didn't answer, but she listened to his message as soon as he left it. He just wanted to know when she'd be home. If she was cooking. There was no worry in his voice. No *Where have you been?* No doubt.

If she doesn't call him back, she's pretty sure he'll assume she's working late again, and be just fine with reheated Reza's and leftover shows on TiVo. If she does call, her own voice will crack when he asks how she is and she lies, "fine." She'll want to scream at him through the phone when he is completely imperceptive, when he doesn't wonder where she disappeared to this morning, when he doesn't know about her dad. When he doesn't ask.

She won't call. She just can't go through it.

She closes the warm, steamed-wet foam containers and dumps everything but the fries into the trash can on the corner. Then gets back in the car, wipes her hands, and goes through the IDs once more, all the while keeping tabs on the Continental.

She wouldn't stay in the bar: that's what she promised the bartender who was not, as it turned out, Drew Hickenlooper. Nor was he too bright. Called himself Bug; when Sloane checked his driver's license she decided he wasn't as menacing as he'd have liked. His name: Bernard Drupe: a not so big, not so bad twenty-three-year-old with a nice North Side address that would certainly ruin his hard-shelled image.

Bug went a few rounds of dumb with Sloane: he wasn't there on Monday night, he didn't know how to get photocopies from "the fuckin' thing"; he couldn't tell her how to get in touch with "the fuckin' manager." Sloane might have gone another round or two with him—he seemed crackable—but she couldn't stand the music. She made him turn it down and it still sounded like guitar sacrifice. When the screaming started again, Sloane was finished: she wielded her phone—a weapon—and told Bug she'd shut the place down while she waited for her team of forensic technologists to show up and dismantle the whole fuckin' operation.

Bug didn't like that idea.

Sloane told him she didn't like it, either, since there was no telling when the tech geeks would arrive. Could be an hour, she said; could be all night. Unless Bug had a decent takeout menu, better music, and maybe some playing cards, she warned that she might not be much fun.

Bug didn't like any part of that.

She knew he wouldn't. Lucky for him, she said, there was a second option: he could let her get at the fuckin' thing, which, she told him, is technically called the Z22 Counter ID Scanner, and is surprisingly easy to use. She also said that since he didn't know how to use it, and that he couldn't find his fuckin' manager, that he'd be smart to step aside and let her take what she needed. She promised to leave just as soon as she was through.

Bug didn't really like that option, either, but by that time, the clock read five minutes to happy hour, so he told her to go ahead—and to hurry up.

It wouldn't take too long, so she took her time.

While she waited for the evidence—every ID scanned on Monday night, only twenty-four of them, total—she asked Bug a few questions. Actually, the same question over:

"Is Drew working tonight?"

"What do you want with Drew?"

"That's his business. Is he working? Tonight?"

"I don't know who you mean."

"Come on, Bug. Drew Hickenlooper. Working. Tonight."

"Hickenlooper?"

"He's not in trouble. This is about a customer of his. Telling me if Drew will be here tonight doesn't make you a rat."

"I'm Bug." He said this with perfectly equal parts conviction and desperation, and Sloane couldn't decide if he really was dumb, or was really good at playing.

Then he asked, "Are you finished?" about the scanner, just as she took the last copy, and Sloane decided he might not be bright, but he was no dummy. He wasn't going to speak for anyone else, and he didn't have to. He wasn't a suspect. He was just Bug.

"Thank you," she said, and left her card on the bar. "If you see Drew, tell him I'm looking for him."

"I think you got the wrong person."

"I know you do."

Now, sitting in the Pilot with the scanned IDs, Sloane feels like the dumb one. She's got no chance with Drew, since Bug probably fired a warning shot as soon as the door hit Sloane in the ass. She's got nothing from Heavy, or the Meyer-Davis case. She does have twenty-four pieces of evidence for Holly's side of the story, but she's got nothing more on the suspect than the *Sun-Times* does.

She goes through the IDs one more time. There's Holly's license, of course, and her gay pals Jason Delgado's and Nate Savage's—both white-smiled and white-skinned enough to put them on the farthest end of the would-be-Hispanic rapist spectrum.

Then there were twenty-one. Twenty-one other patrons recorded Monday night; minus the women, eight left. Eight men, all of them either more Bug than bad guy, or more likely to be after each other than to go after Holly.

Sloane files the men's photos—she'll run them through I-CLEAR tomorrow.

She tries Heavy again, and when she gets his voicemail realizes it's after hours, and he's the one who should be annoyed now. When it gets to the beep she says, "Hey, Russ," and is surprised at herself, her formal address. "Sorry." She doesn't know where this comes from, either, but she says, "I didn't see you today, and I thought I should tell you. About my dad. Call me when you have a minute." She hangs up, just as stunned as she was this morning, when Carolyn left her a voicemail.

Sloane has never felt so overwhelmed, the way things keep moving: fast-forward, relentless, and all toward busting apart. Without work, she doesn't know what to do.

What can she do?

There's really no reason to sit out here; so far, only four people have gone into the bar and none of them had potential. First came a threesome of thirsty-looking suits, their ties loose, tongues about to be; next, a young, way-tall slender woman whose black-and-white striped, long sleeves and boy haircut only made her look taller and skinnier.

Watching that girl, all limbs and style, makes Sloane self-conscious: she's not getting any younger. Or taller. And she probably shouldn't eat the rest of the fries.

She sits there and eats them anyway.

JUST AFTER SEVEN, SLOANE is looking for parking outside Eddie's on Kingsbury. She thought about going to the Paramount Room, the place where Holly had her blind date, but she couldn't snap back after the call to Heavy. Guzman wouldn't let her hear the end of it if he found out she'd been working after hours, and anyway, she doesn't have much to go on.

She's exhausted. She needs a shower. A place she knows and familiar noise. And she needs to try to get some sleep.

Of course she can't find a parking spot anywhere near Eddie's. She goes in circles for a half hour before she gets a meter four long blocks away on Kinzie, by the Merchandise Mart. It's the last place she'd choose, since she'll have to move by 6:00 A.M., but she just can't go around again.

She plugs the meter until 9:00 P.M. and walks by the East Bank Club, where Meyer-Davis gets her Zen. As she passes the entrance, she sidesteps all sorts of people who are coming and going in workout gear, none of them looking particularly thrilled either way. Maybe because the smell of the rich dark chocolate that Blommer's Factory cranks out across the river is heavy on the wind, a tease. Or maybe because all these people go from sitting in a car to sitting at a desk to sitting in a car again until finally, the gym, where they don't even notice the near sickening chocolaty air because it was so hard to find parking and now they have to hustle for the treadmill or stair climber or spin class, creatures of habit.

Sloane's glad her only habits are bad ones.

As she crosses Grand Avenue, the wind whipping through its corridor from the river, her phone vibrates, coat pocket, and the UNKNOWN display sends a surge of fear straight through her. *Dad?* Her hands are already sweating when she answers.

"Hello?"

"Is this Sloane?"

It is. She thinks she says *it is*.

"Hello? Is this Detective Sloane Pearson?"

"Just tell me."

"Uhh, okay? This is Kurt Lutz. *Sun-Times?*"

Sloane's exhale nearly brings her to her knees. "Kurt."

"Uhh, yeah. I'm returning your call?"

"Where are you?"

"Just leaving my office."

"You wrote up the Rogers Park rape, right?"

"I did."

"Who's the lead dick?"

"I'm sorry but you probably know I can't reveal my sources."

Sloane turns around, heads back to the Pilot. She says, "You lie to your friends, I'll lie to mine, but let's not bullshit each other. Meet me?"

"Why?"

"I think this thing is serial."

"I'll get a cab. Where to?"

12

SLOANE THOUGHT ABOUT MEETING Kurt Lutz at the Paramount Room: kill two birds, all that, but she decided it would be better to pick a place on his beat. She wonders if he'll think it's strange that the address she gave him is in Rogers Park, and is not a bar or coffee shop, or even a building; 1050 West Pratt is, in fact, a beach. It isn't exactly beach weather.

She drives up Lake Shore, curls around Loyola's campus past her dad's old apartment on Sheridan, and turns right on Pratt. *God,* she thinks, *it's been a while.* She hasn't been this far north since before she left Area Three. Not intentionally, anyway. Not since Hook broke his ankle and broke her heart and left.

Kurt said he had to stop home, his dog, so Sloane arrives first. She zips up and gets out of the Pilot. The wind is immediate, but different up here: mild. Longer. She walks across the cul-de-sac and onto the sand, boots sinking, toward the water. The moon is low, almost full, and bright enough for her to see the entire beach. It hasn't changed much, not that a beach does; through the tides and the weather and men's plans, it remains. *Like a memory,* Sloane thinks. Hers swelling here.

Hook.

Sloane had been spending the better part of six months crashing on her dad's couch a few blocks south, saving money during officer training and using the space to study and sleep; her dad was working on an extensive renovation in Wilmette, and rarely home.

One Friday night, she couldn't sleep—surprise—but this time she was stressed about a big test on Monday. She was stir-crazy; she'd spent all day in self-imposed exile studying, and cooking and cleaning while she studied.

By the time her dad arrived, late, she was totally wound. She served the pot roast and sat down across from him, so glad for someone to talk to instead of herself; she'd recited over half her study guide by the time she realized he wasn't listening, or eating.

Panicked, she fired a line of questions: *What's wrong? Are you okay? Are you sick?*

She doesn't remember him answering. She only remembers him asking for a beer.

Immediately, she knew: his mouth, slow. Eyes, pink-rimmed. He'd already had a few.

And balls enough to come home with a good buzz. Push away his plate. After she'd been in the kitchen half the day. Fucking pot roast from scratch. Fucking clutter everywhere. Not fair: it was Friday night. She was twenty-one. She should be the one going out for beers. She should be the one with a life.

She doesn't know what of any of that she actually said, but the only thing her dad said, when she was done, was *Go.*

She went.

Her first mistake was a ten o'clock show at the Village North, a theater that ran oldish movies. On the ticket guy's recommendation, she saw *The City of Lost Children.* He didn't tell her it was subtitled. Or that it was about someone trying to steal kids' dreams and winding up with nightmares. For some-one who had looked for her share of lost children and hated to sleep in the first place, it wasn't exactly entertainment.

Her next mistake was a turkey-and-cheese from the White Hen. She took one bite and thought the mayonnaise wasn't right; she spit the second bite in the trash can on the corner of Sheridan and Pratt just as a group of Loyola students passed by, three guys and a girl, all either completely wasted or terrible cheerleaders, their arms up over their heads, wait-ing for his or his or his or her turn to yell, *The Oooo!*

Two doors up, Sloane figured out what they were on about: the Oasis, a storefront bar. After the spirit team went inside, she walked by, looked in the window: the place was dead, save for a string of big guys, sports types, along the bar. The guy on the far end was really good looking. And caught her looking. Mistake number three.

Sloane kept walking; she went all the way to the Evanston border. Past it.

By the time she walked back past the Oasis, the windows steamed by the packed-in crowd, she couldn't see inside. And thinking of her dad, she got the balls. Went in for a beer.

Two sips in, she saw him. This time, she caught him looking. Her beer was gone by the time he came over, introduced himself: Hook.

Hook?

Yep. Last week they called him Captain. Before that? Pirate. Worst was Beach Boy. Then there was Yay-go, Diego, Cali. California.

And now Hook?

He said Sloane could call him whatever she wanted.

She told him she'd like to be called *Nice meeting you, goodbye*. But she smiled when she said it. She wished she wasn't interested.

He said his name was Wes Oropeza.

They were pleased to meet.

He was in the middle of Northwestern's football tryouts. He was a transfer student; a sophomore on scholarship. Hoping to get a cornerback position. Hoping he could make the team, be done playing designated driver. Really hoping he could get on the team so he could afford to go to Northwestern, because he wanted to be a scientist.

Hooked, Sloane thought, the rest of the place falling away.

Five hours into that Saturday morning, as daylight was about to make the drunks proud, Hook and Sloane ditched out. Walked a block and a half to here, this same sand. Talked. Didn't want to stop talking—and didn't; started something.

When the sun came up, Hook kissed her. He straddled in the sand to get down eye to eye, and put his hands on her arms so gently, and barely kissed her.

Some system in her brain wanted to file the kiss—the exact moment—and in the process it occurred to her how badly she'd hurt her dad's feelings the night before. It was because it was August sixteenth. Exactly thirteen years ago, on a Thursday, her mom died. It was the first time Sloane had forgotten.

"Detective?"

Sloane turns, finds the guy who must be Kurt Lutz standing at the edge of the beach.

She wipes the tears she finds under her eyes.

"Kurt?"

"You weren't kidding when you said private." He trudges over, a tall, skinny kid; she can see his ankles wobble. He stops a few feet from her, unsure, sticks his hands in his pockets. "Should we even introduce ourselves?"

"Let's walk." She starts out ahead of him, toward the pier, taking another few moments to shake the nostalgia.

"I should've brought my hat," he says, his scene-kid hair

cut mostly short except for a few places where it isn't. Over his right eye, for one.

"This won't take long."

When she reaches the pier she waits until he catches up and says, "This could be trouble for us both," and she smiles at him, because she thinks maybe she picked this beach because it has always been trouble, for her. Not to mention the fact that it's in Eddie's district. Any one of his guys could come by, be happy to see her, and still want to know what the fuck she's doing in their beat.

"No trouble," Kurt says, "I told you I don't reveal my sources."

"If I give you too much, my name will be all over it."

"Same here," he says, reaching into his inside pocket, "but we both need information." From his faux army coat: a brand-new notepad. Already.

Sloane says, "You can make a career on this case. Is that why you're here?"

"No, I mean, I hadn't looked at it that way. I didn't know it was a headline."

"It isn't." Sloane has more to say, but just now, decides to size him up: he's younger, and by default, happier, and that's just fine. What's not fine is the pencil-skinny jeans that, one, he put on when he went home to walk the dog, which is probably no bigger than a Chihuahua, or, two, wore to the office, his interpretation of business casual. His notepad even looks like he bought it at a clothing store, some sad, sketchy art on the front. She can't imagine his bosses would be pleased, with him here on the *Sun-Times*'s dime, looking so tragically hip.

Sloane knows observations about his appearance are petty, but when his entire outfit seems like a put-on, she can only wonder about the rest of him.

She says, "I'm here because of the victims. I am trying to the find the monster who hurt them. And because I need information you have, I'm willing to give a little of my own. But if you're planning on using all this to get a bigger byline, I'm sorry to waste your time. I won't be someone who hurts these women, too."

It seems Kurt's tongue is stuck somewhere behind his teeth, so Sloane leaves him there, starts down the pier. Lets him work on a response.

"Hey," he calls after her. "I know this could make your career, too."

She turns around.

"I looked you up. You've been under the numbers since the Zookie Truman case."

Sloane wishes this didn't flip her switch, but she's at Kurt so fast he backs right off the pier's edge and nearly eats sand. While he stumbles to stay upright she tells him, "I've been under the numbers, Kurt, because I am, as I said, working for the victims. Not for my career and certainly not for my reputation. You don't know Zookie Truman. Don't talk to me about Zookie Truman. We're done here. Walk away."

Again with the tongue at his teeth. *Little shit.* She pivots and goes.

Ten steps in, she hears Kurt: "You think I want to hurt these women?"

She keeps walking. If he's serious, he'll have to follow.

Twenty more steps and he's almost caught up. "Detective? Stop. Hey—come on. I'm here because you called me. *You* asked me to meet. What do you want me to say?"

She slows, but not to a stop. Why does she always find herself in some compromised position with guys like this?

"Seriously," he says, beside her.

"I don't trust you."

"Why not?"

"You won't stand up for yourself."

"How do you know?"

"You've got weak ankles."

"What, are we going rollerskating?"

"Sure, kid. For your birthday."

"Stop," he says, and does.

She doesn't.

"Fine: walk away. Walk right off into the lake, I don't give a shit. But wait, I want you to know: can you hear me?"

She can, barely. She stops. Doesn't turn around. Waits.

He says, "The reason I got to cover the rape? Because nobody else gave a shit. Nobody. So don't talk like *you* know *me.* I'm not the one who's asking for a fight."

Over her shoulder she says, "He wanted to fight?"

"Yes. And the victim? She did. She got away."

Sloane turns, a concession. "Why didn't you report that?"

"Because if this guy wants a name, I'm not going to be the one giving it to him."

Sloane retraces her steps, softer this time, and thinks of an apology. By the time she gets there, to where he's standing, she decides against it. Instead, she says, "Here's what we can do. You can tell me everything you have on your victim, and I promise I'll only use it for my investigation. Not as evidence for the case. Then I'll tell you everything you need for a headline."

She can tell he's game, because she sees the notepad again.

"Okay," he says, "but how about you tell me first?"

"Don't think so."

"Keep it even, then? Piece for piece? It's only fair."

"Fine," she says. "But no names, no places. No questions. No plans for future contact."

"Feels like a one-night stand."

"How would you know?"

"Should we go somewhere?" he asks, against the wind. "I mean, somewhere less exposed?"

"The dunes are fenced off. The crack whores have dibs on the sheltered spots." She knows this. She's interrupted more than one blowjob.

"My car?"

"Let's just walk." If he's going to take notes, he'll have a hell of a time keeping up.

"I've got two white females," she says, starting out toward the water again. "Professionals. Loop girls."

"My girl is a student at Loyola," Kurt says. "Twenty-two. She interns for an alderman in Humboldt Park? She wants to be in politics. City government. She works a paying job, too, and has a full load at school—"

"These women were on foot," Sloane says, staying on track. She doesn't care too much about his vic's personals; she's steering toward the suspect. "Both of them were surprised by the attacker from behind."

"My victim was on foot, too. She was the one who surprised him, though. She was walking home from the Granville Red Line stop. She noticed an SUV—a Hummer—parking lights on, in the west alley off Winthrop. Had a bad feeling. Her guard was up."

Sloane wonders about the Hummer. If it's the suspect's, or another piece of evidence the girl's clinging to so she sounds like she knows what she's talking about.

She says, "These women didn't see any type of SUV, nor did they have a clue they were going to be attacked until the guy had his hands around their throats."

"He choked them?" Kurt scribbling on his pad for the first time, furious-fast.

Sloane says, "No questions."

"Right. Sorry. It's just that the guy tried to choke my victim. She's super-fit, though—starting forward all four years on Loyola's soccer team. As soon as she felt his hands on her she swung, full-on with her backpack. Hit him in the head, put him on his ass. She thought she knocked him out until he started laughing. Said he hoped she'd fight. So she kicked him, a direct shot to his jewels. Sprinted back toward Broadway, went into the first public place, called nine-one-one."

"These women fought their attacker. They didn't get away."

"Did they . . ." he starts to question. "They didn't," he tries again. "So both of them . . ." He stops. "Damn, it's hard without questions."

Sloane knows exactly what he means; she's dying to ask about his vic's description of the suspect.

They keep walking, slower now; he matches her pace, and he's probably rearranging his words, too, trying to find a way not to ask.

Sloane finds one first. "You don't want to make a name for this guy, but his MO is very distinct. It might as well be your lead-in. Unfortunately, these women, the victims, don't remember much else about him. We need to give your readers something more. Something to watch out for."

"I don't know his MO," Kurt says. "My victim got away."

They keep walking, though the conversation is at a standstill.

They're near the end of the pier by the time Kurt says, "You said your victims worked in the Loop. So does mine. Well, sort of. She studies down there, and she cocktails on

Rush Street. But she's in the Loop a lot, I guess. If that means anything."

"You seem to know an awful lot about your victim. I don't think that's your story."

"I'm telling you what I know. I thought *you* were going to give me a story."

"I guess there isn't one." At the end of the pier she stops, looks south, sees the buildings downtown; Trump Tower still a surprise, the newest fixture on the skyline. *Everything so fast,* she thinks; then feels a sudden ache, her heart. Her dad. She hardly realizes that she says, "I guess we're done here." She starts back toward the beach.

"Wait a minute," Kurt says, "you said this was serial."

"I said I *think* it's serial."

"I can't believe this. You're totally screwing me."

"I'm not doing anything to you," she says. "I told you what I know."

"You told me nothing."

"You haven't exactly helped me, either. If I wanted to know what your vic ate for breakfast, you'd be the first person I'd call. But the traits all these women share are stereotypical: single, white, female. The suspect found them coming from very different locations and my victims didn't mention any type of SUV. As far as I know, none of them knows him personally, or can give more than a vague description, and we can't find this guy based on the fact that he's Hispanic. If that's all you've got, you can't print it. You have to find something more."

"You said he has an MO."

"I did. He does. You want me to tell you? I thought you didn't want to give him a name. Make him get off on fame."

"If we give him a name, we can generate public interest."

"This guy is picking out women with no discernable plan. You're not going to generate interest, you're going to create fear."

"He might not have a plan, but he's got a pattern."

Then, another surprise that had been building all along: Kurt might be onto something. What he said about all the vics being in the Loop isn't so out there. If she can't get a line on the suspect, maybe she should figure out what all the vics have in common.

"Where does your vic study, exactly," she asks, "in the Loop?"

"I thought you said no questions. No names. No places."

"Do you want his MO?"

"The Harold Washington. And Hugo's. She cocktails at Hugo's."

"Okay, get your pen ready. Your girl wasn't the only one this guy wanted to fight. That's his thing. That's how he gets off: the fight."

"The fight," Kurt says, wheels turning.

"Can you write it?"

"Are you kidding?"

Kurt is still writing who knows what when she snatches his notebook and pitches it into the lake.

"Hey—what the fuck? What the *fuck?*"

"Oh come on. You don't need that and you didn't need me. Write this. Just do me a favor, and remember: it's for the victims."

He's still watching the black water where his notepad sunk, lost treasure, when Sloane says, "Nice not to meet you," and heads for the beach.

13

IT'S JUST AFTER TEN when the doorman buzzes Sloane up to Eddie's. On the way downtown, she thought about continuing south to the hospital; instead she rang the charge nurse in the O Corridor who told her James Pearson was fine, and asleep, and would be through the night, with the meds they gave him.

Sloane wishes she had called earlier.

Carolyn's cell went straight to voicemail and when she answered at her home number, voice listless, Sloane hung up. She was just checking, to see if Carolyn had stayed at the hospital with her dad; they really didn't have anything to talk about after that. Carolyn, of course, would have had plenty to say: She's probably been on the phone with friends all night, her story more polished and pathetic with every pass. *I thought I was going to lose him,* she'd say; *things were touch-and-go.* And *Oh gosh, no,* she'd say, *I couldn't eat.* Someone would suggest a hot bath. She'd be in the tub when she'd confide in the next caller. *I feel like it's my fault.* The friend would object, but Carolyn would still be sick about the whole thing. Then, in a warm robe and slippers, she'd deny another sympathizer's offer to help. *Oh no, I don't need anything. Really. Just prayers.* And she'd have been through the story enough times to tell it once more, with tears, while flipping through the pages of a crappy women's magazine and sipping on a glass of overpriced white wine. *I nearly lost him,* she'd say.

Sloane keys Eddie's lock and takes off her boots inside the front door. He left all the lights on from there to the deck, and she can hear the TV, but she'll bet he's passed out in front of it. Today was the first shift of his four-day rotation, and ever since he and another cop started working out at some chain gym near the Twenty-four station, he's usually zonked before he makes it off the couch. It isn't that much different when he skips the gym, though, because that means one of his favorite pro teams is in the midst of a race for a pennant or title or bowl. Then, Sloane will find him passed out on the couch smelling like sweat and beer instead of just sweat.

She goes through the kitchen, tonight's sausage deep-dish

left out, the pizza's cardboard box grease-glued to the countertop. Usually she'd grab a slice, go over and switch from whatever channel Eddie'd been watching to one that might annoy him, and bug him to give her some room, to move over, to go to bed. Tonight, she sees his socked feet hanging over the end of the couch, and she doesn't want to wake him. She wants a shower. She wants to be alone, and to fall asleep, the TV still going in the other room, an old comfort.

There are no clean towels in the closet. Sloane's been slacking on the laundry lately, among other things. Apparently Eddie hasn't noticed. The still-wet one hanging on the shower door, the one Eddie's been using all week, will have to do.

She runs the water, hot as it'll go. Her hair is still damp from the lake wind; the shampoo lathers thick, and quickly. She feels better, finally rinsing off the hospital. Feels like some of her attitude goes down the drain with it.

She finds Eddie's facial hair stuck between the blades of her razor, and wants to be pissed, but isn't. She wonders if the breakup will mirror the way they came together: his shock, her feelings already stripped to nothing.

It can't be exactly the same. When they started dating, Eddie was in shock, but he was thoughtful. Sloane spotted him in the only empty corner of Twenty-four's St. Patrick's Day party at Hamilton's, a full beer, empty stare. He was the kind of handsome that every woman notices and immediately shies away from. He wore his hair longer then; it was soft, darker than chocolate. He was incredibly, naturally fit; defined from the jaw down. And obviously very, very sad.

Sloane knew sad. She went over, brought him a healthy pour of Jameson, found him with a sick heart.

His younger brother had died a few weeks before—an out-of-nowhere heart attack at thirty-five. Eddie was all fucked up about it, and since Sloane had been an expert in all things grief since the age of eight, it was like she already knew him. She knew what it was like to feel responsible and irresponsible; selfish and helpless; numb and angry, and every once in a while, almost relieved by feeling just plain sad. Her understanding, to Eddie, was like magic; the more room she gave him to grieve, the closer he wanted her. And when her lease on Wrightwood ran out last July, he insisted she move in. He told her he loved her. She loved him, too, but didn't say it back, in case it was grief doing his talking.

Last fall, she realized the grief had warped him. It was the day she lost Zookie Truman. She thought Eddie would be her magic, this time. She didn't expect sympathy, exactly, but she wasn't expecting—

"Slo?" From the other side of the shower curtain.

—she wasn't expecting the New Eddie now, either. Even in the steam, her hair is on end. "I'm almost done."

"'K."

She waits until she hears the door close and steps back from the stream of water, pulls the towel over the curtain rod, dries her face. If he's awake, now, she's going to have to try real hard not to fight.

She turns off the water, towels off. Body lotion, a comb, hair balm.

The New Eddie has no sympathy. The night Zookie was murdered, Eddie couldn't understand why Sloane was upset. He added it up, black and white, and the death simply evened a score. Gangs, God, who gives a shit? Somebody else assumes control. "Assumes," he said, because nobody's really got control. Not in this life. Some consolation.

Clean underwear, T-shirt, and socks; then tweezers.

The New Eddie? He thinks a person can spend life a saint, like his brother, or like Zookie, a no-good little banger. Doesn't matter. They'll still go, fair or unfair, good or bad, right or wrong. Who gives a shit?

Floss, toothpaste.

The New Eddie: playing off the world's indifference by *not* giving a shit. So immersed in what's wrong with the big picture that he doesn't see what's wrong right in front of him. Doesn't see, or doesn't care to see; Sloane is afraid it's the latter.

Eye cream. Then takes off the socks; toenail clippers.

New Eddie, he lives day by day: not much gained, a little more lost. Sloane wonders, now, if he's always been this way. If it's always been plain to other people that his star is just a piece of metal, his heart part of a cruel trick on his head. If he's the kind of handsome that every other woman notices and purposely avoids; the kind of guy who, no matter how you add it up, is just another asshole. Just like he says.

Lotion, socks again.

The New Eddie Nowicki: still so good looking, not much else good left. Bitter. Sarcastic. Self-convinced. Thoughtless.

And waiting for her in the bedroom. She can't stall any longer.

Sloane opens the door and finds Eddie's put out all the lights except the one in the hall. She flips it off, and starts for the bedroom, and hears, "Slo." From the main room.

She backtracks, and pads through the kitchen; finds yellow light flitting and angling in the living room, from the windows. From the city. So Eddie's opened the blinds: He knows she likes the lights from the dark.

He's on the couch. "Come here," he says, just enough *please* in his voice to balance need. She goes there.

There's no *Hello,* no *It's been a while* when he pulls her on top of him; not a single kiss. He jerks her underwear aside and pulls her down on him, his hands at her waist. She doesn't fight. Fighting is pointless if the connection is lost. And anyway, this is better than fighting.

Each time he pulls her down to him, she sees the city lights against his eyes. Sees him looking up at her, over her, desperate. She wonders what she must look like to him, if he's convinced himself that this is it. That this is life.

When Eddie is finished, it doesn't take long for him to fall asleep. Sloane stays there, in front of him on the couch; his arm draped over her grows heavier with sleep. Still, she stays, looking out at the city. The sky is clear this late and below it, everything else slow-blinks. This is Sloane's favorite time of night: when she can feel a pulse.

That system—the one in her brain that wants to file specific moments—kicks in, and she knows she's nearly finished here. She can't stay, tonight, this place, forever; even if she could, she wouldn't remember it as clearly as her time with Hook.

His rental in Evanston. The old house. Its sagging structure. Rusty doorknobs. The gravel drive. The back entrance; the rickety screened porch; the shared wood-paneled kitchen. The apple-cinnamon air-freshener. The staircase up to his room.

There: daylight through the A-frame window, always some gray or blue, cold as it was outside. The dust-dry smell of his books. Gas from the space heater. The box spring and mattress on the floor, no frame. The sheets always clean. Crisp, under so many layers of old knit blankets.

His player-sized Wildcats sweatshirt. Big and purple and past her hands, nearly to her knees. His body: warm, strong, and so sore from training for varsity. His skin specked by moles. Bruised from practice. Too pale for California. His arms a bear's.

She never slept so well as she did in that room with Hook.

It should have lasted longer; it certainly shouldn't have been called on a dirty play, but some receiver went up for a catch and came down on Hook's Achilles. And if Hook couldn't play, he couldn't stay. He was smart enough to know that. He couldn't afford it.

He called her and invited her over, and in a few words, the night before she started the Job turned into the night before Hook went back to San Diego.

She stayed that night. They slept; just slept. There was no reason to do anything else. It was over. And when Sloane woke up in the middle of the night, she left. Hoped it was better that way.

Hopes it's better now, too.

IT'S MY FIRST DAY back at the City Hall pressroom and even though I've been gone a week, nobody seems to have missed me. I get the feeling it's because my boss doesn't believe I was sick in the first place, and she must have said so out loud, the opinion spread around the office quicker than any virus could have clobbered me.

I was sick, and I did get clobbered. And if anyone bothered to ask, I would say I think I'm holding it together pretty fucking well.

I've been sitting at my desk all morning—even came in early—and I'm almost done playing catch-up: familiarizing myself with this new ordinance, that new issue. It's ridiculous that I have to read nine-tenths of it, since only the last tenth will ever be news. Still, I have to get the gist of it all, and it's a good thing there's no test, because I'm a little preoccupied. And, I have to get up to go to the bathroom every ten minutes.

The fourth time I'm in there, last stall, it burns so bad I'm pretty sure I've got a full-blown infection. I'm thinking this over-the-counter stuff isn't working so well. I reapply the cream anyway, and decide to spend my lunch hour at Walgreens. Maybe talk to a pharmacist.

I pull at my turtleneck where it's tight—where I'm still swollen. I hope the weather stays cold for a while so I don't look like an idiot, sweating under high collars while everybody else starts wearing short sleeves.

I'll probably never wear short sleeves. The way my elbows are healing, I'll have scars.

I'm washing my hands when the boss comes into the bathroom and it doesn't seem like she has to go. In the mirror, we can both see it looks like I'm up to something so I lean over, splash some water on my face. Then, I look wet and up to something. Doesn't matter: I'd tell her my cat died and then I'd go home and get rid of my cat before I'd tell her the truth.

The boss asks me if I'm still sick and she doesn't listen when I say no; she says if I'm still sick I shouldn't be here. I say I'm just fine because I can live with an infection, but I cannot live without a paycheck.

She says if I'm just fine, what's with the bathroom routine? There's a rumor I'm pregnant.

I'm not pregnant, I tell her, because I'm pretty sure I'm not.

She says if I'm not sick and I'm not pregnant then she needs me on the floor, stat, because the phone's off the hook about this girl, Anna LaJeunesse.

Okay, so I follow her out to the news desk. Who's Anna LaJeunesse?

She slaps a fresh copy of today's *Sun-Times* in my hands and the first thing I see is a photo of this chick, her *I told you so* smile. Then, next to her, there's a sketch of a Latino guy, shaded shady, and I start to get this not-so-good feeling, which must look something like confusion to the boss because she points her index finger at the headline and says we need a counterstatement.

Read it, she says.

I can't believe it.

Would-Be Attacker Picks Wrong Fight
by Kurt Lutz

klutz@suntimes.com

Anna LaJeunesse is a model Loyola student: senior honors, varsity women's soccer captain, Spanish Club president, Student Association for Political Action secretary, and ESL literacy outreach volunteer.

And two nights ago, Anna LaJeunesse proved that she is also a fighter. After being excused early from her Rush Street cocktailing job, La-

Jeunesse headed for her Rogers Park apartment to study for her last round of finals. That night, she never cracked a book. She never made it home.

Just after 8:00 P.M., as she walked from the Granville Red Line station, LaJeunesse noticed an unfamiliar sports utility vehicle idling in her neighbors' alley off Winthrop Avenue.

"It was like a military tank," she said of the vehicle, believed to be a GM Hummer. "I've been living on this block going on four years now," she added. "I know when [something isn't] right."

That sixth sense might have saved her life. Her guard up, LaJeunesse was ready when a man she described as middle-aged, average height, and Hispanic tried to strangle her. A combination of keen awareness and quick reflexes helped LaJeunesse defend herself. "He told me to fight him. So I did." She knocked him down, ran to the Granville Anvil Bar, and called police.

"I had so much adrenaline," LaJeunesse said. "I just ran to the first safe place I knew."

"Sam" Francisco Ortiz, the Anvil's bartender that night, nicknamed LaJeunesse "La Luchadora." "That bad man messed with the wrong senorita," Ortiz said. LaJeunesse agrees, insisting she is not a victim.

"I volunteer for Alderman Van der Meer in an extremely impoverished area [a western section of the 26th Ward] ... I have seen what it truly means to be a victim. I want those disadvantaged people in Humboldt Park, and others like them all over the city who don't have voices, to know that I fought my attacker, and I will fight for them."

LaJeunesse hopes this incident will give her the chance to bend the mayor's ear. "I would tell him that crime like this can happen anywhere if we abandon our people. We need the city to stop using TIFs [tax-increment funds] as development Band-Aids. The poor people are bleeding through them."

Lead detective Tim Finch says there have been no similar incidents in the area and believes this was an isolated event. However, an unnamed source in Area Five believes LaJeunesse's case could be tied to two other similar incidents under investigation there. "This might be serial," the source said. Whatever the case, or cases, LaJeunesse does not blame her attacker. "His circumstances must be far worse than mine," she said, adding, "I hope he's caught, and that the media will remain interested in this case. In *his* case. Maybe that will get the mayor's attention."

When asked if she's considering a career in civil service, LaJeunesse said, "I would definitely like to continue working with the alderman after graduation. First, I have to ace my poly-sci final."

You can bet, come graduation day, Van der
Meer will be the first in line to hire this courageous young woman.

I read the article three times and the parts about the attack three more. I still can't believe it. I was strangled. I was
told to fight.

I fought, too. But I didn't get away.

I'm still standing there trying to recognize the suspect in
the sketch when the boss asks if I'm just going to stand there.
She says this thing's got Van der Meer written all over it, and
if he thinks he's going to use this little luchadora to fight
about the TIF, it's on.

The boss makes a call, says, "Yep, nope, absolutely," then
hangs up and tells me to send out a release stating he's in
D.C., Olympics, e.t.c., n.f.w., which means I should write
that the mayor is in Washington, D.C., meeting with foreign
diplomats and national officials to introduce plans approved
by the Olympic Committee and cannot be reached for comment at this time. All true, far as I know, except the part
about his being unreachable. For this office, he answers.

I take the *Sun-Times* back to my desk and sit there and
type out the release and probably look like I'm concentrating
but really, the news, the sketch, this girl? All of it has hit me,
blunt trauma, C3 vertebra. I'm stunned.

I'm not the only one.

God damn it, Stephen.

A week and a day. I was raped exactly eight days ago and

every second since I've been trying to erase it, because I won't
be a victim, either. I can't be. I thought it through a million
times and in as many different ways. My memory might be
like smashed glass, but the pieces are all stained a familiar
color and the edges are so sharp they cut to the truth.

I just didn't want to do it. I didn't want to come out and
say Stephen is the man who raped me.

Yesterday I'd worked my way around to thinking that I
just wanted to think Stephen did it. For justification. Because
otherwise I'd have fought harder, right? And I wouldn't feel
like I deserved it. Or started to think maybe I wanted it. Liked
it, even.

I thought it was Stephen. And I decided I could live with
that.

I look at the suspect's sketch again: he's Latino-ish, blue-
collared, blank-eyed. He could be Stephen or the maintenance guy who's fixing the copy machine in the corner or
just about anybody.

But just about anybody wouldn't have attacked me and
this other girl, this girl who works for Van der Meer. Van der
Meer, the alderman who's fighting Stephen's company for
city property. The company Stephen defended so adamantly
after I published a press release about its questionable background. Boy, was Stephen mad at me. I wonder if he's been
dating this girl LaJeunesse. I wonder if she pissed him off real
good, too.

I don't know how long the boss has been standing there
talking at me, but I must look like I've been listening because

when I tune in she's going on about making this so-called luchadora sound like *está jodida por* Van der Meer. I know there's a question in there somewhere, by the boss's eyebrows, so I think I smile and I say, "Yeah, I think I get it," and she says, "Good, draft it," and goes back to the news desk.

I watch her walk away, as calm as multiple mood-disorder prescriptions can make her, and I figure the *Sun-Times* counter she wants has to be something juicy, to knock the article off the media radar.

I didn't know what to do before, and now I've got less than a clue.

I open a new document.

I think of Stephen.

I wish I didn't love him anymore.

14

"SON OF A BITCH," Sloane says, her dad's copy of today's *Sun-Times* telling her everything she needs to know about Kurt Lutz and Anna LaJeunesse, the journalist prick and his perfect vic.

Heavy called a half dozen times already this morning and Sloane put him straight to voicemail. Since there are only two possible unnamed sources in Area Five and Heavy's the other one, she figures his first call was to make sure she'll be at work, 8:00 A.M. prompt, to secure the number-one spot on Guzman's shitlist. The rest of the calls were probably to bitch about being the automatic second.

Before she calls him back for the inevitable, she needs a positive angle on the story, so she makes herself another cup of Folgers and sits at her dad's kitchen table to read some more of the paper, rethink things.

She can't remember the last time she read the paper, but she knows why she doesn't. Not much is news. She can't remember the last time she made instant coffee, either, and she's surprised she still likes the shallow, syrupy flavor. Must be because her taste buds were conditioned to the stuff at such a young age. Sloane wasn't quite twelve when she was put in charge of the grocery shopping, and the first time she bought Folgers, the checkout lady remarked that Sloane was quite the grown-up. She went home and tried it and hated it and kept trying it and hating it until she added chocolate Quik. Once she ran out of Quik she learned to like it black. The way her dad did.

Sloane reads the *Sun-Times* article again, and curses Kurt Lutz twice more. She knew he had more to go on than the notebook she gave to the lake; she would have never guessed he already had the fluff piece written and just needed a good headline.

Kurt even got a full-color, feature-style photo of LaJeunesse, posed right there on the scene-of-the-crime sidewalk, arms crossed, smile firm, a winner.

Then, the sketch. Last night, Kurt might've let on that he spoke to LaJeunesse direct, but he never mentioned anything about the suspect. It's kind of fishy, the guys in Three letting him run a color sketch on a one-on-one assault, especially when the suspect has been drawn as plain as his Hispanic, middle-aged descriptors. So plain, in fact, the guy isn't half-bad looking. Sloane bets more people will recognize the artist than the sketch: she can always tell Theo Skinner's work by the dense Elvis hairline. He's drawn the face even-toned, clean-shaven, and symmetrical; nothing much distinguishing about it.

The suspect's shirt, however, is drawn very much like the one Meyer-Davis described. It's collared, light blue, striped. Sloane assumes that if the shirt pocket had a name patch, LaJeunesse didn't notice it. The girl doesn't seem to hold anything back.

But Three might.

Then there's that bit about the Hummer. If this is the same guy, he's either a dumbass with cash who drives his own cars to commit crimes, or he's a smart thief, an opportunist. Sloane tries to talk herself into calling the station, having the dispatcher check the citywide database for any recent Hummer thefts.

She doesn't pick up the phone. Ever since she got out of bed she's been trying to talk herself into calling Heavy. Or at least her voicemail, for messages. It's just that every time she scrolls through the calls, she wishes more than none of them were from Eddie.

She wonders where he is. If he slept out there, on the couch—and if he's still asleep when he should be on his way out the door, the morning traffic a bitch to get from River North to Twenty-four. It's her fault if he slept in; she forgot to check if the alarm was set. Not that he'd hear it from the other room. *Fuck,* she thinks. She should call. She wants to call.

Except what she really wants is for him to call. Not to find out why she didn't wake him or if she's working late or what's for dinner. She wants him to call to ask what happened. To be asking about more than last night.

When the stove clock turns seven-thirty, Sloane's still sitting at the kitchen table, paper tossed aside, the last few sips of Folgers getting cold. She knows she should get her ass out the door if she wants to be at the station anywhere near on time. Why is she stalling?

It's my MO, she thinks. Classic Deputy move from way back: her dad already off to work, the bus here and gone, first-period class under way. If she stalled long enough, she'd have to skip. And why not? Her dad wouldn't be mad. He agreed that every time she transferred, the new school low-balled her placement, and besides, if she stayed home, she'd spend the day reading one of his technical manuals or a book from her mother's literature collection. School was not Sloane's challenge. While the kids were eating the cafeteria's rubber-ized lasagna, copying each other's notes, and talking smack about the latest social outcast, Sloane was learning to build a charcoal foundry or reading *The Brothers Karamazov,* her homemade lasagna in the oven.

School was not the challenge. Nor was coming in, middle of the year, the new girl; explaining where she'd been before this, and before that—and then there was the whole thing about her mom.

The real challenge, for Sloane, was being a kid. She hated wearing her stupid thick bifocals; it was already plain to see the simple, curious students; the perpetually concerned adults. A boy would tell a parent, the parent would complain, a teacher would call: Sloane's dad needed to be made aware that she said things unfit for a young girl. Or, that she was too young to be taking the city bus alone. Or, that her clothes were ill fit for her age. Her dad always stood his ground: it was Sloane's age that was the bad fit.

Things aren't much different now, except for the glasses. Seems like everybody needs some justification for Sloane's behavior. Seems like she's always got to drag at least one heel for people to keep up.

She puts on her boots and coat, gets the rest of her stuff, and dials Heavy on her way out the door. If she wants his help on this case, she's got to try to get him to keep up.

He answers right away: "Sloane—" is all she lets him say—

"Look. I'm the source. Everybody's going to figure me for it so I admit it, okay? But that rodent I talked to, at the paper? He did us a favor, really. You know those guys in Three were never going to work with us—with me anyway. And now we know what they've got, which is a whole lot of nothing, if you ask me. You there?"

"I'm here—"

"Did you read the article? That straight A-merican vic is going to keep the dicks up there working by the book, you know? Miss Courageous, mouthing off, wants to talk to the mayor. Is she kidding?" Sloane clicks the Pilot's locks and shoves her stuff onto the passenger seat. "You know who's really going to be in trouble today? Three. Not me. Finch, and those guys in Three. Right?"

"Sloane—"

"I know, I'm sure Guzman will have his dick in a twist, but I'll tell him: Now the camera's on Three. That means nobody's going to be looking our way. Maybe not even the suspect."

"Sloane—"

"You agree with me, right? We've got room, and we've got to move." She gets into the Pilot—

"Sloane."

"Yeah?" Keys the ignition—

"Stop."

"Where?" Checks her mirrors—

"I'm not calling about the case. I'm calling about your father."

All engines: stalled. She remembers, now, that she called her partner last night—called him Russ, even. Made it personal.

She curls her fingers tight around the steering wheel. Thinks, *Fuck.* Says, "He's okay." Knows that isn't enough.

"Are you okay?"

The Pilot's check-engine light glows orange, waiting for reignition. *Of course I'm okay,* she wants to lie. But she just spent the first part of the conversation failing to prove it.

"You might be hardheaded, darlin'," Heavy says, "but your heart's not made of Kevlar."

"Neither is my dad's." Saying so is too much like a confession. Her heart feels slow, bloated.

"I called Guzman," Heavy says. "I told him I'm the one who leaked the story about the serial."

"He knows better than that."

"He knows what I told him. And I'm telling you: forget work. Forget the case. Your life is more important."

"Heavy, this case is all I can do."

"Actually it's the last thing you can do. I told Guzman you're taking another personal day."

"You can't."

"I did."

"I can't."

"You will."

"God damn it, Heavy. I can't lose a day."

"Come on, Sloane. I can handle the case."

"Yeah? Real quick, then, catch me up on your end. Have you talked to Meyer-Davis lately? Have you checked the databases for a stolen Impala? Considered the new Hummer angle? What about the scene on Sangamon? Have you been back? Or to the West Town Tavern? The East Bank Club? How about H&R Block? And what about her client list? There's nothing like tax time to strike a guy with the urge to force-fuck his accountant."

"I'm on it."

"I checked the file yesterday afternoon. You haven't done a thing."

"I'm doing you a favor."

Sloane feels her rational hold slipping. "You want to do me a favor? Then work this fucking case like I am." Sloane thinks she should hang up right then, but she doesn't. And neither does Heavy.

She starts the car, U-turns, and drives a jagged route northeast, side streets toward the Loop. She waits for Heavy to say something and the longer she stays on the line, this stalemate, the more she wants to get right back to arguing. But she'll ride it out. Has to. Same as when they're on the street together and some disagreement unnecessarily escalates— she's driving too fast, he's driving too slow, s/he doesn't know where s/he's going, what s/he's doing, how basic policework is done. Soon the only thing they're able to agree about is disagreeing—which is not the same as agreeing to disagree, because the latter implies a mutual clue as to what in God's name the other person is thinking—and since they'll still be partners tomorrow, silence is the only respectable option.

Until Heavy says, "Supposed to snow today."

Silence, or the weather. Because nobody's ever right about that.

"I heard the forecast on the radio," Sloane says, relieved.

"Temperature probably won't drop long enough for it to stick. It'll be messy, though."

"Told you not to get new carpet."

"The carpet's not the trouble. My wife says if I bring home one more stray I'm going to be the one who needs rescuing, and if I remember right, you're the one who advised me on the canine situation as well."

"But you're keeping Kedzie, right?" They found the pit bull last week, in the alley behind Treat Restaurant, fighting mange and starvation. Heavy named him and claimed him before they were back on the avenue, making him dog number five at the Coburn home—after Austin, LeMoyne, Sheridan, and Mugwump. That last one was the first one, pound-found. The others were named after the streets where they'd been scrounging.

"Of course we're keeping him," Heavy says. "New carpet or not, you know Sharon can't let anything die . . ."

The silence that comes this time starts on Heavy's end, and it's because one person shouldn't mention death when the other is denying its reality.

So she says, "He's not dying, Heavy."

"Maybe you want to talk to Sharon? She could help."

"He doesn't need hospice."

"I mean she can help *you*."

"I don't need hospice either." Sloane crosses under Roosevelt Road at Canal Street, into Area Five's territory. "Look," she says, "I'm five minutes from the Loop. I'm going to call the hospital, and they're going to tell me my dad is fine, and then I'm going to work the case. Starting where all our girls did."

Heavy says, "I hope you're right," and he isn't talking about the case. She can practically hear him shaking his head when he hangs up.

SLOANE'S PARKED IN A lot on the north side of the Harold Washington Library by the time she gets through to her dad's room at the hospital. Carolyn answers. "He's still pretty out of it," she tells Sloane, "but the nurse says once the medication wears off he'll be feeling pretty good, and they'll release him. Sometime this afternoon, she said."

"Call me. I'll come get him."

"You don't have to come all the way down here again, Sloane. I'm perfectly capable of springing him."

And taking him to your place to play nurse, Sloane thinks. "He needs to go home. To his apartment. His meds are there."

"That's the plan, honey."

Honey. "I want to be there."

"How about if I bring Jim home, and you bring dinner? That'd be a big help."

Jim, she says. *Bring dinner,* she says. "Call me," Sloane says, and then she hangs up, because otherwise she'd say a whole lot of other things about being a big help that wouldn't be any help at all.

Sloane gets out of the Pilot, gives the parking attendant twelve bucks and her keys, and heads for the library. Her instinct tells her not to bother, and that if LaJeunesse was followed from anywhere, it'd be Hugo's Bar; but a wide-open case has a better chance, all the farthest corners swept. The process of elimination is not fun, but it's better than hanging a case on one guy, letting the state's attorney take it out, one shot, one overlooked possibility.

She takes the elevator to the third floor and shakes hands with Deedrea, the snip-haired, thin-boned librarian behind

the information services desk. Along with her star, Sloane
shows Deedrea the *Sun-Times* article.

"I remember that girl," Deedrea says. "She's a regular
visitor here."

"She was here the night she was attacked, and now I'm
here for any information you can give me about other visitors
or employees who might have some idea what happened."

"I'm not sure what I can do."

"Let me take a look at the check-out records from Tuesday night, and an employee list."

"I'm not sure I can do that."

Sloane could go the whole bully-warrant route, but when
Deedrea pulls at a thin snip of her hair, nervous, she looks
very young, and very much like a potential victim.

So Sloane offers a few additional bits of information about
the case: just enough for the savvy-square librarian to picture herself losing the fight.

Deedrea says, "Give me a few minutes."

"Of course." Sloane takes the elevator to the top floor and
works her way back downstairs via side trips through the
stacks. When she nears a block of windows, she hears the
business of the street-level morning commute; the chaos is
muted up here, the space insulated by thousands and thousands of hard-covered reasons not to rush.

She takes the escalators down to the sixth floor, and then
she's stuck: a yellow construction partition blocks the next
descending escalator. Sloane leans over the rail and catches a
glimpse of a maintenance worker's legs: the knees of his navy

pants, tips of his work boots resting on the half-flight. She can't tell anything more about him, since the dividing wall blocks his upper body. How many men like this would be completely invisible if not for making themselves impossible obstacles?

"Excuse me," Sloane calls down to the legs. The legs don't respond.

She passes the floor's social sciences and history research desks, the librarians on both sides quietly busy, and takes the elevator one flight down.

On the fifth floor, the escalator running down is also blocked off, but this time Sloane gets the maintenance guy's top half: he's got one of the treads pulled off and he doesn't like whatever's going on with the drive gear below.

He notices Sloane, pulls his gigantic, oily hands out of the machine and smiles, though he's unable to clear the job's frustration from his throat when he asks, "Can I help you?"

His skin is nearly as black as the oil, his tight curls a shade darker, and his work shirt is the kind of practical green you wish you didn't paint your bathroom.

"I don't think so," Sloane says, considering him eliminated. "Thanks."

She takes the elevator, makes a mental note to ask Deedrea about the employee uniforms, and arrives at the third floor convinced that she's already spent too much time here. The library is a bust.

Deedrea greets Sloane with an official smile and Sloane knows the news will be just as official.

"I'm sorry," she says, "we want to provide the freedom to read to anyone who chooses, and even if your suspect was here, there's very little I can do."

"That's better than nothing."

Deedrea looks over her shoulder at her empty office, comes around the desk, and gestures for Sloane to walk with her, toward the public computers. "You'd asked about Tuesday," she says, her low library voice perfected. "We do have a list of cardholders who came here that day, so long as they checked out material or logged on to one of these." She sits down in front of a monitor at the far end, where there are no other users; Sloane stands behind her, hopeful.

"Unfortunately I would need a warrant to release that list," Deedrea says, "and I would be able to give you names only. We do keep cardholders' personal information on file, and I can give you that information for anyone who's applied for a card since we computerized our system, but in that case you'd need a separate warrant for each name." Deedrea logs on to the computer, says, "I have a current employee list, and Tuesday's schedule. You want those on paper? I'll need—"

"A warrant," Sloane says. "I get it. Anything you can tell me without a judge's magic ink?"

The library page comes up and Deedrea clicks through, on a mission. "I worked on Tuesday. I can tell you what little I know."

"It's the littlest things that get bad guys caught."

"I know, Detective. I read mysteries."

Except that real life isn't structured for a happy ending, Sloane thinks. She says, "I'm listening."

"I was here from twelve to six," she says, clicking to another library page, and another. "We had the usual staff. I wouldn't call all of them friends, but I wouldn't call any of them criminals." She takes an eighth of a piece of paper and a half pencil from a small tray next to the computer and jots notes from the current screen, then clicks through. "It was slow that afternoon, and I spent most of the time preparing to close early—there was a black-tie gala event in the rooftop garden that night for the Library Foundation." More jotting, another screen. "When I left, I saw the event coordinators—all of them dressed like royalty—you can imagine, those are the people who pay for Chicago's paper-and-ink palaces." She returns to the library homepage, logs off. "I saw the caterers, too, and the servers in cheap tuxes. My understanding is that the only employees of ours who stayed past six thirty were security and emergency maintenance." She hands Sloane her notes. "Those are the names and numbers for the heads of those departments, and for the Library Foundation, as well as the contact person at the caterer."

"You can do this?"

"I can be a wealth of information when it comes to people who are famous, fictional, dead, or netizened. You could have found them online just as easily, if you knew who you were looking for."

"The hard part wouldn't be finding the suspect, if I knew

who I was looking for." Sloane tucks the paper in her pocket, says, "Thanks."

"I put my cell number on there, too," Deedrea says. "Please, if there's anything else I can do . . ."

"Just be smart," Sloane says. "Be aware—and don't walk alone. I don't need any more victims."

Sloane leaves Deedrea there, pulling at that same snip of hair, looking as helpless as she was helpful.

At the exit, a security guard politely and thoroughly checks Sloane's bag, and by the time she gets back outside, she's decided that there are too many variables at the library. There's no easy way she'll find the suspect working LaJeunesse's case without talking to Tim French or better, the little luchadora herself. But that means the guys in Three could put each of their brain cells together and figure out Sloane was Lutz's source. The last time they ran an anti-loyalty campaign against her, Sloane went from promising homicide detective to "a fuckin' liability." Word spread, and Five was the only place that'd take her—and that's only because of Guzman—he remembered when they were both in the Twentieth District, and loyalty killed a cop.

Outside, it's already colder and the wind isn't kidding around. Sloane walks up State Street and wishes she had more than her coat; she'd have to go back to Eddie's for her hat and gloves. She's thinking about ducking into one of the retail stores—if she keeps heading north, she could hit up Filene's—but when she's waiting on the light at Monroe, she sees a Dutcher and Grey Realtor's sign, a beacon just a half block east. She'd yelled at Heavy, just an hour or so before, about following up on Meyer-Davis's client list. She never thought about Holly's.

Fifty East Monroe wouldn't be one of Holly's properties, though: it's a high-rise, the top floors of the building advertised as newly converted condos with half-million-dollar base prices. Dutcher and Grey is the Realtor, but from what Holly said about her A-plus sister, it would only be right that the older, wiser Dutcher acts as the listing agent.

Sloane looks up: the building's hard angles and cold steel are unkind to the skyline. She crosses the entrance corridor to get a closer look at the Realtor's sign:

MONROE PLACE: GET IN THE LOOP.

CLASS AND COMFORT AT THE CORPORATE LEVEL

SKYLINE VIEWS. FITNESS CENTER, SPA, AND SALON ON SITE.

1, 2, AND 3 BEDROOMS WITH EUROPEAN KITCHENS

FROM $500K: LEASE NOW TO CUSTOM BUILD

The fine print says that when the redevelopment is complete, the amenities will include a four-star rooftop restaurant and ground-floor dry cleaning, house cleaning, dog walking, maintenance, and postal services.

Must be nice, Sloane thinks: being able to afford all this and a four-star dinner. *Must be nice,* she thinks again, being able to afford all this and enjoy a four-star dinner because even though you've got people for everything else, you can't find your way around a European kitchen.

She could never call a place like this home; all these corporate types in and out the same front doors, long wool coats
over their expensive suits, big-money deals over cocktails.
Sloane steps aside so they can push past each other, valuable
stock market seconds ticking.

She isn't quick enough, though, when some asshole with a
fat briefcase and a sharp elbow has to get where he isn't, and
even though he knocks her a good one, he doesn't turn to
apologize. She watches him push through the first set of
doors and give the same elbow to a twenty-something black
kid who's cleaning an inside window. The kid wears a light
blue maintenance shirt. Collared. Striped.

Sloane goes in, first set of doors, working up a quick story
to get the kid talking, but some other asshole comes by, wants
the kid to pay special attention to the Lexus he's double-
parked on Monroe. Slips him a fiver.

Sloane's about to follow the kid outside, but notices one of
the businesses that may or may not still occupy the commercial spaces etched into the foyer wall: ALLIED MORTGAGE.
Holly's old employer.

She goes over, takes a look at the rest of the alphabetical
list.

The second one she recognizes: H&R Block. Meyer-Davis.

She counts Dutcher and Grey as the third strike, goes
outside, and asks the kid where to find the building's man-
agement. She slips him another five and makes for Zimmerman & Company, thirty-fifth floor.

15

"THAT PROPERTY IS INCLUDED in the fund, sir." Stephen Carvalho is on the phone—actually, on a wireless headset—and has been, even as he introduced himself, welcomed Sloane into Zimmerman & Company's waiting room, settled her in with a bottle of water and a table full of architecture magazines, and returned to his desk. Sloane has no idea who's on the other end of the call, but between Stephen's casual eye contact and the smile he wears like part of his suit, she might as well be in on the conversation.

"Yes," he agrees.

An obvious reason Sloane feels included is the headset. It's fixed on his ear security style, slim and concealed; if she didn't know any better, he'd have to be talking to her. She's the only other person in the room.

Another reason is the way his desk is set up, strategic: his flat-screen is angled so he can view the monitor and Sloane at the same time while he clicks away at his keyboard, fast as a court reporter. There's a file open on the desk, too, its contents occasional priorities. Sloane finds the whole operation unnerving; this near-perfected multitasking.

Then there's the part about Stephen himself. He's a young model exec, custom-built to impress. Firm handshake: check. Tailor-made suit: check. Top-of-the-line looks: check. He's a man with a boy's rough edges; a worker bee with what the boss probably calls optimism and appetite. And that smile? Equal parts promise and delivery.

Sloane recrosses her legs on the suede vanilla loveseat; the couch is too wide for one person, though more than one would be a tight fit. The room is also too big, just for waiting; the few pieces of smart furniture and low, solid-wood tables seem important in so much space.

"The Pulaski Corridor permit will be approved," Stephen says, a glance at Sloane, his conspirator. "The contractors have submitted the final plans, and they're under budget review." He says this with nothing but respect, but his expression is discordant. More cocky than confident.

Sloane figures she should open her water or pick up one of the fat, glossed magazines sitting in front of her, but for some reason she's fascinated by the fact that the only other thing moving in the room besides Stephen's mouth is the art: a shocking-red, sheet-metal mobile hangs in the corner, oscillating, his kinetic compliment. Sloane guesses it's one of Alexander Calder's, since it is similar in form and color to the Flamingo sculpture a few blocks over, in Federal Plaza. What she can't guess is how much it must've cost.

Stephen says, "We're waiting to finalize the numbers. Mr. Reyes will have the most current figures with him tomorrow. Yes, American. Tonight. DFW."

Sloane's waiting on this guy, Reyes. He's supposed to be the one to talk to.

"He's at the Adolphus," Stephen says. "I've made lunch reservations for you at the French Room—will you hold just a moment?" It's as if he predicted the office door to his left would open: he's there, an instant escort for the stacked woman who appears in the doorway. He says, "Great to—"

As the wowie-wow brunette says, over her shoulder, "See you—"

Stephen says, "Dayna. Great to see you."

"Always." Dayna's smile for him is wild, like she's just been fucked or—if she kept to business—just did the fucking.

Stephen closes the office door and follows Dayna, her cleavage and four-inch heels three reasons she's in the lead. As they cross the room for the exit to the elevators, Dayna like she's on a catwalk, Sloane feels like furniture on clearance.

She picks at what's left of the dark polish on her thumbnail, figuring there's little chance that Mr. Reyes is an old man with hair in his ears.

Sloane checks her cell, surprised no one's called, until she realizes she has zero reception. Makes no sense, being so high up and not getting a signal. *Just like at Eddie's,* she thinks, the comparison joyless.

She cracks open her designer water bottle, takes a sip, re-screws the cap; the water is room temperature, and the room is too warm. She'd love to unzip her coat, but her Kevlar and star underneath feel like cheap jewelry. It's rare that a case brings her to a place where the assistant's dental work is probably worth more than her Pilot.

She sits there, alone, long enough to feel like she's supposed to take a hint, but that doesn't mean she's going any-where. The elevators are right outside the door, so Stephen must have taken a ride with Dayna. Sloane wonders what the hell the woman does—for a living, that is—to get such attention.

At Stephen's desk, an intercom beeps and a man says, "Esteban." Just like that, Stephen appears at the entrance, hustles to his desk, reaches over to answer.

"Yes," he says, his back to Sloane. "Lunch. The alderman, sir. Yes. Right away." He presses a button on the phone console and says, "Mr. Reyes's meeting is running long and he's got to be on a plane this afternoon. Can we push lunch?"

Bullshit, Sloane thinks; she can't stop the star part of her that knows this is all nonsense.

"Monday would be ideal . . ."

She gets up and approaches the desk: let Stephen try to brush her off if she's right there—

Except that she never gets right there, because Stephen pivots, ducks, and steps sideways, the move so fluid it seems more dance than defense.

"Okay," Sloane says, stepping back, same way she would from a stray animal.

And for the briefest moment, his smile is wolfish. "Sorry," he says. "Reflex."

"Esteban," from the intercom again.

"One o'clock Monday works. Thanks," Stephen says, one index finger up for Sloane, the other back at the console. "One o'clock Monday," he says again. "Yes, I'm bringing her in now."

Next thing Sloane knows she's in an office twice the size of the waiting room, the buildings northwest spread across its panoramic window, some close enough to see other people working, others far enough away to see their spires.

"Detective?" the tall, dark, and etcetera man who's already up from his giant desk asks. "I'm Maurice Reyes—call me Mo."

When Mo shakes her hand, Sloane knows where Dayna got her smile.

"Please," he says, "have a seat. And tell me how I can help you." A quick look at "Esteban" is his dismissal; they've probably been through this routine a million times.

Though a couch and a pair of suede chairs sit near the window, there is just one slim, wooden-armed chair set in front of Reyes's desk. It doesn't look comfortable.

Reyes remains standing, politely waiting for Sloane to sit,

but when she considers the single chair, she doesn't find much polite about it.

"I'll stand, if that's okay," she says, "and I'll be brief."

"It is okay," he says, "and you have as much time as you need." He doesn't sit, either—or fold his arms, or stick his hands in his pockets—or do anything else to downplay his power position. He says, "My assistant tells me you're here looking for someone?"

"Yes," Sloane says. "I am investigating an assault and I have strong reason to believe the man responsible works in this building."

"Hijo de la chingada," he says, bringing his hands together now, spinning his gold wedding band.

Sloane's heard Guzman say the same thing on occasion, never on a good one. She says, "The suspect wears the same uniform as the men who work maintenance in this building."

"Isn't that quite a stretch? There are thousands of men— and women—who wear those uniforms in this city. The country, even. We're talking about a national company, eh? A company with something like a quarter of a million employees of their own. I hope you have more to go on than a uniform, Detective."

"If you read the *Sun-Times,* you'll know I have a description—"

Reyes opens a desk drawer and shows Sloane the front page. "You have a Latino man who looks as much like me as any other." He dumps the paper in the trashcan. *"Me llamo*

Mauricio Alejandro Escavar Reyes, Detective, and I don't take kindly to those kinds of generalizations."

"I don't make generalizations," Sloane says. "Neither do my victims."

The phone on his desk rings and Reyes eyes the console; midway through the second ring, it stops.

"Victims," he says. "Is it true? There's more than one?"

"Yes."

"Jesus." Reyes rounds his desk, walks over to the panoramic window.

Sloane says, "If you'll give me an employee list, I'll check it against our cases, and our databases, and if there are no hits, that's as far as I'll take it."

"What about the uniform distributor?" he asks, still looking out the window. "Or the dry cleaners? We give our employees the option to use our professional cleaners."

"I'm not limiting my investigation, Mr. Reyes, but I feel like you are trying to."

"If I give you my employee list . . ." Reyes says, his voice trailing so that the rest might as well be in Spanish.

Sloane joins him at the window. "What did you say?"

"Zimmerman and Company is a major participant in the mayor's Workforce Reentry Program. At least fifty percent of our men downstairs are ex-offenders. If you shine a light down there, you might as well drop a bomb. They'll all be gone."

"Mr. Reyes," Sloane says, "I'm an advocate for the mayor's program. I believe that bad guys can make good, and trust me, nobody at the department wants to make waves for a business that gets those guys out of our system. But this guy? He's still a bad guy, and if he's downstairs, I'm going to find him."

Reyes looks out at the city, down at his hands, his ring. "Detective," he says, "please understand. I came here, to the States, from nowhere. I have worked every day of my life to make a place for myself, and for my family, and now, places for others. I can afford to help the men who need it—the immigrants and less fortunate, like those men downstairs. Men who work as hard as I do, for less than I do, and for no respect. I used to be one of them. So you see, it is difficult when you put me in a position where I am forced to doubt the men with whom I have been able to build this business. Especially now—at a critical time for Chicago's Hispanics."

"Not all Chicago's Hispanics," Sloane says, "just one."

"Just one," Reyes repeats, same way he might say *bitch*.

Sloane doesn't want to bring the vics into this, tell Reyes two of the three women worked here. She also doesn't want to waste a week on a warrant, which is about how much time it'll take, if Guzman even lets her work the case anymore. She's estimating what damage she'll cause either way when outside, above the buildings, a thick cloudbank creeps over the sky and turns the panoramic window into a mirror. In the reflection, Sloane sees Stephen behind them, lingering just outside the office door. Watching. *Watching her?* Reluctant to turn around and lose the image, she tries to define his expression: curious? Patient? Impatient? Then the right word hits her, instant and electric: *interested*.

Stephen is the one who breaks the connection. He says, "Mr. Reyes, your car is here."

"Tell him to wait." Reyes leaves Sloane at the window. She watches Stephen disappear.

When she turns around, Reyes has taken the *Sun-Times* from the trashcan. He turns to the local news, hands her the paper, says, "Maybe you only read the front page, eh? Look at this."

He points out the lead Metro story:

City of Chicago vs. Edificio Chicago, Round Two: The Humboldt Park TIF

> City officials were at odds again today over the proposed construction of a commercial and retail development in the Pulaski Corridor. Developers Zimmerman & Company began the south Humboldt Park tax increment financing [TIF] plan with community support until 26th Ward Alderman Alan Van der Meer objected to the developer's hiring practices. Public record shows that Zimmerman & Co. employs ex-offenders through the Mayor's reentry program—

"Wait a minute," Sloane says, at Van der Meer's name. "Yes?"

Sloane isn't sure how the players team up, but she certainly won't talk through this with Reyes, so she backs up to focus on the obvious. "You're employing these workers all over the city, and one of them might be assaulting women, and you're trying to convince me I should look elsewhere so you don't offend these guys?"

"No," he says, like she's the most beautiful idiot.

"You want me to back off because you're afraid I'm going to ruin some real estate deal."

"No," Reyes says, like she's just an idiot.

"Listen," Sloane says, "I'm running out of time to be polite. This guy is attacking women. Choking them. Holding them down and force-fucking them. So he wears a uniform you can find anywhere. So he's an average-looking Hispanic. He is also a pathetic man who only wants what he can't have, and picks fights he knows he can win."

Reyes doesn't say anything, but the way his expression changes as his eyes search the room, and the unimaginable, reminds Sloane of her Lasik surgery. She thought her sight was fine with reading glasses, and was adamant about it; the department made her go because of her eye test. Once "fixed," she was briefly amazed by all she'd been missing, but she didn't like much of what she saw. She spent weeks after wishing she could get the fuzzy edges back.

"I don't expect you to understand," Sloane says, when Reyes's eyes finally settle on her, disheartened.

"Detective," he says, "I am sorry about your victims. With the paper, I was only trying to explain that we already have two strikes against us. I do not want our Edificio project to fall apart because of a single worker's indiscretions." He goes to his desk, says, "Esteban" to the intercom.

"Yes."

"Get a copy of the employee records for the building. Make note of the men working maintenance, and anyone else with an Aramark uniform. The cafeteria. The engineers. And get the list of everyone we hired through workforce development. In fact, put together a list of all the men we interviewed."

Watching Reyes go from passionate advocate to humbled human to levelheaded businessman in the space of a minute, Sloane finally figures out one good reason people pay for great high-rise views and forget to look out: sometimes, there's too much going on inside.

"Is that all?" Stephen asks.

"No. The detective will also need the contact information for our supplier at Aramark," Reyes says. "I can't remember her name—you know, the new girl."

"Inez."

"Inez. And get Mercedes's extension in the laundry department. Find out who's scheduling deliveries now." He lets go of the intercom, says to Sloane, "For some reason, their delivery department has quicker turnover than a *tortilleria*." He cracks a boy's smile.

"Is that all?" Stephen asks again, over the speaker.

Reyes ignores the question; he's checked his watch, and is on his way to the coatrack. "I'm late for a meeting," he tells Sloane, retrieving his leather coat, a slim leather wallet from the inside pocket. He says, "Esteban will help you from here on out. You want a name, a number, a tour of the guys' locker room, a ride home? He's your boy." He hands her his card.

"What's this for, then?"

"Sometimes, you can't send a boy."

He opens the door and leads Sloane back to the waiting room where Stephen is again multitasking.

"Esteban," Reyes says, en route to the elevators, "make sure the detective has everything she needs."

Stephen nods, though he's listening to whoever's in his ear.

At the door, Reyes says, "And, Detective, don't let him give you any trouble."

Stephen says, "Will you hold please? . . . Mr. Reyes, are you out for the day?"

From the hallway, Reyes says, "You can reach me on my cell."

"Have a safe trip."

As the elevator door opens, Reyes reaches into his pockets, pulls on his gloves. "If there's anything else he can do,"—with a nod toward Stephen—"don't hesitate."

As he steps into the elevator and the doors close, Sloane says, "Not for a second."

"This is going to take some time," Stephen says, behind her. "Do you want to wait?"

"My cell doesn't work up here. You have a line I can use in the meantime?"

"In Mo's office."

Mo? Sloane turns; Stephen's already reclined his chair, loosened his tie. She says, "As soon as the boss is gone, I see."

"He's particular." He gets up, pushes the office door open. "There's booze in his bottom desk drawer. Cazadores."

Sloane is only good for about a beer and a half and never the hard stuff but she asks, "What if he comes back?"

Stephen smiles. "Don't worry. I've replaced the tequila twice already."

Sloane walks away from the temptation and into the office. She tries reaching over the desk to use the phone, knows straight away she won't figure it out upside down, and goes around to Reyes's seat, but she doesn't sit. It's just as bright and uncomfortable in here as it is in the waiting room, and probably worse—probably wired to Stephen's earpiece. She's got to call Heavy, and she's got to make it quick.

When he answers she says, "I've got something. It's a lot of work, but it's something."

"Where the hell are you? We've been trying to call."

"I'm at Fifty East Monroe. I'll explain later. Can you meet me?"

"I can if you're coming here and bringing the suspect."

"What?"

"That article caused quite an influx of calls. Wannabe victims, maybe-were victims, nut jobs. Guzman had a team just to take the calls. Probably fifty tips came in. Since I opened my fat mouth to the reporter, Guzman said I had to field the reports. All of them. Even though, technically, they're Area Three's."

"Are you kidding me?"

"Do I sound like it?"

"Tell him that's all bunk. Tell him I've got leads, and you've got to meet me."

"I've been trying to call you to tell you that I've got *the* lead, and we've got to bring him in."

"Well, shit, tell me. Who?"

"Call came in about one Caspar Mercado. His ex saw the article and said he'd done the same to her. She knew details. I didn't talk to her, but Guzman confirmed with the dispatcher, made him our first priority."

"Because of a phone call?"

"Mercado's got priors. Couple of gang raps. An assault."

"Shouldn't we put him in a real photo lineup? Show the vics?"

"After they've seen his face in the paper?"

"I don't understand why Guzman is in such a rush."

"Order came down from Wojciechowski."

"Why does Pee Wee care?"

"I don't know, Sloane, why do you?"

Sloane sits, and immediately notices the blonde in the silver-framed photo on Reyes's desk, presumably his wife. The woman looks back at her, heavy black eyes, and for some reason Sloane doesn't like it. She turns the frame away, says, "This all seems too easy."

"We haven't even found Mercado yet. Let's bring him in,

and his ex, and then decide about the other vics. We've got orders; can't you let it be a little bit easy and follow them?"

She takes one of Reyes's pens from a leather cup, asks, "Where am I going?"

"I've got a patrol unit waiting for the ex. Name's Rosalia Verdez—she's also his baby's mama. She's picking up the kid, getting a sitter, then she's coming in to talk to us. In the meantime, we know Mercado is probably either holed up in his apartment over by Galewood Park, or hiding out with some woman down South. His sister, I guess. A Little Village address. So, you go one way, I'll go the other? Your choice."

"You're over there, I'm down here. How's that a choice?"

"You can also choose to remain unreachable. Let me run this."

"Forget it. Give me Little Village."

"Lillian Slusser's her name. 2524 South Keeler."

She takes down the info, the pen's ink thick, bleeding through her cheap notepad. "Do we have a description?"

"Don't you read the *Sun-Times*?"

"I mean the woman, goddamn it."

"Oh, Sloane, come on now. You can stand a little of this heat."

"Withstood," she says. "Slusser, two *s*'s. She have a record?"

"No hits in the system. Nothing on file."

"2524 South Keeler. I'm on it." Sloane hangs up, returns the pen to its place, and repositions the photograph. *He's particular,* Stephen had said.

The woman he's particular about is quite worthy: her smooth-curled locks and thin, antique-white sweater blend into the background of the soft-lensed photo, pulling focus to the string of pearls that hang off-center between her tanned cleavage, and also to her nipples: two perfectly positioned pearls themselves, ready in her sweater. Her expression would seem accusatory if not for the way her swollen, bronzed lips are just barely parted: *yes*.

Sloane brings her rough fingertips to her own mouth, wondering if her beauty, or her desire, ever seems so natural.

Sloane exits Reyes's office and she doesn't care who's in Stephen's ear when she goes out to his desk, says, "Gotta run."

"I'm not finished," he says.

"I'll have to come back."

"When?"

"Who knows. Sorry for your trouble."

Stephen hands her his card. "It's no trouble. Call me?"

"Could be tomorrow."

"I can meet you. Grab a drink somewhere."

She says, "That's not necessary," and she doesn't know why she says, "I'm working."

"I can meet you," he says again, more to it.

Admittedly, she wants more.

"Your boss warned me about you," she says. "Causing trouble."

"What's the trouble with one drink?"

"From the boss's desk?" She gives him her best attitude.

"Come on. I'm serious. One drink, no trouble."

"You can't promise both those things." Sloane can't believe she's being so forward, but it works: she gets that smile, promised and delivered.

"I'll call you," she says. As she makes for the elevator, her cheeks are hot, as if she'd actually had a shot of Reyes's tequila.

She doesn't look at Stephen's card until she's in the elevator, on the way down. *No trouble,* she thinks, the card clutched and sweaty in her hand.

16

SLOANE DRIVES WEST UNDER the fat clouds that are finally letting loose, light snow falling to instant slush on 26th Street. She passes the county clink on California Avenue, enters Little Village, and takes a trip down another memory lane.

She and her dad lived here, on South Lawndale. The year hospital bills caught up with them. The year they went broke. Her dad took a job as a janitor at the jail, and Sloane took just as much garbage from the kids in her fourth grade elementary class. The school was primarily Hispanic, and though the lessons were in English, it wasn't the first language on the playground, or in the cafeteria, or in the hallways. Sloane knew only a little Spanish and didn't care to learn more, especially when the boys would run circles around her, calling her names she knew were bad just by the way they said them.

After Sloane punched one of those boys, the teacher called her dad to suggest that if Sloane learned Spanish, she might have an easier time assimilating. That pissed him right off: he told the teacher that Sloane didn't need to learn the damn language if she didn't want to and she didn't need to go to that damn school, either—which wasn't true, because that damn school was the only one he could afford. He was never mad after that, though, when the teacher called to report Sloane truant.

The days Sloane did go to school, silence was armor. Boys, girls, teachers, parents; nice or not, eventually they'd ask, *What's wrong?* or *¿Por qué tan callado?* and *Are you okay?* or *¿Que coño te pasa?*

What did they really want to know? How come Sloane was so quiet? Or did they want to know about how barely a year ago, she'd watched her mom turn skeletal, and with hollowed, smiling eyes, tell her, *You two will take care of each other.* Her mom meant her dad and Sloane knew that, but she didn't know why she said it, or why her teeth had turned so yellow, gums gray. Then someone said *cancer* and soon after, they were sneaking wine into the hospital room and she was coughing, and gurgling, and blathering nonsense while she tried so hard not to die.

But she died anyway and that was worse. Those people at school, did they want to know what dying sounded like?

Because Sloane could still hear her mom fighting, every minute until she lost. *That's* what was wrong.

Sloane and her dad stayed in Little Village a year. She never did learn to speak decent Spanish.

Across South Kedzie Avenue, Sloane drives the strip of 26th that's always and never the same: there's the *fruteria,* the *carniceria,* and the *supermercado;* the half-dozen *quinceanara* dress shops, twice as many currency exchanges, and twice that many convenience stores—most of them blasting blown-speaker *banda* music out at the street, advertising their presence. Not today, though: the snow is a blanket over commerce. Usually, there'd also be street vendors, tamale carts, *elote* carts, and taco trucks; men selling papaya popsicles or *picocito*-flavored shaved ice, or Sloane's childhood favorite—coconut ice cream—from refrigerated pushcarts.

Brr, she thinks, even though she's decidedly starving. She cranks the heat, takes Pulaski up to 25th, then drives a few blocks over to Keeler, a one-way south. At 25th she passes the Epiphany Church, and since it takes up most of the block, she's pretty sure Slusser's address has got to be the single house at the end.

Except that the house is a rectory. If Lillian Slusser actually lives there, the Catholics have finally lost the message.

Sloane drives through the next intersection, checks the first mailbox: 2540. That puts 2524, Slusser's supposed address, on the map at Epiphany—right around the church's confessionals.

Sloane reverses all the way back to the church, double-parks, and gets out; she takes a quick walk up the next block to 2425, in case she got the numbers mixed up. There, a side street and an empty corner lot are the only things between 2431 and 2417, which again proves the hypothesis that the phone tip is bullshit.

On the way back, steely specks of rain take over for the snow, and by the time she reaches the Pilot, her hair is surface-soaked. She uses the last of the napkins left over from Feed to dry her face, and redirects the heat vents toward her hair.

Then she redials Heavy. "I'm sitting in front of Lillian Slusser's," she says. "It's a church. So is this woman Verdez full of it, or what?"

"Not completely full of it, no," he says. "I'm at Mercado's apartment. It's on the nice side of Galewood Park."

"I'll bet."

"I met the landlord. His name's DeLincoln and I didn't catch his last name because it took me too long to get his first one right. He says Mercado's the only one on the lease, but that they all moved in last year—Mercado and Verdez and the kid, too. He says Mercado and Verdez had a couple of good fights, but that it was the kid who did most of the screaming. The last time DeLincoln saw Verdez was back in July or August. She split with the kid and a suitcase and some big guy with a cat tattoo for a shirt."

"That was last summer? And she hasn't been back?"

"DeLincoln says Mercado brings the kid by once in a while, but that's about it."

"Guess he's been busy fighting other women."

"DeLincoln was surprised I was there for Mercado. Said Mercado is a stand-up guy."

"So what, I'm supposed to go into the church, say a prayer for him?"

"I'm sorry, Sloane. I don't know who screwed up the address. Will you hang tight for a little bit? I'll call patrol, see where they're at with Verdez."

"I'd like to get back up north," Sloane says, the rain coming harder now. "I'm in for a crap drive."

"Isn't it always? Why don't you go down to Twenty-sixth Street, get some lunch. And don't try to tell me you ate already."

"I did," Sloane lies.

"A half hour, darlin'," Heavy says. "Occupy yourself." He hangs up before she can argue.

She is hungry, so she follows Heavy's orders and drives south. She opts for a taco at Taqueria Atotonilco, the place her dad used to frequent the year they lived here. When he worked overtime, he'd bring home dinner: *tacos al pastor* and *carne asada* for himself, and for Sloane, a strawberry shake. She'd have dry Rice Krispies or saltine crackers for a side dish; she had a weak stomach in those days.

She darts through the rain, hoping to get in and out just as quickly, but winds up at the back of a packed to-go line. She'd decided on a couple chicken tacos on the quick drive over, but the smell of hot grease and wet people is not an appetizing combination. She knows she'll carry it in her hair, the humid meat odor impossible to wash out, same as the morgue.

God, that fucking place. She's been to the morgue too many times, and the time that tipped her makes even the simplest reminder take her right back. Every body in the county without a doctor-signed death certificate sent there, hoisted onto a metal gurney, stripped and gutted, weighed and bagged. Every body in the cutting room coated with the dull film of inertia; the remaining fluids already leaked to the floor, slippery and spoiled, mopped to the drain. Every single body's life, however it was before, reduced to a toe tag and an indefinite stretch in the cold warehouse stacks: every body a nobody.

Last time Sloane was at the morgue, for Zookie, she stopped to talk to one of the cutters who was sitting on top of a picnic table splitting time between a 7-Eleven, white bread, chicken-salad sandwich, mayonnaise squeezed out the sides, and a Newport cigarette. There was no wind; the ashes were all over his scrubs. He was a big black man and his little nametag said *ASK ME,* so Sloane did. She bummed a smoke to get the death out of her nose. Then she asked if he was the one cutting Zookie.

"The kid? Nah." Then he said, "Listen, the way I figure? We all the same. Our bones is white, blood's red, and when we dead, we all blue—an' you know what? We all smell like the same bad mothahfuckah. Anything smell that bad," he said, still chewing, "ain't worried about much now, so neither am I."

"Oh," Sloane said, sorry she asked.

Ask Me looked up from his sandwich and his left eye floated, its focus off toward the parking lot; his smile followed. The mayo in the ridges of his gums stayed right where it was.

At that moment, Sloane wished she believed in God.

At this moment, Sloane steps up to the grease-smeared counter to order her tacos, and feels like she might vomit.

Next thing she knows she's outside, the parking lot, the freezing rain, her chin up, the beads of biting-cold water hitting her face. She wishes they'd come faster. Sting. Wishes the rain would fall hard and fast and soak her to her white bones and make her feel something—instead of in between something. She's never been so afraid; this limbo. Between victims. At the end of a relationship. Holding on to a life.

She drives back to the church and double-parks in front of the entrance. She checks her watch, but can't remember what time it was when Heavy gave himself a half hour.

"Get lunch," he said. She tried.

"Occupy yourself," he told her. She'll try.

She turns on the radio, flips through her programmed FM stations, doesn't find anything. Never finds anything. She listens for traffic and weather on AM 780, and they tell her what she already knows: traffic, yes of course; weather, more of it. Of course.

When they cut to news, the top story is something about the mayor seeking approval for his Olympic stadium construction plans, and Sloane thinks of Reyes. She picks up the

Sun-Times from the passenger seat, opens it to the article he showed her, and skims until she finds where she left off:

> *City officials at odds . . . development in the Pu-*
> *laski Corridor . . . Alderman Alan Van der Meer*
> *objected . . . Zimmerman & Co. employs ex-*
> *offenders through the mayor's reentry program . . .*
> Now, it's come to light that the developer may
> have been overlooking some offenders' records.
> Van der Meer also believes the company has side-
> stepped a federal no-match letter, which requires
> immigrant workers to provide valid social secu-
> rity numbers.
>
> Van der Meer's latest press release states: "Hir-
> ing workers who have not and will not abide by
> the law is unacceptable. In this struggling com-
> munity, we need exemplary projects that not only
> meet, but exceed standards in development and
> in business."
>
> Thirteenth Ward Alderman Jerry Watt has
> been a staunch ally for Zimmerman & Co. "Hum-
> boldt Park needs them," Watt told reporters after
> last night's City Council debacle. "Industry has
> moved west. Public transportation is ailing. The
> economy is awful. And for Van der Meer to ap-
> prove the big-money Springfield [condo develop-
> ment] instead of saying yes to a resident friendly
> project like Edificio? That's a slap in the face to

every working family in this neighborhood. This
TIF isn't a trust fund."

Sloane folds the paper over when a Volvo hatchback nearly sideswipes the passenger side of the Pilot and pulls in front, parks, hazard lights. A slender woman about Sloane's age with better skin and worse boots—big, wooly, tan sheepskin jobs—gets out, driver's side.

From the bootstraps up, the woman quickly comes undone: stretch pants unfortunately stretched, store tags left hanging from the arm of her spring green jacket; her brown curls matted and forced through a rubber band, still wet. Sloane thinks the woman could have used a few minutes with a mirror.

But then she opens the Volvo's back door and retrieves a twoish-year-old boy from a car seat, hair curling at his ears, his wooly boots just as too-big.

Of course, Sloane thinks. A mom. She has no extra time, and if she ever does get a minute, she probably doesn't waste it in a mirror.

Sloane half watches the woman help her son up the church steps, her patience and his boots making the process rather lengthy. Sloane has little patience, and loses interest halfway up. She goes back to the newspaper, finds her place in the article:

> ...TIF isn't a trust fund." Watt believes the
> Zimmerman & Co. project falls in line with the
> Pulaski Corridor TIF's original plan, implemented

in 1999, which aimed to help West Humboldt Park hold on to industrial business.

Since the TIF began, taxpayers' money normally allocated for schools, parks, and community services has gone into the fund. Unfortunately, gangs have taken up the slack, causing crime rates to rise, property values to fall, and businesses to seek refuge in the suburbs.

"Of course I support growth," Van der Meer said last night. "But I will not allow taxpayers' money go to [Zimmerman & Co.] who supports illegal activity. Next thing you know, they'll want to build a pharmacy that employs drug dealers. Watt is the company's political prostitute, and I won't stand for it."

Plans for Zimmerman & Company's four-block retail and residential complex include a community center, an employment recruiter, and a child-care facility.

"This project covers all the bases," said Watt.

"This project covers up our problems," said Van der Meer.

Sloane closes the paper, turns to the back page to find out which Cubs player's going to make or break the season this week—not that it matters to her, but it might determine Eddie's mood later on. If the news is good, maybe here won't seem so bad.

She's triple-checking the reception on her phone because she hasn't heard a thing from Heavy, or Carolyn, or Eddie either, and it's after two o'clock. Outside, another mom—this one better dressed and apparently less patient than the first—carries one little girl and drags another toward the church steps, both of them resisting. When they get up the steps, the church door opens, and a woman in a black business suit and a nun's veil offers a hand to the child on foot, and greetings to all.

As the women coax the girls inside, Sloane decides that if she did believe in God, she'd thank him for small favors.

She's pretty sure firearms are a no-no in church so she stows her .22 in the glove box, .38 under the seat. Then she silences her cell, arms the Pilot's alarm, and runs up the church steps. If the address Verdez gave the tip line is correct, maybe what got screwed up in translation was Mercado's *sister*.

A homemade poster in the entryway reads GOD BLESS MOMMIES! TODAY'S LENT FOR LITTLE ONES WILL BE HELD IN THE APOSTLES ACTIVITY ROOM.

Sloane is about to go in, ask one of the people kneeling in the back about the Apostles Room, when the mom in the wooly boots comes around the corner from a right side doorway, the echo of a screeching child her shadow. There's something territorial about the way the woman eyes Sloane, and she leaves a space so distinct between them on her way out that she might as well growl.

When another mom appears, same doorway, similar vigilant reaction, Sloane figures there's not much she can do; she must smell single.

She avoids eye contact with the next few moms as she heads upstream, following the sounds of overstimulated children to the Apostles Room. And active it is: there are about a dozen toddlers, three nuns, and one mom; based on Sloane's calculations, that makes each adult one hand short of any possible control. That leaves about four kids a few moves shy of trouble, and Sloane picks them out right away: the boy who's cranking knobs on the baseboard heater's control panel; the girl with a brown crayon and a Bible; the boy whose afternoon snack is the host bowl of communion wafers, and the boy next to him, who has found the blood of Christ.

"Hey," Sloane says, but the kid's already got the silver cruet balanced on a low craft table and, assuming it works something like a really full sippy cup, dumps the good juice all over himself. Tears ensue.

God knows why all adult eyes fall on Sloane, but she hasn't made any friends yet, so she shows her star and announces, over the purple-and-red-faced traumatized boy and the rest of the chaos, "I'm looking for Lillian Slusser."

Two of the nuns cross themselves; the mom looks sideways at the third one.

"Sister Slusser?" Sloane asks that one.

"Sistafriend!" one of the girls at her feet squeals, outing her.

The nun nods at Sloane and comes forward, dutifully

taking the brown crayon from the little girl and the host bowl of wafers from the boy on her way.

"Where it's quiet?" Sloane asks.

"My pleasure."

She takes Sloane down the hall and into a room that looks like it's been worked over by a bridal party, cluttered with forgotten silk flowers and safety pins, worn nylons and clear nail polish, aerosol hairspray.

The sister takes off her veil and looks years younger than she did with it; Sloane pegs her at forty—maybe even younger in street clothes. She puts the veil aside and says, "I never did like this thing. I have a lot of extra heat to let out up top." She sits on a folding chair, invites Sloane to sit, too, and places the bowl of wafers on the card table between them. "Hungry?" she asks, a shrewd smile. "It's God's way in there," she says, fingers pulling the hair at the back of her neck where her red hair's gone soft white. "One of our kids' groups' sisters caught a devil's cold this morning, and about five minutes ago I remembered why I never wanted the toddler classes. Those little monsters are going to get me scheduled for the big event sooner than I'd planned."

"I'm sorry?"

"Don't be sorry. I'm not dead yet." She rolls her head from one side to the other, stretching her neck. "Now first things first: please, call me Lil. Sister Slusser has a hard time selling seashells, if you get my drift. Hah."

"You can call me Sloane."

"Does that mean this is an unofficial visit?"

"That means I'm here about someone you know. Caspar Mercado."

"Jesus, Mary, and Joseph," Lil says, crossing herself. "I've been waiting for this."

"Will you tell me where he is?"

"What? I thought *you* were here to tell *me* where he is."

"I was told he might be here with you."

"I don't know who'd say that. He doesn't come around since he met Rosie."

"Rosalia Verdez?"

"Isn't she a beauty?" Lil cracks the same shrewd smile, except she doesn't mean it. "I tried to tell Caspar that she's not a good influence. But he insisted on doing the right thing for Casimiro."

"His son?"

Lil nods. "Name means 'peaceful.' I don't think Rosie's smart enough to know she was being ironic."

"Mercado is suspected in a string of assaults."

"Caspar may be a lot of things," Lil says, "but he is not a fighter."

The way Lil says "fighter" strikes an obvious chord. Sloane says, "He's got a record."

"Oh sure he does," Lil says. "How else do you think he came up in this neighborhood?" She puts an elbow on the table, points her index finger to the heavens. "Let me tell you something about Caspar. When he was a kid, gangs were God in this neighborhood. And Caspar? He was a baby on the sidelines—nine years old, ten at the most? He and his

mom had just come up from Guanajuato and, boy, he saw
the worst of it there. These gangs up here were like sports
teams to him with their colors and their rules. I remember
the first time I saw Caspar; it's still so vivid in my mind: one
of the Imperial Gangsters had given him a black and pink
bandana, and he tied it around his face like an Old West
bank robber. I used to jog, back in those years—you'd never
know it now—I even walk like a penguin. My knees are like
rusted bike gears."

Sloane's afraid the nun's storytelling skills are rusty, too,
so she says, "If Mercado was an IG, he was a fighter."

"That's the *something* about Caspar I want to tell you." Lil
pushes the host bowl out of the way, folds her hands on the
table. "I came here from San Francisco during the nicest
Midwest spring I've ever known—Lord knows I wouldn't
have stayed if it'd been like this one. It was the same spring
that a group of the IGs made our corner their headquarters.
At first it didn't seem so bad; they were just kids with nowhere else to go. But there'd be no gangs without rivals, and
pretty soon it was a war zone.

"It was kind of funny, watching the high-stakes street
business, seeing the boys step up, acting like big men. After-
ward, though? They'd be signing themselves, kissing their
flashy gold cross necklaces. Funny, those boys, thanking
God, thinking He'd saved them every time."

Sloane says, "Mercado was one of them."

"Caspar was a kid, yes. And like I said, he had to be in the
gang. But he wasn't a fighter and he wasn't stupid, either. I

told you, I used to jog? Well, Caspar came to me one Saturday morning and said, 'Sister, I don't want you to run around here.' There was another boy shot and killed the day before, so I thought he was concerned for my safety. But then he said, 'Please, sister. They told me to tell you not to run.' And then I was so angry, because the gang was putting my safety on him. So I said, 'Caspar, you tell your gang that this is my neighborhood, too. And just because I'm a cute white girl doesn't mean I'll be pushed around. I'll run where I like. And I will not be afraid, because God has already saved me.'"

Lil unfolds her hands, flat on the table. "The next morning," she says, "I put on my tennies and went outside, right out the front doors. And there stood Caspar, and this big bully—JuanCarlos Castelleno—one of the IG's leaders. I said, 'Boys,'" she raises her right hand to slap it back down, "'You can have this corner, but unless you're here to break my legs, you will not take my morning run.'

"They looked at each other and Caspar said, 'Sister, we're going to run with you.' When I asked why, you know what JuanCarlos said? He said, 'Because nobody messes with a nun.' How about that?"

"Sister," Sloane says, short, as always, on patience, "that's quite a story, but I'm afraid all you've given me is a pretty good reason why you'd want to protect Mercado now."

"You didn't let me finish," Lil says, standing up. "The two of them ran with me every day until JuanCarlos went to jail. A year or so. Then, by the grace of God, Caspar's mom got her act together and got him out of here." She goes to the doorway, apparently so acutely aware, she knew a little girl from the Apostles Room had tiptoed down the hall and been sitting just outside the door. She grabs the girl's hand and pulls her into the room.

"Sistafriend!" the toddler screams, delighted, as Lil picks her up, not so delighted.

"Caspar got his GED," Lil says, "and a decent job at UPS. Last I heard, he's enrolled in night school at Roosevelt for his associate's degree." She detaches the toddler's sticky hand from her hair, says, "Caspar always says I steered him right. The truth is? I didn't do anything but get him into shape."

"Do you know where Mercado is?" Sloane asks, standing up.

"No." Lil bounces the girl on her hip, says, "Shhhh." She reaches over with her temporarily free hand and picks up her veil, then puts it over the girl's head: peekaboo.

Sloane says, "You can find out where he is."

"Probably," Lil says, her voice sing-song, for the little one. "But I won't."

"Even if he's innocent, I still need to find him," Sloane says, following them back toward the Apostles Room.

Lil turns back, says, "May the good Lord be with you, then." As she turns, the toddler watches Sloane with big, brown, wonderful eyes, and they step back into the chaos.

17

FIRST THING SLOANE DOES when she gets out of Epiphany Church is jam her hands in her coat pockets. The temperature has fallen far and fast, and she left her gloves in the Pilot. She tucks her chin, shielding her face; the cold is dry, now, and the wind so brittle it seems like an entirely different day. She clears her throat, wonders if she's trying to catch the flu.

Once in the Pilot, heat cranked, she checks her voicemail. As soon as she hears her dad's voice, she's making tracks to the Edens, the quickest route to the hospital.

"Deputy," he says. "I guess they're about to let me out of here." Carolyn chimes in from the background and he fumbles with the phone, says, "Hang on, what?"

Sloane waits for her dad to translate whatever Carolyn's saying, her tone bossy. Sloane's knuckles go white around the steering wheel.

"I know," her dad says, languid; he must still feel the nice blush of hospital-grade drugs. "Sloane, I'm supposed to tell you Carolyn's taking me home. And that I've been misdiagnosed. I'm afraid they think I'm some kind of rabbit. You should see this diet—"

Carolyn cuts in again, and this time takes the phone. "Listen, Sloane honey. We should nix the dinner idea—"

Now Sloane's dad is the one bitching in the background, something about starving to death.

"Oh, baloney," Carolyn says to him. "Listen Sloane, honey, his diet is pretty restricted, and they say he's going to be pretty wiped out by the time I get him home. So how about we nix dinner? I don't want you to go to all the trouble. I'll just pick up something on the way. We'd love for you to stop by, though. We should be there by six, fingers crossed—"

Sloane *honey* deletes the rest of *fucking* Carolyn's message. It's Thursday night and her dad just survived another trip to the hospital. The last thing he's going to eat for dinner is some pseudo-gourmet microwaveable meal that's no more appealing than lime jello and cottage cheese.

Sloane gets off the Edens an exit before the one to her dad's apartment, fights for a parking spot in the Jewel lot, and snags a shopping cart that's loose between spaces. On the way to the entrance, the cart's wheels turn in different directions; as she fights the awkward pull, she decides her life is this way.

At the entrance she ditches the cart, hooks a basket around her left arm, and dials Heavy—voicemail, of course. At the beep she says, "Detective, since you never called and you won't answer, I hope you have answers. I found Slusser. She's a nun and she makes Mercado sound like a saint. I think Verdez is the one we need to talk to. Call me and I'm there in ten." She hangs up after that last bit—a lie; even if there was no traffic, she's at least forty minutes away. If Heavy thinks she's within striking distance, though, he'll call back. He'll have to; it's close to quitting time, and he won't want her to show up, get them stuck there all night.

Inside the Jewel, the soft yellow-white lights and farm-stand display make the produce look better than it probably is, and some New Age–glazed love song makes Sloane feel like buying and consuming a half gallon of ice cream. She sticks to her mental list, though, and breezes through the produce section for a head of garlic, a bunch of parsley, grape tomatoes, a cucumber, and a Vidalia onion.

On her way toward the back of the store, Sloane spots a bushel basket of kiwi; still thinking of dessert, she stops to squeeze a couple.

"Can I help you?" asks a guy in a blue apron with a face like a butternut squash, swollen and pale and well past ripe. Sloane's spent enough time talking to helpful people who can't do a thing for her so she defers the question to the mom by the apples, the one who's talking on her Bluetooth headset

while her toddler is doing his own shopping, a fistful of Fruit
Roll-Ups swiped and homebound if mom spends the rest of
the trip gabbing.

"Ma'am? Can I help you?"

Sloane ditches the kiwis and makes for the aisles. She
picks risotto over pasta and olive oil spray over the real stuff,
but skimping ends there. She asks the butcher for three of
the best-looking sirloin steaks, picks up a carton of brown
eggs and a package of goat cheese, and finds a fifteen-dollar
bottle of cabernet with a silver-eyed wolf on the label. Someone told her any cabernet between fifteen to twenty dollars is
decent; apart from that, her only other basis for comparison
is the bottle's artwork. She's drawn to the wolf, his firm re-
pose, a dignified predator.

She's in the frozen section, the sorbet window's glass
fogged from indecision, when Heavy calls back. She puts the
pint of chocolate back on the shelf for the third time and answers. "Heavy. Finally."

"Verdez didn't show."

Sloane says, "God dammit," and slams the freezer door;
her one-two combination startles the wool-capped guy in
front of the frozen potatoes and he jumps back, hands up,
his dark-scruffed face handsome even as it's stuck at *what?*

Sloane feels her own face on its way to an amazing shade
of red; she tips her invisible hat, shows him her phone. His
response is a perfectly crooked smile, sweet as any dessert.

Heavy says, "Cool off a minute and listen, darlin'," no

idea how perceptive he is. Sloane opens the freezer door again to hide behind the fogged glass.

She says, "I'm listening."

"Good. Verdez didn't show, but she called. She said she doesn't want to be the one pointing the finger."

"She *is* the one pointing the finger—"

"But she gave us a fail-proof location for Mercado. To-morrow, eleven forty-five, at the public elementary school on Potomac. He'll be there, picking up the kid."

"So we're on hold until kindergarten's over tomorrow?"

"I've got plenty to do. Guzman gave me a pipe cleaner in Skinner Park and a couple happy endings at a massage par-lor out west on Foster. You're welcome to come in early to-morrow, take one of them."

"What about *this* case?" Sloane asks. "Can I move on my end? Can I follow up on the list I'm getting from those Loop suits?" She peeks around the freezer door, sees the wool-capped guy nearer now, but he cuts away, pretends to be interested in the popsicles.

Heavy says, "Guzman suspended everything until Mer-cado's in here and in cuffs or on his way back to Mexico."

"Why's Guz being such a broken record?"

"I told you, word came down."

"So Pee Wee's the broken record? I don't get it. I don't like it, either."

"Well hey, you're welcome to come over, give them back all the flak I've been taking for you today."

"I'm sorry," Sloane says, and she means it, imagining the other dicks on the floor going at Heavy all day, telling him he's covering for Sloane because she's a piece of ass. Because he wants some of that ass. Because they think he's already getting it.

She closes the freezer door, finds the wool-capped guy with a skinny, harsh-eyed, brunette-capped beauty on his arm, and feels like a completely different kind of ass.

Sloane turns away from the couple and says, low, to Heavy, "I have to go. I'm making dinner."

"How's your father?"

"He's fine. It's his girlfriend I can't stand."

"As long as he's happy, right?"

"I wish I could chalk that up to one of his thirty-two medications, but he hasn't been taking them."

"Maybe he's happy to let things run their course," Heavy says.

Sloane opens the freezer door to just get some dessert already, but in her mind's eye, she sees her dad's face: his once rough and weathered skin gone thin and spotty, his original teeth stained in contrast to last year's bridge, his eyelids fallen over his lashes. And his smile: always difficult. And wanting. No—*wishing*. Maybe Heavy is right, and her dad is tired of trying.

Sloane has no idea which flavor sorbet she finally takes as she slips back into autopilot and hears herself say, "Heavy, I don't think my dad's been happy for a long time."

———

AT HER DAD'S APARTMENT, Sloane fries two eggs over easy, pol-
ishing off both before she feels less than delirious-hungry.
As soon as she eats, she feels nauseated, and thinks maybe
she's been all over the emotional place because her body is
fighting some kind of sick. She doesn't think she has a
fever.

She washes the dishes and the couple of others she left
this morning; separates all but one of the remaining eggs;
slices the tomatoes, cucumber, and onion; and chops the
parsley. While she's timing the risotto, she thinks maybe she
should eat something else, so she opens the açaí berry
sorbet—not the flavor she'd have actually chosen—and not
very good, either. It's gritty, and it tastes more like raisins
than any kind of berry. She puts it in the empty freezer to
keep the ice company. Carolyn will probably love it.

The same someone who told her how to choose a decent
red also told her it's supposed to breathe. When she searches
through all the kitchen drawers and can't find a corkscrew,
she rummages through her dad's toolbox, attaches a relieved
spiral bit to an electric drill, and completely shreds the cork.
She punches what's left of it into the bottle and pours a little
of the wine into three juice glasses; she uses the rest to mari-
nate the meat.

She's sharpening the steak knives when Eddie calls. She
thinks about letting him go to voicemail, to put him off just a
little longer; she should set the table, get the steaks on. *Stalling*

again, she thinks, though there's no reason. It's not like she'll answer and get right to the thick of it, tell him *forget it, it's over.* She has never been, and never will be, the one to give up.

The thin of it is another story. She answers.

"Hey Slo," Eddie says over some other guys in the background. "Pocahontas had a blood spatter class down at the academy today, so we're going for a couple beers at Union Park. Meet us there?"

Pocahontas: Gina Simonetti. Demoted from detective; only reason she didn't get fired was because no one could prove she actually slept with her suspect. Sloane was sympathetic, since all a male cop in the same situation would get from his bosses would be an unofficial rank up.

Then Sloane saw Gina out at Union Park. The little cop with the littler waistline loved the attention. The speculation. Even the nickname. She might as well have worn a feather in her hair.

"You there?" Eddie asks.

"I'm here—"

"I know Union Park's not your favorite, Slo, but not for nothing, all we've been doing lately is sleeping together. I'd like to see you."

"Awww," one of the other guys teases, starting a round of the same.

"You there?" he asks again.

Awww.

Headlights flash in the front apartment window and

Sloane looks out: it's Carolyn's car, doing a U-turn, parking. "I have to go."

"Slo, come on. What gives?"

"It's my dad," she says, up and on her way to the kitchen. "His heart."

"Oh, God, Slo, why didn't you tell me?"

"I'm telling you."

"Where are you? I'll drop these guys and come—"

"He's okay now, E. You don't need to come."

"But I want to." The guys in the background have gone silent; she knows this is no good, his audience.

"I didn't tell you because I wanted to have answers," she says, knowing she's just used Carolyn's line and feeling shitty for it.

"I don't need answers, Slo. Except to know you're okay."

Make that shittier.

"Listen," she says, "he's just getting home. Can I call you later?" She lights the stove, sprays the skillet.

"You don't want me to come over there," Eddie says. Not an answer, or a question either.

Sloane can't believe he said it, let alone sensed it. Her reply is a terrible argument. "This isn't about us, E."

"I know," he says. "It's about you."

"It's my dad," she says, knowing she sounds desperate.

"You know where I'll be," Eddie says, and hangs up without waiting on a good-bye.

Sloane's hands shake as she pockets the phone, moves the risotto to the back burner, and puts the steaks on.

"Deputy," her dad says, first one in the door, slow on his feet. He's no quicker with his scarf, or his coat, but Carolyn isn't any help, squeezing past him, peeling off her coat and deciding what she'll object to first.

"Sloane honey," she says, ears perking to the skillet's sizzle, "I thought you weren't going to cook." She rolls up her sleeves though Sloane knows she'll be no help in the kitchen, either.

"Please, sit," Sloane says, pulling out a chair for her dad. She asks him, "You hungry?"

Carolyn sits down across from him, waiting for his answer.

"Is this what I think it is?"

"It *is* Thursday night," Sloane says, and passes them each a juice glass, cork pieces floating in the wine. She holds up the third to toast.

Carolyn says, "Jim, you shouldn't."

But Jim doesn't even look at Carolyn when he says, "We had a club." He raises his glass. "To Village Quarter Road."

"To Larkin Avenue."

"To South Lawndale."

"West Addison."

"West Montrose."

"North Maplewood," Sloane says, "my favorite."

"Then you went to Oak Park Avenue."

"And then I crashed on your couch at North Sheridan."

"Then when you were at Halsted, I was at Euclid."

"Then I went to Wrightwood."

"And I went out west on Diversey," he says. "And you're where now? Kingsbury?"

Sloane nods. "And you're at Halsted."

"To the long way here," he says, raising his glass.

"And the long way to go," Sloane says, unable to mask the doubt in her voice.

"Oh, I see," Carolyn says, though no one's offered, an explanation. "What about South Ellis Avenue, Jim?"

"Cheers," Jim says, tipping his glass to them both.

They toast, Carolyn's lips too crunched in a scowl to get much of a sip; Sloane and her dad don't sip at all; they never have. It was Sloane's mom who liked cabernet, the one they snuck into Sherman hospital—rather, the thermos of "tea"—because they wanted her to enjoy at least one thing in the little time left.

Sloane puts her glass down next to her dad's, and goes to the stove to flip the steaks.

Dad says, "Smells delicious."

"Steak," Carolyn says. "You think that's a good idea?"

"Best idea I've heard all day."

Sloane thinks he's drawing a line of sorts, and she knows the safe side is the silent one. She minds her own kitchen business, seasoning the steaks with pepper and the leftover marinade, whisking together the vinegar and sugar for the salad, and waiting for Carolyn to decide which side she's going to take.

"Jim," Carolyn says, finally, "I can't compete with memories."

Then Sloane is eleven years old again, the meat cooking too quickly and the eggs still raw, timing always the challenge; and no matter how many Thursday nights or how many times she followed the same recipe—even with the same ingredients and the very same cookware and even when the timing was exactly right—she could never make steak and eggs taste like her mom's.

Sloane never thought of cooking as a kind of competition. Or that she'd put herself in an impossible contest with her own memories.

Sloane never thought Carolyn had a clue, either. Until now.

Dad says, "I've got to use the john."

He gets up and makes his way out of the room and Sloane wonders if that's her cue to say sorry to Carolyn, but she wouldn't know where to begin. The hospital? The precious memories? The token dinner? The day they met? She lights another burner, sprays a second skillet, starts the eggs, and decides to stay on the safe side.

Without her dad in the room, the tension falls hard in her corner. Of course she should say something. Anything. She should just take a breath and step over to the other side, join Carolyn there, let her into the club. Instead, Sloane dresses the salad. Turns the eggs, one easy move. Flips the steaks. Stirs the risotto. And feels like she's stuck there, the god damned safe side. Thinks simply turning around would be an apology, now.

She folds the single yolk she saved into the eggs, then plates the salad and risotto. She wishes her dad would hurry up already. Her timing is right, this time—but only as far as dinner's concerned.

She turns off the eggs and calls, "Dad, we're on," and she's relieved when she hears the toilet flush and the bathroom sink run. She plates the steaks and puts the eggs on top, then adds parsley, goat cheese, and a healthy sprinkle of pepper over everything.

She waits for the bathroom door to open and then turns, two of the three plates and a smile ready for the table; she isn't surprised to find Carolyn's empty glass, but she certainly doesn't expect to see her dad coming into the room with her hairdryer.

"How come your stuff is in the bathroom?"

The plates are sudden stone weights. "I thought," she says, "if it's okay with you, I thought that I'd stay here a while. Help take care of things."

"What about Eddie?" her dad asks at the same time Carolyn asks—

"You didn't tell her?" From wine-stained lips.

"When was I going to do that?" her dad says, wrapping the cord around the hairdryer like he's about to pack it. "You took the phone when I was leaving her the message."

"We talked about all this. You could have told her before, Jim."

Sloane puts the plates down and says, "I'm standing right here, Carolyn."

Carolyn picks up her empty wine glass and toasts the room. "Sloane honey, your father is going to come stay with me."

"Oh," Sloane says, and can't look at her dad so she turns back to the stove to get the last plate, and to right herself, though she is as shocked by this loss as she was by the possibility of her dad's passing.

She hears him asking, "Dep, what about Eddie?"

And she looks down at her plate and she wants to knock it off the stove and say *What about me, Dad?* but she's a grown-up now, so she can either sit down to dinner and pretend this is all okay, or she can't.

Or, she can reach into her pocket, take out her phone, and say, "Shit."

"What's wrong?" her dad asks.

"A lead," she says. "I've gotta go."

Her dad offers the usual protests: "You should eat first," and, "I'll bet you're the only cop in this city who puts the job before red meat," and while she's packing up her things he's telling Carolyn, "When she was in homicide I used to be able to tell her the case wasn't going anywhere." Meanwhile Carolyn wraps Saran over her plate and Sloane says equally plasticky good-byes and she wears her busy-cop face as she gets into the Pilot and waves, *love ya,* and heads north. She snakes her way alongside the Dan Ryan until she finds she can't stand the smell of the meal she cooked and stops in front of Jane Addams High School, gets out, tosses the plate in a Dumpster.

Once outside, and on her feet, she is not emotional; even as she thinks of Eddie at Union Park, a table full of empty beer bottles and Gina Simonetti making him feel better.

Even as traffic thunders on the expressway overhead, one semi following the next's taillights. Even as a group of teenagers chase each other through the school's south parking lot, jump into beater cars, and take off, the fastest boy leading the chase. She can handle these things. There is a logical order to them.

Just like working a case.

She dials Stephen Carvalho.

18

SLOANE SITS IN THE Pilot outside Stephen's loft building on Eighteenth Street. It's a mid-rise structure, the only one over ten stories in the area. On its face, from the riverside, it looks brand-new. When Sloane drove past and turned back to park, she got a good look at the busted-out black windows in the back, and decided it's just another old factory rehab-in-progress.

When she came over the bridge, she wasn't sure she had the right place; there were only a few windows registering any sort of light, or life, and the rest of the block—the once-industrial space between the river and Canal Street—is either torn up, torn down, or empty.

Eighteenth Street is still a bridge here where she's parked, as it crosses over the south branch of the Chicago River and makes its way back to ground level behind her. Sloane's already been out of the Pilot, binoculars over the guardrail, casing the terrain underneath; Stephen told her to park down there in one of the empty spaces. Apparently, residents pull into the entrance and descend a circular ramp to a ground-level parking lot that's half covered by the building, unlit and unprotected, its pavement a nice touch. When Sloane got back in the Pilot and pulled up, she stopped at the flashing light just inside the building's auto entrance. She thought maybe Stephen forgot to tell her about an access code, and then she saw headlights: another car coming up the ramp, apparently meant for use in both directions.

She backed out and down the street against a sudden pack of eastbound traffic and parked in a tow zone. No way she'd park down there, only one way out. Even though she's on the open street now, her hazard lights a testament to her temporary stay, the fat clouds overhead that sit, awkward and idling, make her feel trapped just the same.

She knows she shouldn't have agreed to meet Stephen here, but she couldn't make a big deal out of it, either. When she called him, he said he was just finishing up at the gym—a place called the Rumble Arts Center on North Avenue in Humboldt Park. In Sloane's beat.

Sloane had never heard of the gym, but told Stephen it was probably because nobody had been sexually assaulted there in recent months. He laughed. She laughed back.

She suggested meeting at a café close by the gym on

Division Street, a place with good coffee and even better iced cookies. He said sure, but he'd have to go home to get the list first. He estimated his trip would take forty-five minutes, traffic or none.

Forty-five minutes, Sloane said, and the café would be closed. Stephen told her he wasn't much of a dessert guy, anyway. So they haggled over another suitable place to meet: his suggestions all back-alley, in-the-know booze joints; hers all open to the public, well lit, and stimulant free. The longer they went back and forth, the more inappropriate Sloane felt. It wasn't like they were going on a date, and she was about to say so, but he threw her off track when he said he could really use a quick shower—and said it like she should join him.

That gave her the idea that he had the wrong idea so she said, "Okay: you have the information I need so I'll make it easy. Just pick a place and I'll come there and pick it up." He asked, "Really?" She said, "Yes," and then he said, "Come to my place."

She talked herself right into that one, damn, and she couldn't back up an inch. Because no cop should have a problem going to someone's residence for important information, no matter how flirtatious and handsome and potentially intense that someone happens to be.

Anyway, if Sloane were a male officer and some sweet young thing offered free, on-the-job candy, she'd be there and gone already, about to tell a fake-casual, highly exaggerated story to the boys: how hot and bothered the girl was, just how sweet, just how young.

Only thing Sloane could say at that point in the conversation with Stephen and still be the least bit cool was, "Give me the address." And she's been out here, in front of his place, trying to decide if she should be official, carry her gun and star inside, ever since.

Another burst of traffic comes from behind Canal Street, and Sloane thinks it's just about time for Stephen to arrive, so she picks up her cell and pretends she's on a call. An important call. "Yes, I know," she says, feeling as ridiculous as she does clever. She caught a murder-one suspect once, though, same trick: He thought white girl was caught up on her cell outside the Sports Authority on Clark Street, but it so happened she was following him, and waiting for him to use the deal-marked cash he'd taken from his victim. He bought himself a Pistons jersey. Probably won't ever get to wear it.

While she's "talking," an SUV twice as tall as hers pulls up and stops, its passenger window flush with hers, though a good two feet higher. She waves the vehicle on; it's not like she's in its way. But then it kicks out of gear, and the passenger window comes down, and Stephen's face comes from darkness.

"Hey," he says, his smile barely a flash compared to the window's gigantic metallic frame. "Follow me in?"

A car lays on its horn behind them and Sloane hears herself say, "Okay," and she curses all the way down the one-way ramp, especially when another car turns in right behind her, headlights glaring in her rearview, much brighter than this whole idea.

Sloane parks in an uncovered spot that's just far enough from Stephen's to establish a businesslike indifference, but not too far to force an awkward approach. The car that follows Sloane's turns out to be a cab, and it idles in the lot, nobody in or out, the passenger probably taking care of the fare.

Sloane decides on her gun, not her star, and to be on point, but not to be on. She gets out of the Pilot and heads straight for his SUV, a Hummer H2, according to the back tire. Sloane makes a mental note about the plate: Illinois, QUIM806.

The Hummer's brake lights go off and Sloane wishes she'd brought her flashlight as she rounds the back, to darkness. Another light angles at the pavement when the driver's door opens, and Stephen gets out.

"Hey," he says again; this time his smile is plenty big. And there he is, by the door's light: dressed in some kind of big black coat, dark pants, and—who knows why—flip-flops. His feet are blue-white. He opens the back door, another door light by which Sloane sees him retrieve a black duffel bag. Then, just as quickly, he closes the door and electronically engages the locks. He asks, "Think it'll snow?"

"Hope not," she says. "For your toes' sake."

"Come on. I was in a hurry when I left the gym, and that was for your sake."

"You didn't break any records getting here. One would think you could drive this beast as the crow flies."

"No way. I drive the *chupada* like it's my big brother's."

"How much bigger is your brother?"

"Big enough." He puts the duffle bag over his shoulder, says, "Let's go."

Sloane follows, notices Stephen's left leg is stiff and his foot falls flat: the slightest limp. "You hurt yourself?"

"Nah," he says, his gait changing, becoming more even. "Just not as fit as I used to be."

They reach the covered portion of the parking lot and walk past an elevator to a steel door; he uses a smart card there, releasing the lock, letting orange light slip out from the concrete stairwell as he steps back into the door's shadow. "After you," he says.

"What's wrong with the elevator?"

"Nothing. It just doesn't take us where we're going."

"You should lead. I don't know where we're going."

"Whatever you say, officer."

He's teasing, of course, but they've had enough back-and-forth, so Sloane resists the urge to go again. She waits for him to pass, and follows his bare white heels up the steps.

Two long flights up and they reach a dim, dry-walled corridor. As they start across, they turn and climb another few steps, and Sloane realizes they're on a balcony above an entrance. They pass another elevator and when Stephen opens the door to another orange-lit stairwell Sloane says, "Something wrong with that elevator?"

"Not that I know of. This way." He starts up the steps.

"This place is a maze."

"Used to be a shipping warehouse. Before that, a cloak factory."

"There was a place that just made cloaks?"

"So I'm told."

"Have you lived here long?"

"Just a couple months. It's actually my brother Quim's work studio. Last year he was commissioned for a project—a series of paintings for this woman in Miami—and he was working day and night, so he brought in a bed, a fridge, some furniture. Then some personal stuff happened and Quim stopped painting. He abandoned the whole thing—the project, the place. When I got the job at Zimmerman, he gave me the keys."

"Where is Quim now?" Sloane asks, trying not to sound winded; Stephen doesn't.

"Last I checked, he went back to Brazil; after that, who knows. Macau, maybe. Or Vegas. Somewhere he can blend in, blow money, and waste time. I don't know what he's going to do when he comes back. If he comes back. I doubt he'll ever paint again. That project really wrecked his head."

They reach the top of a second flight of stairs and Sloane follows Stephen around another corridor and down a long hallway, the lights on the walls soft white and decanted, like candles.

"I'm just up here on the right," Stephen says, taking the key ring from his pocket. When he starts to remove his coat and switches his grip on the duffle bag, his stiff left knee buckles and he catches himself, his free hand on the wall.

Sloane's about to ask if he needs help, but then the coat comes off, and all that comes out of Sloane's mouth is "Oh," same as *Wow*.

His white cotton T-shirt is soaked through, see-through: a second skin, tight against the muscles in his back. The sleeves cling to his triceps; the banded collar is flat around his neck.

He turns her way, key in the lock, and that's when she sees the wound by his eye—a cut, long and paper-thin and new enough to bleed just a little, through the scabbing—stretched from the tip of his eyebrow down his cheek.

"Oh," she says again—this time, same as *Shit*.

"What?" he says, that smile. "Told you I need a shower." He pushes open the door and Sloane follows, wanting to reach into her coat, release her gun's retainer strap—a different urge entirely.

The entrance opens up to high loft ceilings and a gigantic, near-empty room. A bank of windows on the far wall provides faint faraway light, their eastern river view drowning the foreground in black.

"Come on in," Stephen says, his flip-flops going *flip, flop, flip, flop* at his heels as he disappears across at least a thousand square feet of space into the dark.

"I'm kind of in a hurry, Stephen," she says, realizing how stupid that sounds, after this whole trip.

"Let me get the lights," he says.

Then, painting by painting, the place comes alive: along the concave wall to Sloane's left, lights fall on canvas after canvas of a flawless blond woman: She begins fully dressed, black cloak, lipstick-red smile. Next, she's in a black dress; a half-dozen paintings later, through a series of undress, all she has left is the lipstick—and her impeccably curved naked body. The next canvas introduces a man—nude, too, and virile—but his face and genitals are blurs of lipstick-red, as if the woman had kissed him, right there on the canvas, a million times.

The next two canvases are completely red. On those, she notices his signature: Joaquim Carvalho.

"Okay?" Sloane asks, her appreciation for art one thing, her understanding another.

"She wasn't supposed to, ahh, end up like that," Stephen says from behind her. "Quim painted over those last ones to piss her off."

"Is that the woman from Miami?" Sloane asks, tilting her head to look at the red canvases sideways.

"It is."

Sloane tilts her head the other way. "How, exactly, did she end up?"

"Well, officer, I'm not sure that's paint."

Sloane takes a split second to register the statement and spins around, drawing her gun.

Stephen is faster, though: his whole body hits the floor and then he pushes off, one arm, springing up a good six feet away from her, hands over his head. "Whoa, come on! I was kidding."

Sloane coughs, getting her breath. "Not funny. Where's your brother?"

"Seriously? Officer—"

"Stop calling me that. I'm a detective. Where is he?"

"I told you, I have no idea. The other side of the world, for all I know. You want to know the story? About that woman from Miami? She paid Quim a shitload of money and then she didn't want the paintings because she thought she looked fat. Quim won the money and the right to keep the paintings in court, and then he tried to turn them into a series. He had a shot at an installation at the Cultural Center, but whoever was in charge there at the time said his work didn't speak to his heritage. Quim flipped because he had all these *capoeira* prints he'd done before and shelved. The whole thing made him think he sold out before he ever had the chance to make a statement. He never thought he was that good, anyway. He's been convinced people have been blowing smoke since he got out of the Institute." Stephen can't help but laugh. "The *Art* Institute. Come on, detective, my arms are getting tired."

"Why are you limping?" she asks, gun still trained. "And what happened to your face?"

"Street *roda,*" he says.

"I don't know what that is. What is that?"

"It's capoeira—"

"You said that before. I don't know what that is, either. Keep your hands up."

"It's a game. A sport based on strength and form. A fight—"

"You were in a fight?"

"Not a fight, exactly. A strategy. A thinking dance. There's music. It's hard to explain. Look," he says, and in one move, he is a human pinwheel: his body fluid and flawless, gravity irrelevant. When both hands touch the ground, his legs swing one way and back, and from the strength of his torso, he lands right where he started.

"Oh," Sloane says for the third time tonight; this time, it's an admission. She lowers her gun and then realizes that behind him, outside the windows, those clouds that trapped her just a little while ago are spilling snow in aimless globs. Finally.

"You were right," she says, chin to the view.

Stephen turns around, sees the snow, says, "*Maldição*."

"Are you Spanish?" Sloane asks, glad he's turned away so she can holster her gun with some dignity.

"I'm Brazilian."

"Is that why your boss calls you Esteban?"

"He calls me that because he's a domineering prick. My name, in Portuguese, is Estevao." He walks over to the window, looks out. "Come here."

She doesn't move. "Will you please get the list?"

"Come on," he says. "Look at this."

Sloane goes to the windows but stays a good distance from Stephen. "Snow," she says, unimpressed, though it does look amazing from where they stand: a brisk wind chasing heavy flakes around, giving them a little more time to play in the sky before they fall down in fat clumps, temporary ground cover.

"I grew up in Northern Brazil," Stephen says. "Salvador. It never snowed."

"I grew up here in Chicago," Sloane says. "You didn't miss much."

Stephen glances over, shakes his head. "I'll be right back." *Flip, flop, flip, flop* . . .

Sloane waits there, wishing she could be outside, snow blanketing all the noise.

She doesn't hear Stephen when he returns because he isn't wearing his flip-flops, and he doesn't say anything. He just appears next to her, hands her a file folder, puts his hands up overhead again, surrendering, and then leans over and kisses her.

For a long time.

SLOANE DOESN'T KNOW HOW to get back out of the building so she just keeps finding down-stairs. When she finally gets out into the snow, it seems so warm outside; she takes off her coat and throws it in the Pilot's backseat and breathes, and exhales. And breathes.

She looks up at the backside of the old building, black windows between wet, white flakes, and thinks nothing else has ever been so black and white.

She didn't want to leave.

She couldn't stay.

She has nowhere to go.

And right now, she could care less.

The snow keeps coming.

YOU WERE A VIRGIN, before.

You had a boyfriend, sure; all the way through high school. He had the fastest pitch in baseball, and he had a car and his parents didn't care if he stayed out late. And, for a little while, you thought he was the one. You didn't know any other one.

Senior year, you thought you'd be the first girl in your class to get married. Thought you'd have three children like your parents did and cook your mother's recipes and go to every Little League game, even if it was just to watch your husband coach. You thought your days would be spent fast and thoughtless, like dollar bills.

Still, you didn't give it up the night you two were crowned

Homecoming King and Queen of Bushnell High. You wanted to; you just didn't picture it the same way he did: front bench-seat of his car, you in that pretty satin dress, your cheap crown. Both of you with beer on your breath. He turned on the radio to set the mood and the country station was playing George Strait's "We Really Shouldn't Be Doing This." You laughed, mostly because you were nervous. Then he kissed you for a little while and you reclined, so he was on top; when he tried to pull up your dress, though, you said *No* and *Please, just kiss me a little while longer.* He did. He tried to be patient and you tried to talk yourself into it but the way he rubbed against you, his tux pants against your dress—for him, that was that. He said he loved you, and you were just as satisfied.

Then came the baseball scholarship to Mizzou and your easy small-town dreams disappeared, a fly ball over the fence. He left you there with the locals who hung around Casey's parking lot talking about all the amazing things they were never going to do. Those kids were effective advertisements for college. You applied.

You started classes that next spring and you were happy to say good-bye to Bushnell. You majored in communications, worked at the college radio station, and interned at a local PR firm. You worked hard those three and a half years to graduate on time—and with a near-perfect GPA and honors, to boot. You were sure employers would be competing for you but didn't take any chances. While most of your classmates took off the summer after graduation to go back-packing in Europe or Habitating for Humanity in South

America, you went back to your parents' in Bushnell, and to the post office, sending off resumes, every day.

When the call came just before Christmas, you were ready. When you waved good-bye to Bushnell the second time, you couldn't believe you ever had small-town dreams.

You were still a virgin, then.

Yesterday morning, you tried to go on as usual. You went to work. You were a wreck. Every time you thought someone was looking at you or you caught a flash of a blue-striped shirt or any blue shirt for that matter, you died a little. The hair on your arms bristled underneath your sweater when the CE suggested a trip to Gene & Georgetti's for lunch. He tilted his head at you and asked if you were okay and you said, "Sure, just stressed, too much work to do," and took lunch at your desk.

When the office emptied out you started to get paranoid, and while you were listening, making sure no one was there, you started feeling dizzy. You couldn't eat breakfast that morning, and you thought maybe that was the problem, so you braved a trip downstairs to get a few things from the cart.

When you got back upstairs you could not eat or work. You just sat there. Just sat.

Then you heard something and peered over your cubicle and it was a maintenance worker, blue striped shirt. He was black and his nametag said GERMAINE and he told you he was there to fix a leak in the boss's bathroom. Germaine was a big man and mean-looking, but when he saw the banana at your desk he tried to be friendly and said he liked bananas a "whole bunch." In fact, Germaine said, he would "go ape for one right about now." He laughed after that, slow enough to convince you he was kind of slow himself, his lips wet with spittle. Still, his laugh made you cry and your crying scared him, so you lied and told him you were upset because your grandmother was in the hospital. He said he was sorry and so were you but you were still crying when the CE came back from lunch, so you told him the same story. He said, "Of course, go home."

You went home. But not home-home. Because if either of your parents even so much as heard your voice they would know something had happened. Then they would come here and you would have to tell everyone the truth and who knows where that would put you. Back in Bushnell? It wouldn't take long for everyone there to find out you saved yourself for a cold, late night in an empty lot with a stranger where *no* meant nothing and begging for your life meant less.

After, in the vacant lot, his gloved hands around your neck one last time, you thought of your high school boyfriend. You'd heard he threw out his shoulder, the last inning of a Big 12 game, and that was that, too. Heard he wound up a car salesman in Kansas City with a real pretty fiancée and a real regular future. He probably heard you were here, sitting pretty on the big city's shoulders.

How could he, or anyone, imagine where you really were?

You don't know how long you were unconscious after he raped you, but it was the "sister" from upstairs who came walking by and saw you. Saw you there, pantsuit caked with mud, your gravel-skinned knees and your ripped off nails bleeding right through your professional image. Sister took your keys and helped you inside and promised she wouldn't say a word—none of her business, she said. Then she ran you a shower and gave you some pajamas and put you on your couch with a glass of water. It tasted metallic and you said so and she told you that was because your mouth was still bleeding.

She wrapped some ice in a towel and told you she'd stay if you wanted her to and you did. You pressed the towel against your lip and then you told her everything you remembered.

When you woke up in the morning, your first thought was that you'd missed your alarm and therefore the train and therefore an important work deadline and you were confused because you were on the couch and not in bed and then you heard someone else in the room, her heavy sleep-breathing. You thought you were still shaking a dream until you sat up and felt the pain. Your mouth. Your neck. Oh god. Your reality.

And then you foolishly went to work, your emergency lip gloss so ridiculous, your excuse about being so cold even more so—the CE praying you weren't planning on catching the flu before fashion week—his own self too centered to notice you already looked sick. And felt worse. And then the bit about your grandmother and today, you're at home, since the boss was thoughtful enough to give you the rest of the week off of work, presumably because you're headed to Bushnell.

You're in the kitchen talking yourself into eating lunch when sister knocks with the morning newspaper to show you. On the front page, it says another girl was attacked; "Look," sister says, "just like you, but lucky."

You read the article and find the only thing the same is the fight. Sister asks about the Hummer; you don't remember any Hummer. She wants to know, "What about the Hispanic?" The only one you remember is Jorge, and you don't think the man in the sketch looks at all like Jorge. Anyway, if Jorge attacked you, how would he have had a car nearby? When he was coming from the same train? When he got off before you did?

Sister puts the paper on your table and tells you it probably wasn't Jorge because men hardly ever rape strangers, anyway. Rape is a crime of power. Not passion. It's planned. Doesn't come out of nowhere.

Then she clicks her thick plastic palm tree–decaled nails against the table and says she thinks you know who did this. She thinks you were targeted.

You tell her you've only been here four months; you have no idea who would target you. She says, "Think about it. There are plenty of men in your life. Tell me about them."

You tell her about the men at work: they're all art geeks, gays, old guys. White men with too much money or too little interest to bother.

You tell her about the men at 50 E. Monroe, your building: you've only met a few, and they're from the recruiting company on the eighth floor. They have a frat-boy reputation, supposedly because of all the beautiful women who are in and out of their offices for interviews. When your boss scheduled a charity golf outing a few weeks ago and asked you to run an invitation down to them, you figured out the real reason for their rep: you walked in on a pair of associates discussing a woman whose breasts were apparently keeping her in the running for a pure-commission sales job. The shorter, balding man took one look at you and said he hoped you were there to interview for the position as well; his slightly-cute partner agreed that your breasts had equal potential. You handed the short one the invitation, thinking it'd make them both sorry being there on account of your boss and all, but he read it, handed it to his partner, and asked if you'd be his caddy. His partner laughed and there was nothing cute about him anymore. Then the short one asked your name and you told him and then he put a y on the end and asked, "How about you be my nineteenth hole?"

You tell sister you're sure those guys are pigs, but not criminals. Their egos are too humongous. She says, "But hold on, most guys with big egos think ladies want their action." That upsets you because you don't even know what action means, really. She says sorry and tells you to keep going.

The dry cleaners, you say, are a Korean couple who know you by your phone number. You think it's sad that they're the first ones outside work that come to mind because they're good people. They are always smiling and they use just enough starch.

You start to tell sister about the corner market guys and

she wants to know if you mean the store a few blocks up on California. Yes, you say, if she means the Armenian brothers who call everybody "bro," including you. They sell a little of everything that could be remotely considered convenient, though you aren't sure who could need a last-minute Muslim-themed gold-framed painting of the Last Supper, Allah in the middle.

When the younger brother found out you worked in advertising, you became his new consultant. Last time you went in for an energy drink, he wanted your expert opinion of the sign he made: it was a crudely drawn cartoon of a man on white posterboard with black magic marker; the man held a bottle of beer with a 6.99 label. The dialogue bubble over his head happily proclaimed BUD! VAT A DEAL! You told him you really liked the sign; he gave you your drink for free.

Sister says, "Okay, keep going."

Finally, the baristas. You have to explain that's what they call the people who make coffee nowadays, and once a week on Wednesday, your double *cortado*. You can't afford one of those every day. At the place you go, up here by the El stop, the coffee is crap and the baristas are kids, younger than you; down in the Loop, where you prefer the brew and get the double *cortado*, the coffee is crack and the fair-trade people who serve it would never be so unfair.

Sister asks if there was anyone else you can think of, so you mention the homeless guys on the corner by the El station. She laughs. Yeah, right.

You can't think of anyone else. Sister says, "Think," and

you can tell she's running out of patience so you say, "Sorry, but I am not going to report this."

She looks mad.

You ask, "What about this being none of your business?"

She asks if you remember anything else about Jorge or the train ride.

Of course you do. You spent the ride trying to lock away details—the memory exercise. You remember the billboards above the windows. You remember the transit map, and the passengers. The black man and his twisted-up Wendy's bag and his White Sox jogging suit and the whites of his eyes when he looked at you. The burned schoolboy, feet tapping. His uniform. His skin so scarred, and face so old compared to his mother's, who looked so young. So lost.

And Jorge. Gray ball cap, striped work shirt. Thin black duffel bag. He was there, and when you opened your eyes, gone.

You say that's all you remember.

Sister asks, "Don't you want to catch this man? What if he comes back for you?"

You remind her again that she said this was none of her business.

She says, "Yeah, I'll mind my own business all the way up until I see some other girl's face in the paper. Or I wind up in the fight. Listen, girl, I don't want to be a contestant in this game, too."

You never thought about it that way. You never thought you could be responsible for saving someone else.

You're pretty sure sister was annoyed when she left, and it didn't sound like she meant it when she said you should come upstairs whenever you wanted. You would've never gone before, though, so you figure things aren't much different.

When she left you looked outside and you can't believe it's snowing. You start to think you're hungry but then your dad calls, and he didn't expect to reach you at 5:00 P.M. You tell him you've got this really big project and he says he'll be brief. Then talks about the fallacy that is global warming, and also essentially about your rent. You pretend to be fine as you listen and agree, though you're only trying to sound like yourself. You tell him you've got this really big project again and you're waiting to hear from your boss, too, so that he won't try to put your mom on the phone. Because she'll hear right through you. You promise your dad you'll call on the weekend and you try so hard not to cry when he tells you he loves you.

Now, you watch the snow fall from your front window; you can't believe it's April and the ground is ever so delicately being covered. The place where it happened—where you were raped—covered just the same.

You can feel the cold.

19

SLOANE IS JOLTED FROM sleep by the hotel's loud, double-ring telephone. She answers and a robot tells her it's 6:35 A.M. Her wake-up call.

She sits up, shielding her eyes from the lights; she left them on so she could get some sleep. The television is on, too, though she muted it sometime in the middle of the night when loud infomercials insisted she, too, could lose weight, earn her college degree, and clean any surface in just six easy payments. Now, the channel is broadcasting a *Hart to Hart* rerun. Something about the millionaire couple going on a tropical cruise to catch a murderer. Sloane is pretty sure the closest she'll ever get to a luxury ship is a security detail at Navy Pier.

She turns off the TV and starts the double-serve

coffeemaker with half the water, so it'll brew strong. She unpacks her toiletries and runs the shower. Clean, dried, and dressed, she takes the coffee with both packets of creamer and one Sugar In The Raw. It tastes like it's trying, but trying's not good enough this early.

She leaves her stuff half unpacked, and two bucks on the nightstand for the maid.

She hits the ground floor by 6:50, thinking of buttered toast and real coffee at a diner on State Street; she heads right back upstairs when she realizes how much snow fell overnight.

"A foot at least," the bellboy says.

In her room, she adds layers—almost all the clean clothes she has left in her bag—and switches out her thin camel leather jacket for her heavy CPD dark blue. She calls down to the valet to bring her car around; she's got an hour to get to work, but she has a feeling it'll be tough going out there.

She's right. The plows have come through at least twice, but they sure don't make anybody a better driver. Cars are all over the road: a guy in a real nice Mercedes, thin racing tires spinning, is going nowhere fast; a guy in a Jeep who thinks he's all-terrain doesn't defy the rules of ice and goes over a curb, into a snowbank.

She sits in stop-and-slow for six blocks, then cuts over to Grand, to avoid expressway traffic. It still takes her twenty minutes to get across the river, four-wheel drive doing nothing but making all her wheels slide on the ice in tandem.

Once she's out of the thick of it, she can't pass up a real cup of French roast at Sip, so she calls the station and tells

Commander Salamander—a nickname Frank Salamano had to take along with the promotion—that she'll be late. He says she's not the only one, and she better not be stopping for coffee.

The French roast is worth the extra five minutes, and the maple-walnut scone she picks to go with it is decent, but not worth the price—let alone the price of a rear-end accident. When Heavy calls, she taps the brakes and they make like ice skates, locking up and putting her an inch from the back bumper of a delivery truck. Sloane decides she better ditch the pastry, let the phone ring, and keep her eyes on the road.

She gets to the station a half hour later in a trip that usually takes half that. She parks on the far side of the lot behind a UPS truck, hoping to get a few more sips of the good stuff in her system before she goes inside. She can't very well bring the coffee with her, fifteen minutes post-roll; it'll piss off the Salamander. A plow rolls by in front of her on Grand, pushing slush to the curb. *Snow,* she thinks. *In April.* With all the rest of the shit coming down, she guesses it fits.

Swoop, the cop otherwise known as Brian McInerny, pulls in next to her, toasts her with his 7-Eleven foam cup. She regretfully leaves her own coffee, jumps out of the Pilot, and makes tracks for the entrance. Swoop's a cop with a knack for getting in on a case just in time to share credit; the last thing she needs is to be seen with him, to let the rumor mill turn out the idea Sloane has recruited him.

Once inside and up on the floor, she finds the place is already cleared out for the morning. Salamander's hello to

Sloane is from underneath a Kleenex, which he's using to pick his nose. "Detective Coburn, Interview One. With Caspar Mercado."

That's why Heavy called. "He found Mercado?"

"The man turned himself in," Salamander says, looking at whatever he fished out, now on the tissue.

Sloane goes to Room One and looks in, sees Heavy's backside and Mercado's front: the suspect is a smallish man with a crew cut, a clean-cut goatee, and a brown uniform that must match the UPS truck outside. His careful body language and downcast glances remind Sloane of a guy on a tightrope, no net below.

Sloane knocks, watches Mercado jump.

"Detective," she says, cracking open the door. "A moment?" She steps back from the window and lets Heavy make his own excuse for an exit, in case he's on to something with Mercado and needs a lead out.

Next to the door, Sloane notices the red stick figure drawn on the corner of the whiteboard: having finished his beer and taken a leak, he's apparently getting head from a cutout photo of one of the rookies. Sloane bets that'll stay up for a while.

Once Heavy clicks the door shut, Sloane asks, "Is he copping?"

"He doesn't even know why he's here, darlin'. Says he heard from the nun that we were looking for him and wanted to come in and clear things up as soon as possible so he won't be late picking up his son today. When I started asking questions, Mercado said the nun told him Verdez and her boyfriend,

some guy Barreto, were behind this. Mercado said no way—
Verdez depends on him for the child's care, since the kinder-
gartner cuts in on her love life. Anyway dipshit Salamander
booked him on the warrant, so now it's our problem."

"The nun was right about Mercado."

"Or he is a damn good liar. Doesn't matter: he doesn't fit
Meyer-Davis' description and he's got an alibi for the night
she was attacked. If Verdez doesn't step up, we have to let
him go."

"We have to find Verdez."

"I've got patrollers headed back to her place now. If she
won't press charges, we're done here. Until then, I'm stuck in
there trying to convince a kindhearted, God-fearing kid to
stick around voluntarily when he should be at work and so
should we."

"I've got a few things to do," Sloane says, opening the
flap of her briefcase, giving Heavy a glimpse of the *50 East
Monroe Employees* file.

"As far as I'm concerned, you're at your desk clearing other
cases. We've got at least a dozen open, a few of them close to
getting CI'd."

"We'll never get charges on those. You know it."

"The way it's going, we'll never get a charge again. The
state's attorney is going to laugh in our faces on this one. Caspar Mercado. Are you kidding me?"

Heavy lets himself back into Room One and Sloane goes to
her desk, and she does look for a way to clear some other cases.
The cases just happen to be Dutcher's and Meyer-Davis's.

She's got nearly forty names—forty guys who work at 50 East Monroe, all of whom have blue and white striped shirts and, more importantly, criminal records. Running the names through I-CLEAR yields a number of guys who must've done some real good, real quiet time. From petty thieves to pedophiles, gang thugs to drug runners, each one looks a little worse than the next.

Sloane looks at each photo and checks each record for registered vehicles, but none has registered a Chevy Impala or a Hummer. No surprise: guys like these don't put valuable things in their names because if they *do* wind up in the clink, their baby mommas or brothers-in-arms still need a provider. They still need means and wheels.

Anyway, no smart criminal brings his own car to a crime. Sloane's gut says this guy is either stealing, borrowing, or renting cars, the former being the most economical for a criminal.

Next Sloane flags the Hispanics, the whites with dark features, and the light-skinned blacks. Doing so only narrows the slate by seven, so she weeds out men over fifty and trims the number to twenty-eight. *Twenty-eight of the hardest-looking maintenance men this side of Joliet,* she thinks.

"Detective." Salamander. Behind her. An order.

Sloane puts her screen to sleep and spins around in her chair.

"Guzman called," Salamander says, standing over her, arms crossed. At this angle Sloane can see straight up his long Italian nose, snot trapped in his nostrils by thick nose-hair. He sniffles.

"You feel okay?" Sloane asks.

"He tells me you've been a little too compassionate lately. Do you want to tell me what the hell you guys are doing with a suspect and no victim?"

"Commander, sir," Sloane says, standing up so she gets less of the congested view. "We're waiting, right now, for patrol to bring in Mr. Mercado's accuser, but I must tell you, and I think I'm speaking for my partner when I do, that Mr. Mercado simply didn't do this."

"Pearson, you're the police, not the jury." Salamander reaches over her and across Heavy's desk for a tissue. Sloane wonders if Pee Wee puts all the guys who move up through some kind of asshole training because every one of them seems stuffed up, somehow. "I've got orders, which means you've got orders. Now I want you to get Mercado's victim, or you get him out of here and get on with it."

"I don't understand why you keep forcing me into dead ends when I've got leads."

"Leads? Pearson, you've got no case. I don't know how you managed to dance around this long."

"It's called policework," she says.

"I told you: The order came from Commander Wojciechowski. Do you think he doesn't know how to do policework?"

"I think you all know *how*. It's just that none of you want to do anything but ride your desks until you hit a cush job in Sixteen or wait out your twenty."

"While you ride every cop who likes a loose fuck."

Salamander blows his nose, tosses the Kleenex toward her trashcan, misses, and grumbles all the way back to his office.

Sloane lets him have the last word because she supposes it makes Salamander feel better.

She wakes her screen and speeds up her search—no way she wants to be there when Pee Wee shows up. Still, she'll do what Salamander says—she'll put together a six-pack of pictures, including Mercado's booking photo. By collecting the other five faces from the most prime suspects on 50 East Monroe's list, she'll work her bosses' version of the case and her own, same time. She figures if Heavy is going to sit on his half-assed attempt at his case and the bosses are going to sit on their hands, the least she can do is try to get one or another of them to stand up.

She runs through the list again, including only Hispanics and only assault charges. There are three:

Camacho, Manuel, a.k.a. "Pinch." 31 y/o. 5'10, 165 lbs. Criminal sexual assault. On parole.

Flores, Jorge, a.k.a. "Garras." 34 y/o. 6'2, 180 lbs. Aggravated criminal sexual assault, vehicular invasion, criminal damage to property, unlawful restraint. On parole.

Gutierrez, Alfredo. 40 y/o. 6', 200 lbs. Two counts predatory criminal sexual assault, child. Sentence served.

Sloane picks two more with moustaches to balance the group:

Sanchez, Alejandro, a.k.a. "Dirty." 32 y/o, 5'10, 155 lbs. Five counts felony aggravated battery w/firearm. Gang-related. On parole.

Terrazas, Juan, a.k.a. "Raza." 46 y/o, 5'9, 170 lbs. Federal drug conspiracy, distribution. Gang-related. Sentence served.

Sloane dumps the photos onto one page with Mercado's and the info onto another. Then she goes back to Room One, knocks. When Heavy pops his head out, expectant, she whispers, "Pee Wee wants a lineup. Tell Mercado to sit tight and quiet. I'll be back."

"Where are you going?"

"I don't have time to argue, Heavy."

He doesn't say anything because she's right: he'd be arguing.

On her way down the steps, Vince Marchetti follows Pee Wee up, and Sloane can tell the detective is having a one-sided conversation. "It's Everman. He doesn't want to do the paperwork . . ."

"Gentlemen," Sloane says, and gets the hell out of there before anybody else wants to argue.

20

HOLLY DUTCHER TELLS SLOANE she's holding an all-day open house in River North and Sloane gets the address, says she's stopping by. She doesn't say anything over the phone about her case.

The open house is only ten blocks from Sloane's hotel, and after this morning's confidence-busting detour, Sloane wonders why she ever checks in at the station. The building is a multiuse just six blocks north of Eddie's loft in the big old Montgomery Ward Catalogue factory. They call the residents' section the Domain, and the lobby is like a showroom, its furnishings more elegant than anything they ever sold at Monkey Ward's.

The doorman tells her Holly's unit, #2904, is on the ninth

floor. He gives Sloane convoluted directions, and she thinks of Stephen's place, another converted factory that maintained its original, though structurally illogical, skeleton.

Sloane's stomach drops when the elevator starts its trip up to nine and it's because she's thinking of Stephen, now. The way he held up his hands, *I surrender,* and kissed her. The way she put her hands against his chest—felt his damp white T-shirt, smelled a good sweat—and she meant to push him away but she also had to kiss him back. His lips, soft and salty. His breath in clipped sighs; hers, stolen. Then his hands, warm and so gentle, his fingertips lightly at her neck, pulling her closer.

She was already too close so she did push him away and said *No* and he stood there, looking at her, waiting for her to change her mind. She wanted to. He must have been able to tell, because he reached for her and said *Come on,* but she knew if she kissed him again, *no* wouldn't mean anything. So, she backed away, her hand inexplicably feeling for her gun—embarrassing—and then she said *I'm sorry* and she was back in the maze, finding her way through, and completely lost.

Just like this time. When the elevator doors open and Sloane gets out, she's on the ninth floor. There is no #2904.

Sloane finds a fire extinguisher and next to it, the building code's floor map, which shows her how the units are numbered, which convinces her she's in the wrong building. From there it's guesswork, a series of wrong turns, and a resident with a big-pawed, yellow lab puppy. The resident takes the time to redirect Sloane and the puppy uses the time to chew a doormat. The owner goes into training mode: "Sit, sit, sit," and the puppy could care less, so Sloane says, "Thanks," and gets out of there before she finds out whether or not the two have conquered housebreaking.

Sloane follows the directions back the way she came and across a parallel hallway and voila: pink balloons and a welcome sign for #2904.

The door is propped open, and Holly is on the far side of the main room staring out the west-facing window at Goose Island. It isn't much to look at.

Neither is the unit: the owners were definitely sticking with the building's old-factory roots, all the furniture distressed, or metal-framed and machinelike. The wall to the left is unfinished concrete, and the others are painted the same color. Sloane guesses it *does* make Goose Island something to look at.

"Holly," Sloane says. "You aren't easy to find."

Holly turns, chin quivering underneath the smile she's probably been preparing all morning. "Hi, Detective."

"Please, call me Sloane."

Holly shakes her head, eyes low. "You're the first person to come by, Sloane."

"I wondered," Sloane says, because it's a weekday, but she knows doubt is the seed of a vic's silence so she says, "You know, the snow and all."

"In this market," Holly says, "you can't plan for home-buyers any better than you can for the weather. And the sellers? They really want to get out of here. It's too small. I mean—they've outgrown it."

"I know the feeling," Sloane says. She also gets the feeling Holly isn't very good at this job.

"You look good," Sloane says, and it's the truth: Holly's dressed in a black pants suit, high-heeled leather boots, a red scarf. Classy. Professional. A little sexy, even.

Holly doesn't say anything, just rearranges her hair over her scarf.

Of course, Sloane thinks. The scarf covering just a little bit of the truth. And Sloane, the idiot, uncovering memories.

"Look, Holly, you know I'm interested in buying a place and soon. But I didn't come here for the open house. I came here to ask you about Fifty East Monroe."

"What—why?" Holly goes over to the living room table and picks up her listing sheets like she's been thrown off-script.

"You used to work there, at Allied Mortgage, correct?"

"Yes. I told you that."

"I forgot to ask: do you list any of the condominiums that are available there through Dutcher and Grey?"

"No. When Amanda came to help me move out of A.M., she realized another company was buying the whole build-ing with plans to redevelop it for residential use. I told you— she's business-smart—she got the entire listing." She hugs the pages to her chest, a schoolgirl. "I don't understand what this has to do with me, or with what happened . . ." and she doesn't look like she really wants to know.

Sloane assumes a nondominant stance. "There's something I haven't told you, and I shouldn't tell you now, but I think it's important."

"What?" Tears are ready in Holly's eyes.

"There's another woman who was attacked. She used to work in the building, too."

"I read about her. In the paper—"

"This is a different woman."

"Oh my god." Holly finds the couch, its cushions looking about as comfortable as its metal arms. She drops the listing sheets on the seat next to her.

Sloane sits down across from her on something that's either a table or an ottoman. She says, "This might be a stretch, but I've been investigating the possibility that the man who attacked you may work in that building. Have you been to Fifty East Monroe recently?"

"Of course. Amanda has to be there all the time, so that's where we have weekly meetings. Tuesdays."

Sloane's about to ask if it's okay to take out her notebook when Holly says—

"Oh my god. Tuesday was my date with Marc. Tuesday was—"

"Now hold on a second," Sloane says, ditching the notebook idea and moving the listing sheets aside, to share the couch. If Holly fast-forwards to the rape, it's good-bye rational discussion and hello Dr. Pearson. "Holly, let's talk about Tuesday. Do you remember anything about your meeting?

Did you interact with anyone apart from your sister? Men talking to you?"

"Just the usual flirting from the guys on the eighth floor."

"Who are they?"

"A recruiting company. Amanda says they staff tech offices, but they act like they're hiring for *Playboy*. They always tried to flirt with me when I was at A.M. I think they're one of the only companies who stayed through the change in building ownership."

Sloane hadn't yet explored the possibility of a man who worked above ground level being suspect. It isn't that she ignored the idea. It's just that when she averages three days on a case, there's an inevitable funnel: she dumps everything she has into it, and goes with what leaks through first.

"These guys," Sloane says, "from the recruiting company. Have any of them ever been out of line with you?"

"What guy hasn't? I mean, deep down, they're all chasing bunnies, right? And it isn't because they want to be friends."

Sloane isn't clear on the reference, but she finds some wisdom there. "What about the other men who work in the building?"

"I don't really know anybody since the building sold. My sister would know."

"What about the men who work *for* the building? Janitors. Maintenance. Security."

"I think they're all new since I left, too. Anyway, they're paid to be polite, you know? Unless we see them in the building's cafeteria. Me and Amanda meet there sometimes, because they have a really good salad bar. But I swear, it's like standing in line in front of a construction site, the way they stop and stare."

"Did you have lunch there on Tuesday?"

"Oh god." Holly shakes her head. "It was one of those guys?"

"Now I didn't say that, and I'm not trying to lead you to any conclusions, or to sell you a suspect. I'm only trying to help you remember things about that day that you might not think relate—remember? The purple cab?"

"We went through this. And I've been through it myself, really, a million times. It doesn't matter how far I go back. What I remember is what I told you. I'm sorry that it isn't enough."

"Holly, we have someone in custody."

"Oh," is all she gets out this time. She looks like she's choking underneath that pretty red scarf.

"This is a good thing. Listen. I'm near certain that the man we're looking at is not the man who raped you. But, in order for me to keep working your case, I need to clear him, and that means I need you to look at some photographs."

"I need a cigarette."

"Okay," Sloane says, glad she's still wearing her coat as she accompanies Holly out onto the three-by-six balcony.

Holly takes a pack of Marlboro Ultra Lights from underneath the covered grill, strikes a match from the book stowed inside the cellophane, and smokes like a novice: stiff fingers, quick puffs, an eye on the front door inside. Sloane figures one of the advocates offered Holly a smoke, made her part of the club. She hopes they didn't give her any other bad ideas.

Sloane rests her forearms on the metal ledge, lets Holly do her thing. She looks out over the north branch of the river, at the Tribune's press, Kendall College. The sun has made an appearance, glaring off the fresh snow while it has a chance. There are clouds on the western horizon. Sloane wonders how much worse it can get.

"If I recognize him," Holly says, "do I have to go with you? Do I have to see him? Will he see me?"

"Right now all I need you to do is look at the photos. Okay? If we charge him, you'll need to come in and talk to us, and to the state's attorney. I'll do my best to keep you clear of him until trial."

"When is the trial?"

"There are a lot of things that need to happen before that," Sloane says. Like finding the guy who actually did it. Getting some physical evidence. A DNA match. Linking him to more than one victim. Convincing the state's attorney that there are no holes in the case. Convincing the other victims to cooperate. Getting a decent prosecutor. A better judge. A sane jury. A chance in hell. "Let's just take one thing at a time."

"Okay." Holly throws the cigarette over the rail and says, "Show me."

Sloane retrieves the paper from her inside pocket and

unfolds the six-pack, and she knows she shouldn't but she thumbs Mercado's picture, to draw attention to him.

Holly says, "Oh. My. God." She backs away until she's against the sliding glass door. "I know him."

"Show me," Sloane says, her heart racing. It wasn't supposed to happen this way.

"It's him. He sits by himself in the cafeteria and one time another guy said something to him and the other guy wound up with a broken arm. Me and Amanda saw the whole thing—and then the guy said he fell. He was too scared to tell the truth."

"Are you sure the man you're telling me about is the one who attacked you?"

"Yes. No. I don't know? He's . . . said things. To me."

"What kind of things?"

"Not things, really. More like an animal. He growls. He stares and he growls."

"Point to his photo, will you?"

"Oh my god," Holly says again, and she can hardly look at him as she points to the biggest, baddest, worst-looking man in the lineup. He's got straight black hair that's parted in the middle and hangs, greasy, down to his chin. His eyes are black, empty pools, a predator's, and his jaw is strong and angular, an animal's.

"Oh god," Holly says again, shivering.

"Why don't you go inside? I'll be just a minute." Sloane opens the sliding glass door and Holly enters, and then she stands there, watching Sloane, from the other side of the glass.

Sloane checks her notes and finds the man is number two:

Flores, Jorge, a.k.a. "Garras." 34 y/o. 6'2, 180 lbs. Aggravated criminal sexual assault, vehicular invasion, criminal damage to property, unlawful restraint. On parole.

He certainly has the historical chops for a serial crime like this, but Sloane's afraid she screwed herself, playing it this way.

She takes out her cell and she thinks about calling Heavy and asking his advice, but if she brings him in on this now, she's only risking another *no*. She knows Salamander won't buy her snafu discovery and he's made it clear Pee Wee doesn't want this case to go past Mercado. She can hear them: *No. No. No!*

But right now, the only thing Sloane needs is a *yes* from Holly. She tucks her phone away and goes inside.

"Holly," she says, "you pointed out a suspect who is a known sexual offender, out of jail on parole. If you tell me he raped you, I have enough probable cause to bring him in to talk to him. But it's important that you know that's all I can do. You're the one who has to take up the fight after that."

Holly holds out her hands, watches them shake. "What if I say no?"

"I've got no case."

She clasps her hands together. "What if I don't know?"

"I go back, work other leads. Keep my eye on him."

"Will he be there, in the cafeteria, next Tuesday?"

"Not if he's the man who raped you."

"If I say yes, will he know it was me?"

"If you say yes, Holly, you're the first one brave enough to take up the fight."

Holly unlocks her hands, clenches fists. "Go get him."

21

SLOANE RETURNS TO THE station just over an hour later, a pair of young Loop uniforms following, Flores in their custody. Sloane steered clear during the arrest so Flores wouldn't associate her with the guys, or get any ideas about what she may or may not know. Right now, she doesn't know enough.

Sloane parks next to the UPS truck, stays in the Pilot, and watches the two beat cops wrangle Flores from the back of the squad. He is a hulk, and a hell of a lot bigger than the 180 pounds his record claims. He is dressed in his maintenance uniform—the shirt short sleeved—and his wrists are cuffed behind him, trapping his huge arms in a taut V. Or at least he makes it look that way—then, at the perfect moment, he jerks his elbow and pops the shorter cop in the nose.

Blood is immediate, so the cop runs inside. The second one, whose size is more comparable, face less hardened than Flores's, turns him around and forces him against the squad to regain control. It seems to work until Flores sees the first cop disappear into the station, a trail of blood specks fresh in the snow. Flores's head rolls back in a fit of wide-mouthed, uncontrollable laughter.

It doesn't take long before the cop has had enough of the funny business, and he lets Flores know it: He puts a sharp knee into Flores's hamstring, probably aiming for his balls, at the same time barking a command that clearly includes the word "fuck."

Flores's posture goes slack, and then, just when the cop lets down his guard, Flores bucks against the squad, giving himself enough momentum to push the cop away and turn and bark back—literally. The cop drops, and fast, and draws his weapon. Flores laughs at this, too.

Oh, shit, Sloane thinks, left hand opening the door, right on her gun. She didn't want to introduce herself under unfriendly circumstances, but Flores sure doesn't look like he's interested in making friends.

Sloane's out of the car at the same time Buchanan and another uniform named Swigart follow the short cop outside to help.

Sloane gets back into the Pilot and gives them five minutes, to let the other cop dust the snow off his pants, and for the guys to get Flores inside and well into booking. Then she goes upstairs to tell Heavy the good news.

On the floor, Heavy's standing at his desk, zipping his coat.

"Any word on Verdez?" Sloane asks him.

"Nope." Heavy opens his bottom desk drawer, feels around.

"What do we do about Mercado?"

"Hold him for his forty-eight and apologize Monday morning. He seems okay with it, except that he needs somebody to pick up his kid. Did you happen to get that nun's phone number?"

"No."

Heavy opens his middle desk drawer, same search. "Guess I'd better head over there, then, and get the kid. Who knows? Maybe Verdez will turn up. Can't find my gloves," he says to the drawers, though it seems like he's preoccupied by something more.

"It's not that cold," Sloane says. "What are we doing about Mercado's truck?"

"Augh," Heavy says, rubbing his forehead. "Mercado wants me to call his manager, explain the situation. He's a nice guy, but I don't know how I'm going to make this sound okay to his boss or to anybody else. I'm thinking of taking the truck and delivering the damn packages myself."

"I don't recommend that," Sloane says, since Heavy doesn't know north from south, and lets Sloane drive every time they have to ride together. "Hey," she says, "why don't you tell Mercado's boss that he's part of an important investigation, and that we're using him to draw out a criminal?"

"You're telling me to lie?" Heavy tries the top drawer.

"No. I'm telling you that I just went to see Dutcher, and she picked a man out of the lineup I made for Mercado. Jorge Flores. He's downstairs being processed."

"Did you tell *our* bosses?"

"Not yet."

"That's my cue." Heavy shuts the top drawer. "I'll be back."

"Hurry up," Sloane whisper-shouts as he clears the DMZ. "I want you in on the Flores interview."

Heavy holds up two fingers, crossed, and heads out.

A half hour later, Sloane has everything that anybody documented on Flores pulled and printed out.

The first thing she reads is a police report, which tells a much scarier story than the official charges, because as it reads, the aggravated criminal sexual assault, vehicular invasion, criminal damage to property, and unlawful restraint all happened in a single night.

The report was written nearly ten years ago by the first responding officer—some cop named Mark Sikula—who interviewed the victim. What he wrote went like this: after dancing with a woman in a West Side club, Flores followed her home. She refused to let him into her apartment. He broke the door down. He stopped her as she was trying to get out the back door. He tied her up with a lamp's electrical cord and began to force her to have intercourse, at one point ripping off the lampshade and burning her face with the hot light bulb. She claimed he told her she wasn't so hot and threatened to make her eat the bulb. During the assault, the victim's roommate arrived home. When she discovered the situation, she went back out the front door. Flores went after her. The first vic continued out the back door to the neighbors'. The neighbors did not confirm or deny the story as she told it, and said that they did not know Flores.

The second report Sloane reads is a beat cop's who stopped the roommate for running a red light and driving with no windshield. She told the officer that she'd just left her house where a man was trying to kill her roommate, and that the man was now chasing her—her excuse for running the light. The officer noted that another vehicle had blown the light, but chose to pull over to ticket the roommate. Instead of issuing a ticket, he followed her home, and thus joined the investigation.

Those were the police reports.

The court file says something else. In a nutshell: the victim's roommate refused to testify, as did club-goers, neighbors, and friends—apparently the vic wasn't so well liked in her chosen circle. Waiting on a DNA match, all the prosecution had to go on was a one-against-one story, a broken-down door, and a busted-out car windshield, which the roommate later claimed was caused by a large bird.

Apparently, midtrial, the defense attorney complained that the interpreter who was present during Flores's eventual interview didn't explain the situation to him correctly, and led him to a confession under false pretenses. Tapes from the interview proved the interpreter left out words. The jury decided those words were important.

Flores was charged, yes: for aggravated criminal sexual assault, vehicular invasion, criminal damage to property, and unlawful restraint; turns out the proceedings made it sound like it was the victim who aggravated *him*. She was playing a game, someone said. She wanted to be tied up, said another. And Flores had no record; it was his first set of offenses.

By Sloane's math, Flores's sentence for the assault alone could've earned him anywhere from six to thirty years in jail.

He got ten years. Out in eight. The judge must have been asleep.

Another half hour later, Sloane has read it all again and decided on a game plan. She's on the phone with Danielle Garcia, her favorite interpreter, when—

"Pearson," Salamander yells from his office.

"Uh-oh," Sloane says. "The commander's calling. Are you coming over?"

Danielle says, "*Si,*" and, "*Vemos en unos minutos,*" and Sloane says, "Thanks, bye."

Sloane finds Salamander leaning on the front of his desk, arms and legs crossed, lip bit. "Do you mean to get me fired?" he asks.

"Not sure how I'd do that, sir."

"What did I say? I said you deal with Mercado, and then you work your other cases."

Sloane remains in the doorway and says, "All due respect, sir, this *is* one of my other cases. My victim, Holly Dutcher, pointed to the man downstairs. This isn't some anonymous phone tip. Dutcher isn't going to disappear. And Flores? He isn't some reformed gang member with a kid in preschool. He is a convicted felon. Aggravated criminal sexual assault, for starters."

"You pressed Dutcher with your photo lineup."

"You and Guzman pressed me with your hard-ons for Mercado."

"I told you, Pearson, I was following orders. You should try it."

"Sir, I'm onto something here. I think you know that. Otherwise you'd have shut me down this morning. Look. I did what you said. What Pee—what the commander—said. I put together a lineup and it's legit: ex-cons who are all part of the bigger picture. So I was lucky that Dutcher picked Flores. The important thing is, she didn't pick Mercado. We don't have a crime without a victim, and Mercado's ex has us running in circles. Just let me see what Flores has to say."

Salamander unravels his pretzel position and sits back on his desk, hands flat. "This is how we get our reputation. I let you keep working this case, and all your others are CI'd, and nothing gets done. This is why civilians think we prioritize cases—"

"We *do*, sir."

"But where do we draw the line? Are you going to tell me one sexual assault is worse than another?"

"No, I can't. And I can't stop a man from beating up on his ex-lover. And I can't stop a drunk woman who says no and yes and no when her date only hears the yes. But I can stop this man—this serial predator—if you let me keep at it."

Salamander probably doesn't realize it, but his eyes drift left, to the wall that separates his office from Pee Wee's. Then he says, "I can't do it, Pearson."

"Sir," she says, finally entering the room, but just a step. "I'm not sure why you're worried about priorities. We all have priorities. Hell, with all this year's murders and the back-up at the lab, I'll be lucky if they have DNA results by the time my suspect is convicted, incarcerated, and up for parole. But at least I'm working for the victims. Isn't that worth a little time on the clock?"

"You really think Flores is your guy?"

"Honestly? I have no idea. But I'm asking you, sir, to let me find out."

Salamander's eyes drift again. This time he says, "Try not to make headlines with this one, okay?"

When Sloane returns to the floor, Buchanan is waiting for her—though he looks more like he's waiting for a smoke break. He says, "Flores is in Room Three."

"Thanks," Sloane says. "And thanks for helping those Loop boots. I don't think they knew what they were doing."

"Sloane, I'm not sure anyone knows what they're doing with this guy. Do you know he was beating his head against the squad window all the way here?"

"Did someone downstairs take a look at him?"

"Yeah. They think he's got a mild concussion. Swigart thinks he did it on purpose."

"Of course he did," Sloane says. "He's no stranger to the system." Flores knows he's got to talk, and if he's learned English, he needs another way to render himself unaccountable.

Sloane hears flat footsteps, and then sees Danielle Garcia come up the steps: she's out of breath, overweight, and the most unassuming Irish-white woman ever to speak a second language better than her first.

Sloane says to Buchanan, "Do me a favor, B? Get Flores something to eat. No sugar. Just a sandwich, some water."

"Only if you feed it to him," Buchanan says. "I'm afraid he'll eat my hand."

"Deal."

Danielle hobbles over and joins them. Instead of an *hola* she asks, "What is that noise?"

Sloane hears it: a muted, repetitive scraping sound—like someone is rubbing marbles together.

Buchanan points at Room Three, says, "Told you you're giving him the sandwich."

When Sloane peeks in through the window she sees Flores sitting there, cuffed, grinding his teeth.

"Ridiculous," Sloane says, so Danielle doesn't think there's anything to fear.

"Loco," Danielle says.

Sloane gives Buchanan a silent dismissal and asks Danielle, "How's your knee?"

"Ay de mi," she says. "Fucking Carlos thinks I can walk it off. Can you believe that? Walk it off. The doctor said to lose some weight and all of a sudden Carlos thinks he's some kind of fitness coach . . ."

Sloane is trying to listen, but Flores's grinding is so atrocious her own teeth hurt. She says, "I'm sorry. This is really—we've got to get in there."

"Lead the way. I've got no sympathy for insincere Mexicans."

Inside, Jorge Flores, otherwise known as Garras, isn't happy. He sits at the table, wrists still shackled behind him, teeth grinding.

"Give it a rest," Sloane says, when she leads the way into the interview room. She turns back, lets Danielle come in and squeeze past, her wide bottom making the only feasible position the corner spot across from the door.

Sloane says, "God, that's horrible. Please ask him to stop."

"Por favor señor que deje de hacerlo."

Then, while Sloane is still closing the door, Flores is up, out of his seat, and after her: he uses his body to pin Sloane against the wall, and the only thing keeping him from eating her alive is her arm—the right one put out reflexively as he came at her, trying to bite her, jaws snapping within inches.

She's losing the battle fast, her left arm hardly strong

enough to pick up the slack when Flores uses his weight to lean in, his teeth going *snap! snap!* and Sloane heaving, then losing an inch, then heaving—her hands gripping his neck, pushing him away and cutting his air, doing all she can not to crumble completely.

"Dios fucking Christ," Danielle says, looking for a way around them, to open the door and get out.

Sloane looks at Flores's soulless face, straight on. No fucking way she will let him get to her. She heaves again, using all her strength to push Flores far enough to lock her elbows. Immediately, she thinks she made a mistake; she's sure her arms will break, the weight of him.

Then Danielle is back, and Heavy is there, wrestling Flores away.

Sloane's arms are like dead weights, but she pulls her gun and commands, "Freeze! Flores, I said freeze!"

Flores doesn't listen. He's in the middle of a fair fight now, and he's losing: Heavy has him facedown on the table and they're both sucking air, a time-out, until the table leg breaks and they both go down with it.

Heavy gets a good angle and forces Flores onto his knees, pushing his head forward, his mouth an inch from the metal ledge of the table. They jockey for the upper hand, but Heavy clearly has it so he says, "I don't speak Spanish, Mr. Flores, but I'm no god-damned woman, either. Do you want to lose some of those teeth, or do you want to talk to me?"

Danielle pulls Sloane up from the floor, though she hadn't

realized she'd sunk there. She holsters her gun and the two of them watch, stunned, as Heavy keeps at it. "I wish you understood me, Flores, so we didn't need this other bitch in here to translate. It's bad enough having one of them over my shoulder. But two? I don't know about you, but I don't fucking trust women. Not a one of them." He looks up at Sloane, says, "If you bitches know what's good for you you'll get out of here."

Flores's knees splay when he tries to sit back on his feet, but Heavy keeps him there, still reeling. "Am I right, Jorge? The way they twist words? The way they trick you into thinking they want you? Letting you see just a little more than you should when they'll never give up the rest. You know I'm right."

"Ya," Flores says; Heavy eases up, lets him get off his knees.

"Blondes," Heavy says. "They don't listen. It's enough to make you nuts." He looks back at Sloane. "Just get the fuck out of here, will you, Pearson?"

"Ya," Flores says. "Get the fuck out."

Then Sloane gets it: Heavy's making a friend. She doesn't like it, but she's never going to do it herself. Not after this.

"Come on," someone says, and then it's Salamander standing there, and this time he's the one in the open doorway. He takes Sloane's hand and he whisks her out and the door closes and the reporting of the incident begins.

Sometime later, after everyone on the floor has heard about or talked about what happened, made their jokes, said their sorries, and moved on, Sloane crosses the DMZ and stands outside Room Three.

Inside, she can hear Heavy, though his new friend is the one doing most of the talking.

22

WHEN SLOANE WAS HALFWAY through second grade, she asked
her mom where babies came from. Her answer was, to a seven
year-old, cryptic: She said Sloane's dad took her on a trip to
Rome.

Her mom's descriptions of the city were better than Sloane
had ever read in any book, though, and Sloane was spell-
bound: she could picture the sun coming up over the Spanish Steps at the top of the Via Veneto. She could imagine her
parents sharing Fettuccini Alfredo with oversized forks that
once belonged to Alfredo, the man himself. And she shared
her mom's anticipation, even in the retelling, as she described
walking the narrow cobblestone streets arm in arm with her
man. As they turned a corner and discovered the Trevi Foun-

tain. As they kissed, right there in the plaza, and threw coins over their shoulders, into the water, for good luck. *Love changed us,* she said.

Sloane had no idea what any of it had to do with babies, but she liked the stories, and pretty soon decided that Rome was the most romantic place on earth. As soon as her seven-year-old brain embraced the idea, she was obsessed: she asked for spaghetti every time she had a say at dinner, said *ciao* every time she arrived or left, and she watched her mom's copy of *The Nights of Cabiria,* about a woman who searched the city for love, until she nearly wore out the VHS tape.

For her second-grade social studies project, Sloane, of course, chose Rome. She checked out every library book, and scoured every map; she wrote a paper about the Pantheon, made a clay replica of the Coliseum, and brought *The Nights of Cabiria* to show a clip of the Giardino Degli Aranci—a garden with one of Rome's most panoramic views.

Sloane didn't know why Mrs. Lehman shut off the tape in the middle of her presentation, and she didn't know why the teacher called home that night. After her mom hung up, she told Sloane not to worry about it; Mrs. Lehman just didn't understand Italian film.

It was that spring when her mom got sick and died, and Sloane's dad moved her to the South Side. It was there she learned what a prostitute was, and then realized the kind of love Cabiria had been seeking in Rome.

Sloane was heartbroken. Rome was ruined.

One night when she had every reason to sulk, and her dad

still asked why she was sulking, she told him: Her mom was
a liar. Babies don't come from Rome, and love doesn't change
a thing.

Her dad said, *Your mother did not lie to you. You were con-*
ceived there, in Rome. While we were on vacation.

And someday, he said, *love will change you, too.*

Now, as Sloane sits at the hotel's *osteria*-themed bar, the
joint about as authentic as Italian dressing, Sloane decides
love hasn't changed much, except her address.

"Another club soda?" the hound-faced bartender asks.

"Please. And I'd like to order . . ."

She trails off because the bartender looks like he's ready to
serve the guy who's wheeling his suitcase past Sloane a nice
hot plate of *get the fuck out of here.*

Sloane noticed the man, too, of course; first as part of the
business of the hotel lobby spilling into the bar, one of a constant stream of travelers checking his Blackberry. Then he
stopped in to look at the menu, the five-dollar martini special, and at Sloane. And then again, to check out the score
on the bar television. And to check out Sloane.

This time he's back, no business. His suit is wrinkled,
and he looks like he's jet-lagged; when he bellies up to the
other end of the bar, the bartender is right there, a guard
dog.

Sloane chews on the last of the ice in her glass. She came
down from her room to order a pizza, to get away from her
phone and to sit among people, but she's starting to think

she should've stayed in with a painkiller and a sleeping pill. Some Friday night.

It's not like she had other options, though; yes Stephen called while she was still at the station, and left a message that he wanted her to meet him, but he also wanted to know why she didn't come up and say hello when she had Flores arrested. By the tone of his message, it sounded like an official call, and after dealing with Flores, Sloane was pretty much finished being official today.

Heavy called as Sloane was stripping down in the bathroom, about to get into the tub; as soon as she arrived at the hotel and shed her mental cop armor, she realized Flores had really hurt her. Her arms, joints, her head—everything felt sore and stiff, like she'd been in a car accident.

Heavy had saved her and probably her case, and she was sure he was calling with information, so she answered. Turned out Heavy had nothing new on Flores, and just wanted to make sure Sloane was okay. He said Pee Wee put them all on hold because the lab promised Flores's DNA on Sunday, well within Flores's forty-eight-hour custody limit; he also said the commander did not want another suspect brought in until they cleared the other two.

Sloane's dad called while she was in the tub, left a message, but he didn't want anything special. Sloane figured he must be at Carolyn's by now, and he's got no reason to worry, so she didn't want to call him back and give him one.

Eddie didn't call.

"Here you go," the bartender says, serving her the club soda and an empty martini glass, a full shaker in his hand. "The gentleman at the other end of the bar would like to buy you a cocktail. I can't tell you what to say, but I will tell you if I pour this drink, he's going to come over and try to impress you. He's going to tell you he's from Los Angeles—he's an actor, haven't you seen him before? He'll name a bunch of movies and if you've even heard of them, you won't be able to remember which part he played. Then he'll tell you he's just come into town because he's been asked to audition for the lead in a television pilot. He'll drop it there, pretend it's nothing—"

"Why are you telling me this?"

"Because the guy does not have a room here, and the only place he goes with that suitcase after he's scored is back to the city-stickered Volvo he parks in a tow zone over on Hubbard Street. He's here every weekend. He's a scumbag."

"What he's doing is shitty," Sloane says, "but it's not illegal."

"It should be."

"What? Lying? Come on. When people like each other they see what they want to see, and hear what they want to hear. As long as it's mutual, I have no problem with it. Anyway, it sounds like he puts a lot of effort into it. He even looks like he had a long flight."

"Are you telling me you want this martini?"

"Oh, no." She puts a ten on the bar, gets up, says, "Send it back to him. And tell him I loved him in *Nights of Cabiria*."

UPSTAIRS, SLOANE'S MIND GETS right back to wandering, because there are no calls to her phone. Still no Eddie.

She orders a kid's grilled cheese and fries from room service, and channel-flips, but pretty soon her mind has wandered over to Gina Simonetti, and jealousy sucker-punches Sloane square in the chest.

She should call Eddie. She's afraid.

She wonders where she'll go. She can't afford to stay here much longer. She guesses she'll have to find a temporary place and get her stuff out of storage—she put it there when she moved in with Eddie, since he already had furniture. It's not going to be pretty: most of it is junk, bought on the cheap when she was trying to make a quick nest in her studio on Wrightwood for Doug.

She met Doug when she was coming off an almost-relationship with a younger cop. Doug was a studio musician, and he'd stepped in to do sound for an aging rock band at the Park West; he was one of the only people left hanging around when the band's lead singer took his last drink. There was a brief investigation, but everyone from the label's manager to the roadie's girlfriend—who lost everything in her purse when the singer used it as an impromptu barf bag—told Sloane the singer was diabetic, and had promised he'd make this his last tour.

Doug was pretty cool. Sloane wasn't sure she loved him, but she thought she might if he welcomed some stability into his life. Problem was, his idea of stability was a freelance writing job, a constant move from gig to gig, and the partying in between. He'd play music whenever and wherever, and Sloane didn't mind that; he was a good musician. And he was older. He talked about things like philosophy and world politics, and both those were at least ten feet over the head of the cop kid she had inexplicably crushed on. She loved to listen to Doug play, on the other end of the couch, strumming and singing softly—he had the most beautiful voice, and she always felt like when he sang, he sang to her. It only took a ticket to one of his shows to figure out she wasn't the only one: lots of girls loved to listen to him play, and just about all of them looked like he had sung to them before, too. When he'd introduced Sloane, the band guys were as nice as they needed to be without remembering her name, and the ladies in the crowd were sympathetically nice, either because they'd been there before or knew they'd get a shot eventually.

Sloane worked overnights then, so their schedules weren't so different; she'd get home ready to crash, though, and he'd arrive ready to rock. The night Doug left, Sloane worked a murder scene—a party broken up by the discovery of a girl in an alley with the broken end of a bottle of Hennessy in her throat, most of the alcohol in her system. Sloane was the lead on the investigation and she told her guys not to touch anything; that meant she spent five hours listening to the same CD over and over and over. *My milkshake brings all the boys to the yard.* Sloane was so fucking sick of the noise that when she got back to the apartment and Doug wasn't there and neither was his stuff, she was actually happy for the peace and quiet. She already had him figured out, anyway: he liked moving from gig to gig and it didn't matter whether it was work or music or women. That morning Sloane slept six hours straight.

A knock at the door means dinner; Sloane sits on the bed and watches the WGN news while she eats. *More snow,* they say, and she feels like even the earth has lost control.

Then, the Friday-night clock going on ten, Sloane takes the painkiller and the sleeping pill, crawls into bed, and hopes for sleep.

IT'S FRIDAY NIGHT, AND I've got plans.

Yes, I'm tired, but that's never stopped me before. Besides, it's my own fault—I didn't sleep much last night. Couldn't, after I followed Stephen.

I pull the iron through my hair again, hoping wherever we end up tonight is dark; even with my curls straight, I still can't hide the marks on my neck. But I won't wear a turtleneck again. There is nothing remotely sexy about a turtleneck.

I switch the stereo from my iPod, which has been shuffling nicely, to AM 780; checking the news has become a compulsive habit since I've started working for the city. I'm also interested to know if there are any more girls like me. A blonde, maybe.

The radio cuts from a commercial back to the eights so the traffic-and-weather woman is on deck: She says there isn't much traffic, but there will be more snow. It's crazy, this weather. I consider the cold and look in the mirror at my neck and guess a scarf isn't out of the question.

The news guy comes on the radio next, his lead story about some woman cop who nearly got killed by a guy in custody. Then it's on to a West Side shooting, and then Obama, and then the Olympics—the usual cycle. He rounds out the block with a fluff piece about how to handle all this snow. Like we haven't been handling it since December.

My job is done, though, because he never mentions the mayor, or Alderman Van der Meer, or that LaJeunesse girl, either. The stuff she's been trying to drum up about Humboldt Park is off the radar, thanks to me.

It's no wonder I'm tired. It's not easy, shutting people up.

In the mirror, I draw thick, perfect lines of black eyeliner on my top lids. The lady at the makeup counter said the definition would draw attention to my eyes. Once I'm done, I think she was right. I apply the softest pink blush under my eyebrows and cheekbones, then two coats of mascara, and shimmery lip gloss. I press my lips together and think I don't look much like myself, but I haven't felt like it, either, since that night.

I pull on brown patterned tights and zip up my favorite

denim skirt. I hope wherever we're going isn't too fancy; I look good, sure, but I blew a lot of cash on the cab last night. I really didn't expect we'd go all the way down to Quim's.

It wasn't so well thought out, I'll admit. But I knew Stephen would be at the gym—Thursday nights have always been his *capoeira* nights—so I took a cab there. I didn't know where else to find him; I sure wasn't going to show up at his office, and I didn't know where he'd moved, after we split. I thought the best place to confront him would be privately, in public. So what better place than the street?

The cabbie acted like he had another place to be, so we got to the gym early. I freaked, though, when I saw Quim's Hummer parked out front. I guessed he was there to pick up Stephen, but Quim was about the last person I wanted to run into. Quim and me? Like thick, mean oil and water.

I thought fast and told the cab driver to keep going another block, and then let me out. I watched out the back window as we drove away, though, since I had to duck when we passed by the first time. Then, right when I was about to get out of the cab, I saw Stephen: he was leaving the gym five minutes early, and he was still wearing his sweaty workout clothes—and what the fuck?—he was driving the Hummer.

Then I told the cabbie to turn around and follow the Hummer, and I told him he'd see a nice tip, too, though the farther south we drove, the less cash I had to make that happen. But, whatever, I was pissed. Because when Stephen and I were dating, Quim wouldn't let him touch that stupid

Hummer, or any of his other cars. Quim acted like they all belonged in a museum. Not like his art—*ha*.

Stephen and I, we always had to ride the bus or use a Zip car, both of which are fine but not so fun when you know people with rides just sitting around, collecting rust. I still can't believe that Quim would let loose of one of his babies.

But what I really don't want to believe is that Stephen was dumb enough to take the Hummer up to Rogers Park the night he got mad at that LaJeunesse girl.

We drove all the way down to Quim's. I had the cabbie take me down the building's ramp, to the parking lot; I thought that might be the perfect private-public place. But when we got down there, some woman was there, too. A blonde. She had been waiting for Stephen, I guess. I'd never seen her before, but I could see the look in Stephen's eye, even from across the parking lot: It was the same look he had when we started dating. He was interested.

Stephen took the girl upstairs. The cabbie asked me, "Where to?" and I think he got the idea what we'd been doing. I told him to take me to the Loop because I wasn't going to pay extra fare just to wait for the blonde to leave, and I sure wasn't going to run out of money to find out she didn't.

The cab driver dropped me by my office. I gave him all the cash I had, minus a fiver, and hoped he'd forget where we started.

I took the El to the bus and the bus west and the bus took forever, the fucking snow, but I was still high on adrenaline and I didn't want to go home yet, be alone, so I jumped off at

Damen Avenue and trudged up a couple blocks to spend the last of my cash. I ducked into the tavern on the corner of Huron, sat at the bar, and watched a couple girls play dice while I sucked down a Jack and Coke. It didn't help my nerves. I started to freak out again: What if Stephen found out I was following him? What would he do?

I went home and thought it through and that's why I didn't sleep, but I decided there was absolutely nothing wrong with what I did. Stephen is the one who hurt me. I have the right to know where he is—what if he comes after me again? It's not fair. Since the night he found me—even since that night a long time ago, I've tried to be kind. To be the better person. To let go.

Seeing him with that blonde, though? My heart broke all over again. Same as when I caught him with that first girl he said was just a friend. And then, LaJeunesse.

But I was also scared. Seeing that look in his eye, knowing he thinks he can hurt anybody he wants and get away with it. I let him get away with it.

I turn my iPod back on and of course it shuffles to Zuco 103's "Jusarra," our song. One of our songs, anyway. We liked to dance, so we had a lot of them.

I pull on my cleavage-friendly sweater and decide a scarf is the perfect accessory: between the two, I'm strategically covered—and uncovered.

Then I pour myself a second Jack and Coke, and chew an Excedrin. This is my new routine since I discovered there's nothing like the caffeine-acetaminophen-alcohol combination to relieve pain. And, if I have more than one, I don't feel much at all.

When I'm done, I lace up my snow boots—well, the boots I wear in the snow, anyway—they're tan suede and come up to my knees. They aren't waterproof, or very warm, but they're flat-heeled, so I figure fashion is nearly equal to function, unlike the rest of my kicks.

The bossa nova beat takes me, so I dance a little, a slow samba. It's been a long time since I danced, and my knees are the first to let me know I shouldn't be: I'm still hurting. More than Stephen will ever understand.

I get my coat. I know he likes to go to Enye on Fridays, so that's where I'll start.

I won't let him hurt anyone else.

23

SLOANE'S WAKE-UP CALL DOESN'T get her moving right away. Last night's pills knocked her out cold for a couple hours, but by two o'clock she was awake again—the useless kind of awake that has left her with vague memories of a Marlon Brando movie with loud motorcycles and a bunch of yahoos drinking, fighting, and riding around in circles. If not for Brando, she'd have thought it was a nightmare.

Sunlight frames the hotel room's heavy curtains, so she opens them and looks out: There is more snow today, blinding-bright, covering the tops of all the buildings. The streets are plowed, though, and the city is Saturday-morning quiet, all the tourists and weekenders still sleeping off wild nights.

Sloane doesn't want to be late today so she gets dressed,

no shower, moving as fast as she can, though her joints are stiff and her arms hurt like hell. And she's thirsty.

She buys breakfast—peanut M&M's and an orange juice—from the vending machines in the hall, and polishes off the juice in the elevator.

She's still waking up as she drives Grand Avenue and she's sorry when she decides her body feels worse than it did yesterday. Painkiller hangover, probably; it's no wonder people get addicted. Her tongue feels like she left it hanging out to dry.

She stops at the Burger Baron for two bottles of water and a lemonade and makes it to the station right on time.

Inside, up on the floor, most detectives are in various stages of checking in or heading out. Salamander is sitting at one of the property-crimes dick's unoccupied computers, a cup of coffee, an electronic *Sun-Times*. "Pearson," he says, leaning back in his chair. "How are you feeling?"

"I'm fine, sir."

"Good. Because I have no shortage of shit for you to get done today."

"Where's Heavy?"

"Here and gone."

"Already?"

"Well I certainly wasn't going to let him sit on his ass and wait for you, princess."

Sloane says, "Because that would make no sense," sarcasm blunting her words. "He's my partner, and I'm here on time. What the fuck?"

"What the fuck? You guys let shit pile up. You don't have time for each other." Salamander stirs SWEET'N LOW into his coffee, says, "Don't worry. I'm sure you two will be reunited before the day is through."

Swoop stands up from behind his computer monitor, his back to Sloane, and hugs himself so that it looks like someone else is there, hands rubbing his back—the way kids do when they pretend they're making out with someone. Swoop moans, makes kissing noises, says, "Oh, Heavy. You're so . . . big."

Sloane ignores him, asks Salamander, "Are my cases online?" but Swoop starts a trend: other dicks peek around their computers to see her, smacking their lips.

"You are all *so* grown up," she says.

Her acknowledgment only gets a few more of them to join in. Across the DMZ, the homicide dicks pick up on the noise; thankfully, most of them look too busy to enjoy the show. Most of them.

"Sir?" Sloane asks. "My cases?"

Salamander tears himself away from one of Ebert's movie reviews, stands up, and says, "Get to work, ya god-damned slackers. She's never going to sleep with any of you." Then he says, "You get to work, too, princess. Yes, your cases are online."

"Thank you," she says; *asshole,* she thinks.

On her way across the DMZ Sloane sees Mumford come out of the men's bathroom, sports pages under his arm, strutting like he left a stink.

She tries to avoid him but he says, "Hello," and he says it real polite.

"Hello back," she says, just as nicely. She's glad Mumford was in the can a minute ago, when Salamander stated the obvious, because she can tell he still thinks he's got a shot with her.

"Hey," Vince Marchetti says, "Pearson." She didn't see him before, and she doesn't really want to see him now, because he's the best-looking guy on the floor, so of course that means she's fucking him, too.

"Hey Marchetti," she says without looking at him, and beelines for her desk.

He follows her, unclear on the concept. "Detective," he says, "I wanted to say sorry about Nigeria. You were right, I let the wrong bad guy go."

"Well, now you know. For next time." She sits down, opens her online files.

"There's something else," he says, standing over her desk, awkward.

"Always is," Sloane says. Across the floor, heads start turning.

"So, I caught a case just now, body of a young white female up on the Bloomingdale Trail. They're saying the deceased was strangled, and maybe raped. I'm on my way to the scene now, but I took the liberty of looking at your current serial case this morning, and I wonder if you'd come along. Take a look."

"Sorry, Vince," she says. "I keep getting into trouble for

actually working cases. If I come in on yours, the bosses are sure to have my star."

He rubs his red eyes and Sloane thinks he probably has a real hangover. He says, "I just thought, with a body, you know, all the evidence is there."

"A body can't testify," Sloane says. "Are you telling me you think your vic was done by my guy?"

"I don't know, but she seems to fit the profile."

"Young, white, and female isn't much of a profile. The vics in my case were attacked on neighborhood streets and taken to abandoned buildings, and they all lived to tell me about it." Sloane doesn't doubt that Vince might be on to something, but, "Right now I'm looking at three cases I have to take care of today, starting with a guy who's showing his goods to little girls after school. How about you take a ride up there, see the body, and call me if you still think she's one of mine?"

"Okay," he says. "I just thought . . ." but whatever he thought doesn't make it out of his mouth. He goes back to his desk, sits down, and rubs his eyes some more.

Sloane keeps her case files open while she checks on Heavy's notes from yesterday with Flores, which are sparse, and of course in no way organized or summarized. They read:

Flores, Jorge, aka "Garras"=Jaws
Current addy=2120 S. Laflin—Pilsen
Does not own vehicle.

Parole officer= "Martin Valenzuela"?

Flores=English in prison.

"Grateful" for job at 50 E. Monroe. Janitor.

Girlfriend= "Carmen Alverado." Crrntly in Mxco; Flores wants to "get ass" but lives w/C's cousin "Bianca Alverado," aka "Coño Curioso." Flores plans to be w/C when she returns.

Flores: saving money to move to apt.

No alchl/drugs/sbtnce abuse.

Free time=working out=weight gain.

*Hates white girls, esp. blondes. Atty in prev. case lkd like Det. Pearson. Re: case: "bitches set me up." Refer to case?

Flores: "Unfamiliar" with River Nrth, West Town, Uki Vlg.

*Has "friends" in Humboldt Pk . . .

*Intrvw cut short by Cmndr. Wojciechowski, request follow-up post-DNA.

Sloane closes Heavy's report, cursing Pee Wee: he must've shut down the interview at four o'clock sharp. God-damned bosses and their god-damned desk rules. They won't pay for overtime and they won't let a cop work for free, either, so a bad guy sits in holding twiddling his thumbs for thirty-two of his forty-eight.

Sloane brings up her first case, which consists of two police reports on yesterday's flasher: two fourteen-year-old Hispanic girls gave statements about walking home from Wells Academy together and being harassed by a male suspect in a green or olive-colored older-model Jeep, which one girl described as "boxy." They both say the man rolled down his window and asked, "Do you want to see my dick?" The two girls gave their statements separately and to two different patrol officers, and both statements are similar in description of the location, time, vehicle, and suspect. Both state they were on the seven-hundred block of North Armour Street. It was ten minutes to two. Both said Jeep. Both said white male, black hair, and the description ends there, since they claimed he opened his door and showed them his penis, which, as far as Sloane's concerned, is enough to ruin anybody's memory. The girls ran, smartly, down to Superior, and then west on the street's one-way east. They did not see the suspect again, but ran directly to one of the girl's homes and told her mother, who called 911.

There are a number of things that bother Sloane about this. One, it was before two o'clock, and most high schools don't let out until three. Two, old Jeeps' windows don't "roll" down—they're either unzipped or removed. Three, Wells Academy is west of Armour and the girl's address is west of the school, which means the girls were taking the long way home. Fourth, Richard Milburn High is a block from where the incident occurred. Last time Sloane passed by, students had been moved to a temporary facility and the building was being renovated, but that's a second reason it would be of interest to the young ladies.

Sloane knows her options are limited on a Saturday and she gets no answer at the high school's listed number. There are seven different Jeep models but Sloane limits her DMV check to green Wranglers—they're "boxy." It's a long list, no offenders. Then she writes down the two girls' names and addresses—she's going to talk to each of them before she spends any time on the street looking for a green Jeep. She has a feeling one or the other of the girls will spill the truth, and that it will indeed have to do with a male, but it's unlikely he'll be old enough to drive.

Sloane signs out an unmarked and heads back east on Grand Avenue toward the first girl's address. She hopes the girl had a good Friday night, because if Sloane's theory is correct, it might be the last time the girl gets to go anywhere fun for a while.

On her way past Smith Park, Sloane spots that idling unmarked car again. It's parked facing a bunch of dogs and their owners: a Saturday snow playdate for canines. The scene is picturesque, the people dressed in all colors of cold-weather wear, the dogs leaping over or sinking in or just eating snow.

And Sloane doesn't know why she hadn't realized it the first time, but there's no other cop it can be.

It's Heavy.

When she rolls up behind him, she notices something weird—something furry—on the top of his side-view mirror. As soon as she's too close, the thing jumps and scampers for the nearest tree: It's a squirrel.

Sloane cuts the wheel and rolls down her passenger window as she pulls up, parallel with Heavy. His window is down, he's wearing gloves and a knit cap, and he's eating French fries.

Sloane doesn't know what to say.

Heavy says, between fries, without looking at her, "So what? I'm having lunch here."

"It's nine o'clock."

"So what?"

"I don't know." She puts the car in park. "Is there something wrong?"

"I'm a pushover."

"Why would you say that?"

"Because I'm hiding and you found me."

"I thought you were having lunch."

"Oh, for God's sake, darlin'," he says, tossing a fry out the window, in the squirrel's direction. "I shouldn't be a cop. I haven't been a cop for a long time."

One of the dogs barks in the distance, and Heavy tries to smile. He says, "I started out in animal control, you know."

"I didn't know that."

"I had the uniform, the truck, the so-called equipment. I worked out in Huntley. A lot of deer, back then. And I did that for two years, saving cats and killing rabid raccoons and chasing coyotes—until I found out how much the police made. I took the test, on a lark. Just to see. And I passed the damn thing—top of my group. At that time, though, the only place hiring was the CPD. Biggest and best mistake of my life. I never belonged here—in the city, or with a star. But if I hadn't come, I wouldn't have met Sharon."

"You've been doing the Job a long time," Sloane says. "Everybody respects you—"

"Aww come on. You're not that dumb. I haven't gone after a case since 1996. I was in Fifteen and I chased a suspected drug dealer who ate his own coke stash when he was running away from me. He wound up dead. The kid also wound up being a preacher's son, and the whole neighborhood came down on me. I think you can imagine how supportive my bosses were." Heavy tosses another fry into the snow. "You're starting to get it, aren't you?"

"No."

"I was told a long time ago to do my job. And what that's supposed to mean is, you wait until someone else tells you what to do, and then you do it. They don't like you, darlin', and they want me to slow you down."

"You? You would do that?"

"Guzman talked to me, the same day you started this serial thing. He said, 'You know what happens when we upset the community, don't you?' "

"What the fuck does that mean?"

"It means there's somebody out there, in *this* so-called community, who doesn't want you to solve this case. I've been trying to tell you, Sloane: life is more important. People you love are slipping past you because you think you can win the fight, and maybe you can, but the thing is? There will always be another one. Another fight. But there will never be another now, or another you. Your life is more important."

Sloane makes sure the car is parked, because it feels like it's rolling backward.

"We can't stop this guy, Sloane," Heavy says. "We can only waste time with innocent men, or close this thing and move on."

Sloane turns up the heat, and she thinks of Zookie Truman. That case went just this way. Sloane took it all the way to court, but no one could—or apparently *would*—call out Nigeria. He was bulletproof, and the people connected to him were as armed as they were dangerous. Like Sloane said, Nigeria had long arms: long enough to make her witnesses victims.

And long enough to make the law bend.

The squirrel returns, in and out of the deep snow, searching for Heavy's fries.

Sloane says, "I won't quit."

"I didn't think so," Heavy says, "but I already have."

"Are you going to do what they say? Are you going to slow me down?"

"I don't know anybody capable of that, darlin'."

Heavy throws a couple of fries at the squirrel. "How's your father?"

"He's okay."

"Is he responsible for this tough skin of yours?"

"Half."

They sit there, cars idling, watching the dogs and their people. Neither detective says a word; they listen to the dogs bark, the people laugh. The squirrel gets brave enough to jump up on Heavy's hood and look at him through the wind-shield, and Sloane knows they've both spent a lot of time here.

She's already stayed too long.

She shifts into reverse and says, "Marchetti's got a body. I'm going to go check it out."

Heavy is still smiling when she backs up and heads north.

24

THE BLOOMINGDALE TRAIL RUNS quietly around the city, over the streets and between blocks, an old freight-train track. The city has plans to make it a bike path, but right now, it's snow over weeds over gravel, dirt, and leftover ties.

On top of that, just over Hoyne Street, there's a crime scene.

Sloane parks on the north side of the trail, where single-family homes are expensive enough to be set apart on all sides by thin, wraparound yards. An alley divides the garages in back. Sloane walks the alley, an eye out for anything that looks like it doesn't belong.

When she reaches the base of the path she hears the busy, quiet work of the cops and the techs above, each with their own agenda, only a lowered voice here and there, respect for the dead. There is no northern entrance here; scrappy bushes have grown over and through a fence that runs along the path, and the incline is so steep and cleared of brush that climbing would be tough.

Sloane cuts through a residential yard back to Hoyne and heads south.

On this particular stretch of the path, a block of two-story condos runs parallel, and the police have set up camp there: they've parked squads in front of garages, drawn police lines across front doors. The units all appear to be finished and occupied, except for one with a FOR RENT sign in its window.

Sloane makes her way past the police line with her star, gets access to the path from the keyed gate that's propped open, somebody's baton wedged between links.

The body is a white female, fully dressed, facedown. In between techs who are dressed like the girl is toxic, Vince Marchetti is crouched down at her feet, apparently interested in the soles of her high heels. Not exactly snow shoes.

"Marchetti," Sloane says from just inside the path gate.

He looks over his shoulder.

"Mind if I take a look?"

Marchetti stands up, comes over. "A local guy found her when he took his dog out this morning."

Sloane follows the taped-off footprints as they come from the east, through the snow. "Did you get these tracks?"

"I'm told there are three sets: the resident's, the dog's, and the girl's. It looks like the vic ran up here from Damen Avenue, stumbled, crawled, and collapsed."

"Who is she?"

"Name's Rachel Sayers. She lives three blocks north of here on Hoyne. I spoke to her landlord. Her parents are in London. Salamano's making that call."

"Salamander is here?"

"He's up at the girl's place."

Sloane decides she better make this quick. She approaches the body, asks, "What's the initial cause?"

"The ME isn't here yet, but I'm saying strangulation."

Sloane swipes a pair of latex gloves from a box in the snow, her homicide muscle memory better than if she had to ride a bike. She kneels, tilts her head, and looks at the girl.

The sunlight glare off of the snow provides a perfect examination light. The girl's face is congested, but there are no signs of petechial hemorrhages in or around her eyes. Her pupils are dilated, which means she died in the dark. Her expression is strained, focus up, as though she'd been looking for breath.

There are few signs of manual strangulation on her neck: there are slight contusions but no abrasions, no broken skin, no visible fractures in the neck bones. "Are you sure about strangulation?" Sloane asks, meaning, *She wasn't strangled.*

"Why?" Vince asks. "You see something different?"

Sloane doesn't answer. She checks the girl's clothing as it relates to her position: She wears a T-length polyester trench coat that's slit for style in back and appears to be buttoned in front. Underneath the coat is a collared blouse, also buttoned, and wool pants, belted. The girl's arms are down at her sides, unnatural positioning. If she had collapsed here, she would have tried to break her fall.

When Sloane takes a closer look at the girl's hand, she notices a brown spot on the girl's thin, cream-colored glove where a ring protrudes.

"Was she married?"

"Engaged."

Sloane shows him the glove, says, "There's blood here," and wonders if it's from a fight. She asks, "Have they been over her clothing yet?"

"Not yet."

"I'd check for trace—hair, fibers. I don't think she died here."

Marchetti looks back at the marked-off tracks coming from Damen Avenue. "Somebody carried her?"

"Exactly." Sloane stands up. "I don't think she was raped. If somebody had re-dressed her, she wouldn't be tucked-in, belted, and buttoned."

"I guess this isn't your guy."

"Nope." Sloane says. She keeps an eye on the gate, anticipating Salamander, and knows she'd better start her exit. She peels off the gloves, says, "I don't think she was raped or strangled. I'd tell the ME to check for obstructions in her throat, and find out if she was right or left-handed. And I'd find out where she came from last night, because I'll bet the last person to see her alive was the one who carried her up here."

Marchetti follows her to the gate and she says, "I'd better get out of here before Salamander shows up and accuses me of working."

"Thanks, Sloane," Marchetti says, and offers a hand-shake.

Sloane hands him her gloves. "Good luck."

She makes it back out to Hoyne with no sign of Salamander, but she's parked to the north, and that's where he's coming from, so she doesn't want to take any chances.

She walks south to Willow, planning to go around the block, take Damen up; sneaky.

As soon as she turns the corner, she sees the vacants. Two of them, south side of the street, past a half-block, redbrick apartment building.

She tells herself there are thousands of vacants in the city, but her heart beats faster anyway. She crosses over to the south side of the street and sees both buildings are missing windows, abandoned in the middle of construction.

Behind the chain-link fence that surrounds the buildings, the developer's sign reads IMMEDIATE OCCUPANCY URBAN CONDOS. Sloane remembers a sign like this at the place down on Erie, where Holly was attacked. She gets out her camera and scrolls through the photos she took to be sure, and then finds a second similarity: the sign that advertises PANTHER CONSTRUCTION.

Sloane calls Heavy. "Hey—you remember the construction company that was working at the site where Meyer-Davis was attacked?"

"Nope."

"Can you look it up?"

"Yep."

While Sloane waits, she walks around the properties and finds the gate on the eastern side unlocked.

She lets herself in. Both units are open. There's distinct evidence of entry in both, so she's tiptoeing out when Heavy comes back on the line and says, "Panther Construction."

Sloane says, "I'm onto something."

SLOANE STOPS FOR COFFEE and a bowl of oatmeal at the Earwax Café, because Holly needed an hour to get her shit together.

Before she called Holly, she tried the number listed for Panther Construction. She got a guy who answered "Panther," but when she identified herself, it turned out he didn't speak English very well, and wasn't familiar with the construction company. She asked for his manager and he hung up.

So, she called Holly. Sloane assured her Flores was in custody at the station, and told her he'd stay there until his DNA came back from the lab and the state's attorney came in for felony review. The second part wasn't exactly true, but she didn't want Holly to worry. And, she hoped Holly could help get her onto a *real* lead now, something that would stick.

She told Holly her reason for calling was she decided she

was ready to take advantage of the housing market and wanted to see some places. She had specific addresses, as she had Heavy run a check for city permits for Panther Construction. She included the two units on Willow Street.

Holly said she'd get her listings together and call agents for appointments. Since the buildings Sloane had actually seen were nowhere near finished and unfit for occupancy, she wondered if her plan would sputter out, but Holly called back, excited as a little kid, with lockbox codes and meetings in twenty-minute increments. She explained that on such short notice, she was only able to get four showings, and that the places Sloane was interested in on Willow were a no-go, but she felt the appointments they had would be a good start.

Sloane hoped so.

THE FIRST PROPERTY is in East Village on Wolcott Street, and Holly decodes a box padlocked around the iron fence to get the front door key.

Unfortunately, Holly doesn't know anything about the place except what's on the listing sheet, so they wander through the empty rooms, learning as they go.

When Sloane notices diagonal cracks spreading toward the ceiling from the corners above the bedroom door, she figures it's within reason to ask, "Do you know anything about Panther Construction?"

Holly looks at the listing sheet and says, "Sure: They built this property."

Sloane doesn't know why she's surprised at Holly's obvious answer. "They didn't build it very well." Sloane points to the cracked drywall.

"I'm sure that can be fixed," Holly says, no clue that it's probably a foundation issue, which isn't a quick or cheap fix.

Sloane says, "I don't think this place is my style. Where's the next one?"

"Down on the four-hundred block of Sangamon. Shall I drive?"

Sloane knows those are the places where Meyer-Davis was assaulted. "I'll meet you there."

Sloane shoots down Ashland and gets to the address in less than five minutes. She makes a note on the first place's listing sheet: *poor workmanship. Faulty construction?*

Then she gets out and crosses the street to check out the condo they're about to see: It's next door to the Meyer-Davis crime scene, and Scott Zwick smiles back at her from a Realtor's sign in the front window.

"Oh," she says, wondering how she's going to get around this one.

Holly pulls up, gets out, says, "I hope you hate this place."

"Excuse me?" Sloane doesn't think she heard her right.

"I know this guy, and I'm sorry, I can't stick my finger far enough down my throat."

"Oh," Sloane says again, amused by the small, strange world.

Zwick is waiting inside the empty place with a phony smile for Holly that doesn't hold up when he sees Sloane. "Have we met?" he asks, like he doesn't remember.

"I looked at another place of yours last week," she says, also like he doesn't remember.

"I didn't think you were working with a Realtor."

"I wasn't. Holly is a friend of mine."

"Should we have a look around?" Holly asks, but not because she's picking up on the tension.

"Here's the listing," Zwick says, passing one to each of them. Then he says, to Sloane, "Why don't you take a solo look, come back, hit me with questions? I've got a couple questions of my own for your Realtor, here."

"Okay," Sloane says, feeling dismissed.

She heads straight for the back bathroom and checks her cell reception because she could care less about looking around. She can hear the Realtors' voices echoing in bitter clips through the vents; she tells herself she's doing Holly a favor, too, at this point.

Sloane blocks her caller ID, dials Holly, waits for an answer, and hangs up.

She dials again, waits for Holly, hangs up.

She hopes the third time's a charm.

When she returns to the main room, Zwick is handing Holly her phone, telling her, "It says you've got full bars. Are you sure you know how to answer it?" He looks over at Sloane: *idiot.*

Sloane checks her own phone and lies, "I don't have any reception."

Holly says, "Someone keeps trying to call."

"I just have a few questions for Mr. Zwick," Sloane says.

"If you need to go outside? Maybe the reception is better?"

"You're right," she says. "Could be one of our other appointments."

As soon as Holly is out the door, Sloane shows Zwick her star. She says, "There's a reason I'm not working with the brightest Realtor and it's because I'm undercover."

Zwick steps back, the lines around his eyes working their way through disbelief to amusement to arousal.

Sloane says, "I'm sorry I haven't called you. But I don't know whom to trust. I'm running out of time, though, and since you seem legit, I'm taking a chance. Will you help me?"

"Isn't it my civil obligation?"

"Assuming you're civil."

"Let me prove it to you," he says.

"There is a man who is sexually assaulting and quite possibly killing women, and I think he might be associated with Panther Construction Company. Do you know anything about the company, or can you help me find out?"

"Sure," Zwick says. "Owner's name is Lonzo Barreto."

Barreto. Sloane thinks she knows that name. "You know Barreto?"

"Not really. Last time I saw him he was fighting with a material supplier so I steered way clear. Since then, all Panther's other projects have been put on hold. I think they went broke. This development is the last one they finished."

"How does a construction company run out of money? Aren't they funded by developers?"

"Yes, which means the developer filed Chapter Eleven, or cut them off. I'm not surprised; even in a good market, their buildings weren't easy to sell."

"Why?"

Zwick points up to a section of triple crown molding, says, "Looks nice, until you uncover the problems underneath."

"I noticed problems at another of their properties. How in the hell do they keep getting jobs?"

"Connections, I assume."

"Who are they connected to here?"

"This place?" Zwick asks, opening his briefcase and retrieving a file folder.

As he flips through the file, Holly comes in, asks, "Did he answer your questions?"

Zwick says, "Zimmerman and Company."

Sloane says, "I have to go."

"Why?" Holly wants to know.

"She got a phone call," Zwick says.

"I'll call you," Sloane says to Holly, looking at Zwick.

He nods, says, "You better." A possibility.

When she gets out to the Pilot, she calls Stephen Carvalho.

25

BY THE TIME STEPHEN calls back it's after eight o'clock, so Sloane says, "I assume you already have plans tonight."

"Yes," he says, "but they aren't as pretty. What are you in the mood for?"

Answers, she thinks. "Your call."

"I'm in Glencoe," he says. "Just finished work. How about we meet at the Pharmacy on Chicago Avenue in West Town, say, half hour?"

"Which one?" Sloane asks, thinking it's a weird choice.

"It's a bar," he says. "Green cross sign. Red cross window?"

"Right," Sloane says, feeling stupid. "I thought maybe you were in the mood for bad lighting and an over-the-counter buzz."

"I am," he says. "See you there."

Sloane checks herself in the mirror for the hundreth time.
She's been ready to walk out the hotel door since five o'clock,
after she got back from the flasher fiasco. When she didn't
hear back from Stephen right away, she went back to the station to figure out where she'd heard the name *Barreto*: she
found it in Heavy's interview notes from Caspar Mercado.
Mercado claimed a guy named Barreto was Rosalia Verdez's
lover. How that mattered, she wasn't sure, but she couldn't
figure anything she was sure of, this damn case.

Sloane was antsy then, nothing from Stephen, so she decided to knock the teen flasher off her case list. The first Wells
Academy girl didn't seem like she'd be the leader of any pack,
so Sloane went easy on her, and she stuck to her story; the second one looked older than she should, spoke to her mother in
a tone that should've earned a lashing, and wore her eye
makeup at angles that made her look bossy. Sloane figured
she'd be the one with the boyfriend, and pressed her hard:
*What's that ink on your hand? Is that a tattoo? No? You wrote
that yourself? It's your boyfriend's name, right? Is he a student at
Wells? No? What about Millburn? No? Why did you and your
friend cross Ashland when you both live over here? How would
your boyfriend feel if he knew you were going over by Millburn?*
The girl was in love, and when it came down to it, more afraid
of losing her boyfriend than catching the charges. Sloane got
her to admit there was no green Jeep, no white man, no illicit
exposure. She would have left the girl there, with her mother,

if her mother had any semblance of control. Instead Sloane put it on the girl and had a couple of uniforms pick her up, give her an appropriate scare.

If only adults were as easy to crack.

On Chicago Avenue, Sloane finds the Pharmacy's neon-green cross and drives past, parks at the end of the block. She's glad she found a spot close because she's wearing her thin leather coat and the temperature never warmed up enough to melt snow. She's also glad someone's shoveled the sidewalk, because she's wearing dark red, four-inch heels, and traction wasn't a selling point.

Sloane hopes she's dressed appropriately; when she called down to the concierge for a description of the bar, he said, "It's chill." It took her three outfits to decide whether it was better to be over- or underdressed and she wound up with a combination: jeans, a low-cut, black V-neck sweater, and a triple-strand gold charm necklace with quartz and stone pendants. Her lipstick and nail polish match her heels.

She doesn't mean for this to be a date, exactly, but she knows better. Especially because all eyes fall on her when she walks into the joint and suddenly she feels sexy.

She doesn't see Stephen so she takes a seat at the bar, and is met immediately by a wide-eyed bartender whose thick-framed glasses remind Sloane of the pair she used to wear. "What can I get for ya?"

"Just a club soda," she says. "I'm waiting for someone." And she wants to be sober when he arrives.

The bartender fixes her soda and hands her a drink menu. He says, "If you're interested in eating, I've got a hamburger or a gardenburger, and a basket of fries for a buck."

Sloane says, "Thanks," and uses the menu to get a discreet look around the room. The space is long and narrow, and cut into three sections. She guesses that in the second section, the lighted walls that a pair of girls disappear behind are the bathrooms. The light falls away to flickering candles and she can see a group of guys seated on a band of couches that round the back walls.

In front, an electric PRESCRIPTIONS sign hangs over the beautiful, dark-wood bar. As far as Sloane can tell, it's the only reference to the name apart from the signs out front. Behind her, framed black-and-white photos of rock stars stare down at the low, empty tables. Sloane supposes all those guys had their fair share of prescriptions.

"Have you decided?" the bartender asks when he does a lap past her, probably because he thinks she's been looking at the drink menu since he left it.

"I have no idea," she says. "I'm not much of a drinker."

"You like cream soda?"

Sloane thinks of the stuff her dad used to get her from the Jewel. The too-sweet grocery brand in the blue can. She smiles. "I do."

"You'll like my version."

She watches him pour a healthy dose of vanilla vodka into a glass and feels just a little of her willpower slip away.

Sloane's as careful as she can be with the drink, but it's halfway gone when Stephen walks into the bar, and it's not the alcohol that makes Sloane think *Damn.* She crosses her legs.

He's dressed casual in a form-fitting black thermal, jeans, and dark leather sneakers, and he hasn't had a shave. When he sees Sloane and smiles at her, she has to look away.

He takes the empty seat next to hers, looks at the backlit bottles behind the bar, and as Sloane's gearing up to say something, shuts her up. "You look hot."

"Thanks," her voice catches. She coughs, to cover her nerves, then slides her cocktail over to him and says, "It's strong."

"What is it?"

"Cream soda."

"Forget it," he says. "Too sweet for me." He flags the bartender, tells him, "Bombay Sapphire. Rocks. Lime."

While the bartender pours gin into a short glass with ice Sloane says, "You want to grab a table?"

"Why?" he asks, "Would you feel better with two feet of wood between us?"

She picks up her cream soda and makes getting up her answer.

She selects the table in the front window, farthest from the rest of the crowd, the outside streetlights muted by the red cross painted on the window. She sits facing the door.

"Listen," she says when he sits down. "Things are starting to fall into place with my case, and they keep stacking up right outside your building. I want you to tell me about Panther Construction."

Stephen leans back, crosses his arms, says, "Aww, you tricked me. I thought we closed that case down at my brother's place." He reaches for his drink. "I feel so used."

"No you don't."

"It's Saturday night."

"And last night was Friday night. A girl was killed."

"Oh." He puts down his drink. "You think it was the same guy?"

"It doesn't matter what I think. I need to *know* about Panther Construction."

"Alright," he says, avoiding a sigh. "Panther was set up about five years ago by my boss's brother-in-law, Lonzo Barreto. He was one of the first guys Mo met in the ex-offender program back when he worked for some other developer— Englewood, I think. The program had just started, and back then, every ex-con had a mentor. Mo was Lonzo's."

Barreto again. "How long ago was this?"

"I don't know. Five years? You'd have to ask Mo."

"You know if Baretto dates a woman named Rosalia Verdez?"

"That, you'd have to ask Barreto."

"So Mr. Reyes mentored Barreto. How did Zimmerman and Company wind up financing Panther?"

"Mo gave Barreto startup money on his own and then he got Zimmerman to invest."

"Reyes must've believed in Barreto."

"I don't know about that. I do know he married Barreto's sister, Soledad. So Mo's kind of—tied up in it, I guess."

Sloane remembers the photo of Soledad: the pearls, her breasts, her indifferent beauty.

She asks, "Do you know why Barreto was in jail?"

"You're asking me? You're the detective."

"It's my understanding that Panther might have filed Chapter Eleven."

"I don't know about that either, but they are going broke. Mo cut them off when he found out Barreto was hiring guys he used to know."

"I thought Reyes supported ex-offenders."

"I'm talking about neighborhood guys. Gangsters. But Mo made Soledad mad, when he quit giving Lonzo money. Ever since then, Mo's been pushing for this Pulaski Corridor project. To get Lonzo some legit work without the gang, and to get back into Soledad's good graces."

"I think I need to meet Barreto."

"Wait a minute, I thought we were just talking, here. I wouldn't have said a word if I knew you'd use it against me. You go to Barreto, and Mo finds out I talked to you, and I'm as good as unemployed. I might be a glorified travel agent, but I respect Mo, and this job is a guaranteed opportunity. I do Mo's dirty work for a few years and can do whatever I want next."

"What is it that you want to do next?"

"I don't know. Usually, I only know what I want right now."

Stephen finishes his drink; Sloane hasn't touched hers. The mix of alcohol and sugar and convoluted information has made her feel looped.

"You ready for another?" Stephen asks, getting up.

"Maybe just a beer."

She watches him approach the bar and watches other women watch him, too. Sloane wishes she could make sense of all these loose connections or forget them entirely. At least for tonight.

When he returns, two bottles of beer, two shots, Sloane says, "Oh no. I have to work tomorrow."

"Are you ever *not* working?" he asks, putting the drinks on the table. "You sound like my brother Quim. He can't separate work from life, either. Are you miserable? He's miserable. I tell you, if I took the shit I get from Mo all day home with me . . ." He stops, says, "I won't start. But I will say that Quim's life was wrecked because of work. When that woman rejected his paintings, she rejected him. He's never been the same." He picks up both shot glasses, hands one to Sloane, says, "Let's drink to life."

"To life," she says, and clinks her glass with his; the shot goes down like fire, from her throat all the way to her belly. "What was that?" she asks.

"Medicine."

The night starts to blur, and quick; more than once, Sloane finds herself talking too much. They finish another round of beers and Sloane is denying a second shot when Stephen says, "Hang on," gets up, takes a call.

When he comes back, everything becomes too clear: he says, "I have to go back to the office."

"What?"

"That was Mo. He missed his flight, and I have to book him another one out of Dallas in the morning." He sits down like the alcohol has gone to his head.

"Are you okay?"

"Of course! I'm great. It's ten-thirty on a Saturday night and I'm going *back* to fucking work because I have never made a reservation my boss can keep. I swear, if Zimmerman didn't spend so much money on Mo's last-minute travel, they could probably afford to rebuild the Pulaski Corridor themselves. Corporate money," he says, and he's nearly shouting now. "No matter how much I spend, I barely see a dime."

"I'm sorry, Stephen," she says, reaching out to offer a calming hand.

He pulls away. "I lied when I said I can separate work and life. How can I? I'm Mo's bitch."

Sloane gets up, says, "Stay here. I'll pay the tab."

Stephen stands up, grabs her by the wrist. "Don't be ridiculous. Wait here."

This time, when Sloane watches Stephen approach the bar, he is a completely different person. He's still smooth on his feet, but he's lower now. Alert. Prowling.

Sloane zips up her coat. It is definitely time to go.

When he returns, he asks, "Are you parked nearby?"

"Yep, right out front, actually."

"I'll walk you," he says, and she can't think of an excuse why not.

Once outside, Stephen says, "Sorry I have to cut this short. I thought I was off the hook this weekend, so I didn't bring my laptop home. Seriously? Mo wouldn't know where to find his shoes if I didn't tell him. Half the time he isn't sure who he's meeting or what he's supposed to say. I'm sure you heard about this whole thing with the alderman?"

Sloane says, "Yeah," and stops walking, because they're in front of the Pilot, but Stephen keeps talking—

"It's been in the news. I'm the one who made peace with Van der Meer and got Mo a meeting with him on Monday. I'm sure Mo's going to blow it. I keep telling him Van der Meer is going to bury us—he's not going to lose the run for state's attorney. But Mo doesn't listen to me unless he asks me a question."

"Why would Van der Meer bury you?" Sloane asks.

"Because there's bad blood between them. Some business deal that went wrong a few years back, after Mo helped Van der Meer's campaign for the alderman's seat. You know, I'm starting to think Mo's push for the Pulaski Corridor project is just so he can beat Van der Meer."

Sloane's head is spinning and all she can think to say is, "This is me."

She gets out her keys, unlocks the passenger door, and throws her purse inside. When she turns to say good-bye, she's caught in Stephen's arms—his hands at her neck, and not so delicately this time—and he kisses her, hard. She tries to stall him—"Stvn"—but he keeps kissing her, lips soft but with too much force behind them; the piney smell of gin still strong on his breath.

She tries to push him away, hands against his chest, but she only tips back on her heels, and as he moves with her, he presses her against the Pilot. Then, her discretion alcohol-soaked, she decides this is spontaneity, and she kisses him back.

She raises her arms, just as he had the first night he kissed her, and surrenders; it's been so long since she felt passion that she'd mistaken it for aggression. Stephen wraps his arms around the tops of her shoulders, and she has to bend to his weight; she's still hurting from yesterday's assault, and her position is obviously compromised.

Then, a woman screams—

"Stephen!"

He is at once off-guard; he lets go of Sloane, and only then does she realize he was practically suffocating her, just with a kiss. She finds her breath at the same time the young woman behind them says, "It was you, wasn't it Stephen?" She holds her hat in her hands, tears streaming, a mess.

Stephen backs away from both of them, cautious.

"Was it you?" the woman screams, begging him, and bringing the bartender and one of his bigger friends out of the Pharmacy.

"It was you," the girl says, her voice short now, hysterical.

All at once, it hits Sloane: the cut under his eye. The bad ankle. His brother's Hummer. His job at 50 E. Monroe; his access to employees—and uniforms. His strength and speed and agility and him, always a step ahead of Sloane. "It's you?"

"Yes," the woman says, shaking so terribly she falls to her knees.

"What's the problem here?" The bartender asks, both men approaching.

"Don't do this," Stephen says to the woman.

"I'm calling the cops," the bartender says, his cell phone lit up.

Fuck. Sloane thinks of the alcohol in her system and the star on her belt, her .22 in the glove box and the trouble that's only about to begin. She'd been a complete fool: seeing exactly what she wanted to see, hearing exactly what she wanted to hear.

When Stephen takes a step forward, toward Sloane, she's in the Pilot, passenger side, doors locked. She climbs over the center console and starts the car.

Stephen says, "Wait!" and knocks on the window, his frustration spiked by flashes of anger. Behind him, the men shout warnings, and Sloane shakes her head at Stephen, *no.*

He pounds on the window now, with the heel of his fist, enraged.

"No," Sloane says out loud, looking at him, straight on. "No." There have been too many fights.

She hits the gas and doesn't look back until she's parked in the tow-zone in front of Eddie's.

26

SLOANE IS SITTING IN Eddie's bathtub, water from the shower running over her hair, her shoulders, and around her, to the drain. She has a bar of soap and she is very clear in purpose, and that is to wash her feet. Those fucking red heels.

When Sloane let herself into the loft, she didn't even think about who might be there, besides Eddie. Turned out it was no one. No one at all.

As soon as she got inside and called out to no answer, she locked the door and stripped down, left her shoes right there with her purse, her sweater somewhere in the hall, and everything else in here, getting damp on the tile floor. She washed her face with the rubbing alcohol Eddie uses to rinse his razor. She stopped short of rinsing her mouth with it.

Her tears are cold on her face and she can't make the water hot enough. She lifts her head, lets the water run down her throat. She just wants to be sober. Sober. Normal.

Eventually she can barely close her swollen eyes, all the crying. She shuts off the water and takes a deep breath and thinks she might be okay, now, until she takes a towel from the hook on the bathroom door and finds that it's still wet.

Eddie.

Then she is on her knees, the tile. In sobs.

The next thing she knows she's lying there, flush with the bathroom floor, looking at strands of her hair collected around the base of the sink.

She pulls herself up, the towel around her, and opens the door; the cooler air from the hall is fresh and definite. She goes into the bedroom, the smell of Eddie everywhere, and crawls into his bed. Takes his pillow. Holds it to her face.

She hears her phone ring, faint, from her purse in the hallway. Maybe it's Stephen; he got away, wants to know where she got away to. Maybe it's the police; the bartender or his friend or the girl got her license plate. Why did she flee?

Maybe it's the police; they caught Stephen Carvalho. A serial predator.

Sloane doesn't believe it's true. She has a better gauge, doesn't she?

Prosecution would say she's been debilitated by fear. Fear of change. Fear of leaving an upstanding guy like Eddie. Fear of her father's death.

Defense would say that's all possible, but Sloane always made the Job her number-one priority. She didn't mistake personal fears for her professional problems.

She thinks of Stephen. *You tricked me.*

Her dad. *How come your stuff is in the bathroom?*

And Eddie. *It's about you.*

She sits up, gets up. Gets dressed. She has to leave. They're right: It's always been her.

She's pulling on the jeans she finds in the closet that don't fit when she hears Eddie key the lock. She checks the clock: it's almost two. She hopes he's alone.

It takes him a while to negotiate the lock, and then the door, so she's sure he's drunk. Before tonight, she would have been intolerant. *Why do you have to challenge a twelve-pack to prove you had fun?*

It's been about her. She didn't realize.

"Eddie," she says when he stumbles in. He sees her, but he doesn't believe it.

"What the fuck happened to you?"

She braces herself against the doorframe, the jeans unbuttoned, in her bra. "I'm sorry," she says.

"Why?"

"Because of the way I've handled things."

"Then how come you always make me feel like *I* should be sorry?" He props himself against the wall hip first, then shoulder. Sloane wishes she could take a few steps forward, and fall. Hold on to his legs. Hold on to *him*.

"You're leaving," he says.

"I was," she says.

"It's okay," he says. "I miss you when you're here."

Sloane doesn't take a single step forward. She just falls.

SOME TIME DURING THE night, after Eddie has taken Sloane to bed, she wakes up and knows this is where she belongs. He's snoring, so she pushes him with her knees; he rolls over and throws his arm over her, his beer breath.

Sloane falls asleep and sleeps hard, and she doesn't wake up until daylight comes. She watches Eddie try to be quiet as he puts on his uniform, presses his hair into place, wipes off his shoes.

The familiarity of it all makes Sloane want to burst: she should do this. She can do this.

She pretends to be asleep when he sits on her side of the bed and leans over, his breath still yeasty and minty-sweet, and whispers, "Good-bye, Sloane. I'm sorry."

It takes everything just to breathe.

SLOANE SPENDS THE REST of the morning getting her things moved out of Eddie's, into the Pilot. Her phone rings off the hook, but she isn't expecting any good news.

Her head is splitting. This time it's a real hangover. She has no idea who she thought she was last night. She knows she needs hydration, but even water sounds unappealing; the sweat she breaks during the move is feverish, comes with chills.

When she's finished, she leaves her keys on the kitchen

counter and slips out; she can't bring herself to take one last look around, make it final.

She drives back to the hotel and lugs another suitcase inside to the lobby, where a family of four and a group of bachelorettes wait for the airport shuttle. The bride-to-be is wearing a veil studded with colored condoms and somehow she still looks wiser, more content, than any of her bridesmaids.

A bellhop Sloane hasn't seen before takes her bag, and on the way up to her room, he is perceptive enough not to ask how she's doing, or if she's had a good time in the city.

Back in her room, she sits at the desk's foam-cushioned chair for the first time and finally checks her voicemail.

The first message is from Stephen, at midnight. "Sloane. I tried to stop you, to explain. I'm at the police station now. I guess you won't give me my one phone call?"

Next message, Heavy. "Good morning, darlin'. I'm going to take a ride out on Foster to give that massage parlor a Sunday morning surprise. I'm on my cell if you need me."

Then Guzman. "Detective, it's twenty after eight. I'm waiting for an excuse."

Vince Marchetti. "Sloane; Vince. I'm calling to say thanks for coming by yesterday. We got a positive ID on the body and you were right: she wasn't strangled. The ME ruled the cause of death complications from asthma. Anyway, thanks for your help. Take it easy."

Heavy again. "Sloane, Guzman is looking for you. He sounds pissed. Just a warning."

Guzman. "Detective. I've got an upset mother downstairs who says you put the screws to her fourteen-year-old daughter yesterday. Is there any case you can't fuck up?"

Then, her dad. "Dep, I haven't heard from you since you went chasing after bad guys. Send up a smoke signal, will you?"

Finally, Guzman, round three. "What the fuck," is what he's saying as he hangs up, no other message.

There are no more messages, and Sloane is surprised. Stephen had to have been arrested last night. The girl was there; the bartender. He couldn't have escaped. Could he?

Sloane dials the dispatchers', gives her star number.

"What can I do for you?"

"I'm looking for an arrest last night. I don't have the report number. Suspect is Stephen Carvalho. C-A-R-V-A-L-H-O."

"One moment."

Sloane finds a pad of paper and a hotel-labeled stick pen next to the room's phone. She draws sharp lines around the logo on the paper while she waits for an answer.

"I'm sorry," the dispatcher says when she returns, "I'm having trouble finding that name. Do you know the location of the arrest?"

"I think it might have been in Thirteen. There was an altercation outside a bar on West Chicago Avenue."

"One moment."

Sloane looks at her fingernails, the dark red polish already chipped at the tips from the move, peeling at the cuticles from all the time in the shower.

"Detective," the dispatcher says, "my apologies—I must have misheard you . . . I thought you said Mr. Carvalho was a suspect? He pressed charges against one Tanya Lynch? She violated a restraining order."

"Carvalho had Lynch arrested?"

"Yes."

"He had a restraining order against her?"

"That's correct."

"Thank you." Sloane hangs up, reorders things, and realizes she hasn't been right about anybody—not even herself.

She dials the one person who will understand.

"Dad? Can we talk?"

CAROLYN RECOMMENDED A PLACE near her home and said she wouldn't be joining them so Sloane thought, *Great* and said, "What's the address?"

She takes Lake Shore Drive south to Hyde Park, past Grant Park and the museum campus. She can't remember the last time she's been to the planetarium or the aquarium or the Field or even Soldier Field. Stephen was right: work has been her life.

When she gets to the restaurant, she discovers it's fancy— one of those valet-only places—and she wonders if she should get some nicer clothes out of the back of the Pilot. *Fucking Carolyn,* she thinks as she pulls up and hands off the keys, and for the first time the thought breaks a smile.

The décor inside the place is somewhere between sleek and circus—overdone in Mardi Gras colors, oversized furniture, and overplayed music. Sloane waits at a table for two right there in front, the staff circling like vultures, a tuxed kid filling her water glass after every sip.

Sloane checks out the menu. It boasts "American Classics" and she thinks there better be something classic about a fourteen-dollar hamburger.

When Sloane's dad arrives, he doesn't see her at first, and her heart feels like it fills up with air as she watches him look around the room, unsure of his destination, when she's sitting right there.

"Dad," she says, standing, her napkin on the table, a careful hug. He's always been a big man; now, she feels his ribcage.

"Hi, Dep," he says, and as they sit the tuxed kid is there, his pitcher of water, and so is the waiter.

"Good afternoon," he says. "I'd like to tell you about our specials—"

"Do you have fish?" her dad asks.

"Yes sir, a Cajun-roasted trout—"

"I'll take it."

Sloane says, "Healthy?"

Her dad says, "With fries."—then to Sloane—"Let me enjoy something on my plate. Between you and Carolyn I'll never look forward to dinner again."

"I'll have the burger," Sloane tells the waiter, "medium."

Once the waiter is gone and their water glasses are full, Sloane says, "Nice place."

"It's a little much, I know. But Carolyn? So's she."

"Do you really want to live with her?"

"Do you really want to live with me? What was that whole thing about, the other night?"

"It was nothing," Sloane lies.

"If you and Eddie are having problems, don't you run away."

"Eddie and me? We're fine."

"Aww, Dep. Come on. Your car was still out front when I got here. I saw all your stuff packed into the back."

"We were kidding ourselves."

"That's what love is, don't you know that by now? I was sure I tricked your mother when she fell for me, and I thought I was the luckiest man alive, for a time. We promised we'd be together forever and boy, was she pissed when she found out the truth. All the things she was going to miss. You."

"You said love would change me."

"You don't think it has? Look at you, Sloane. You're a beautiful woman. It's not because of someone else. It's because *you* love. That's what changes you. That's what changed your mother and me."

"What about Carolyn?"

"I don't know. I'm already changed, I guess. And I suppose I tricked her, too, because she says she loves me. But I already know nothing's forever. And Sloane, the truth is? The only thing I'm going to miss about this life anymore, same as your mom, is you."

"You aren't going to take your medication, are you." Sloane says this, instead of asking, so he doesn't have to answer.

He passes her a ring of keys. "I know you already have a set," he says, "but the apartment's yours. As long as you need it. And Dep, Eddie will come around. If you want him to."

When the food comes, they eat; not much to say.

When the bill comes, her dad takes out his wallet and says, "Go on, Dep. You've got unpacking to do."

Sloane sets out, knowing he's handed her the keys all along.

27

ON MONDAY MORNING, SLOANE is sore from sleeping on her dad's couch and worse for trying to make nice with Guzman, who was pissed mostly because he woke up with a sewer backup on account of all the melting snow, and then discovered he had lots of other shit to clear out at the station. He'd cut Flores loose before Sloane arrived, and she had no argument; admittedly, Dutcher's case was dropping heat and without Meyer-Davis, whose tax-day deadline wasn't until Wednesday, the whole thing was getting pretty cold. After all her mistakes—including Carvalho, the one she hopes the bosses never find out about—Sloane realizes there's no way she can keep the case open.

There was a brief tease of hope, right before Guzman
started in on Sloane: it was when Sue Burkhart called, a wait-
until-you-hear-this hello. Sloane was sure the evidence coordinator was calling with results on Holly Dutcher's button.
Instead, she just wanted to say thank you: Madison was the
Girl Scout's top peanut seller, and that meant she was awarded
a giant stuffed zebra and a "cookies and more" charm. Sue
told Sloane her order total was sixty-two dollars, and that
the nuts would be there in six weeks, which turned out to be
about one year and forty-six weeks sooner than Sue could
promise Dutcher's evidence.

Like the button would've made a damn difference anyway. With so many untapped leads and so little time, all
Sloane has left to sell Holly Dutcher is false hope.

The whole trust-each-other-and-fuck-everybody-else promise, as it turns out, is bullshit; the truth is that because they
agreed to trust each other they're fucked. The truth is, Flores
is out, Mercado was never in, and nobody really gives a shit.
All Sloane can do is pretend there's a chance, her twisted
true hope: that there'll be another victim.

Sloane decides against calling Holly let alone spending
another second at her desk when Stag comes up to the floor
to shoot the shit with some of the dicks, sees Sloane, and says,
"Hey, Real Estate, I hear you're on the market again." Of
course he's the one to announce it, and then to take bets on
which cop will get a lease on Sloane next.

Sloane tries to ignore them, finish up some paperwork

and get out of there, but she can't believe it when Guzman comes out of his office, sees Stag cutting poster-paper for a wager board, sees the dicks plunking down cash—odds inexplicably on Mumford—and doesn't say a word. Instead, he looks over at Sloane, disappointed as ever, and returns to his office. Are they all trying to chase her out?

When Vince Marchetti hits the floor, he causes an immediate stir, ruining Mumford's odds. When Swoop squeezes a couple bucks from Marchetti's pocket, Sloane decides she's got to go. She'll drive up to Rhonda Ailers' place, find out what her husband Joe, a repeat domestic offender, did this time. She's packing up her things when her cell rings. The panic that accompanies the UNKNOWN number on the phone's display shuts out all surrounding noise.

"Pearson," she says, praying her dad is okay. Knowing it won't be much longer that he isn't.

"Detective," the caller says, "Kurt Lutz, *Sun-Times*. I'm calling for a quote."

"You've got some nerve," she says. "You think I'm going to let you jam me up again?"

"I just want to know what you think about the fact that Rachel Sayers, the attorney to twenty-sixth ward alderman Van der Meer, was killed this weekend."

"I don't work homicide," she says.

"I know," Lutz says, and she hates him for it. "But you told me you thought LaJeunesse's attack was part of a serial case. LaJeunesse is Alan Van der Meer's intern. Are you willing to acknowledge the possibility that LaJeunesse's attack and Sayers's murder are connected?"

"No comment," Sloane says and hangs up. How did that little shit reporter scoop her again?

Sloane marches over to Marchetti's desk and she doesn't care who sees them talking. "Marchetti, we've got to talk."

Marchetti looks up from his computer monitor, and around Sloane at the bullshit coming from the guys on the other side of the DMZ. "I'm sorry," he says. "I didn't put myself in the running."

"Forget those idiots. I want to talk about Rachel Sayers."

"Here?"

"They think we're going to fuck anyway. Might as well seal your bet."

Marchetti leans back in his chair, an uneasy smile. "I thought you said she wasn't one of yours."

"I'm not looking for the collar," she says. "I want to stop this guy, and I think we can help each other."

"I'll tell you right now I can't help. You were right about Sayers. She wasn't raped or strangled. She had an asthma attack. The ME says that's cause of death."

"What about the position of the body? The marks around her neck? The blood on her ring finger?"

"I worked the case as hard as I could, Sloane. Until the autopsy. You know as well as I do that if it isn't ruled homicide, it's no longer first on my list."

Sloane says, "Murdered or not, Sayers worked for Alderman Van der Meer. So does LaJeunesse, the girl who was attacked in Rogers Park. There's a case here somewhere, Marchetti. Help me find it, and it's yours."

Marchetti smiles for the boys across the way, says, "Well, I guess if we're going to sleep together, I'd better keep you happy." He gets up, gives Sloane his seat at the computer, and says, "Get to work."

Sayers's online case file is open and, of course, thin. Sloane skims her personal information: Sayers was twenty-eight, lived alone, practiced law at Hassett and Klein, LLP, a boutique firm at 32 West Walton. She was engaged to a man named Elliott Flynn, a British banker, currently on his way to the States from London. Her parents, both of whom work for the U.S. government, are on the way here from Taiwan. The rest of her family is staying behind in upstate New York, where Sayers grew up, an only child.

The first on-scene report says Sayers carried no cash, but her purse and jewelry remained with her; the foot tracks were measured and recorded: two people and a dog in, two people and a dog out, just as Sloane thought.

The photos show the position of Sayers's body exactly as Sloane remembered it—as though she'd been placed there; the close-up details of her face and neck hard to take.

The hardest thing to take, though, is the fact that this case will take a backseat because of the ME's report. *Cause of Death: complications from asthma.* Son of a bitch.

When Marchetti comes back to the desk with copies of the file Sloane asks, "Did you pull any trace evidence? There's none listed."

He hands her a copy of the file, says, "It's not online. I figured there was no point since, well, the asthma. We got some fibers from the front of her coat and I got a lucky break at the lab: they came from a Ford Taurus. The manufacturer's database estimates the model to be between 2006 and 2009."

"Wow. I guess that's the rush you get when a young white female with a law degree and government parents gets killed."

"Actually," Marchetti says, "that's the rush I get for romancing Sue Burkhart."

"You did not."

"I did. And let me tell you, I've got enough deluxe mixed nuts to last two lifetimes." Marchetti smiles. "Sayers doesn't have a car, and none of her family or known friends own or drive a Ford Taurus. The city and suburb databases reported no stolen vehicles of a similar make or model. So, I started to check rental agencies for records or surveillance tapes. Didn't get very far before I got pushed—the case I'm on now—an unidentified body under the Kennedy at Belmont. An adult Hispanic male. Bite marks all over his mouth. Some gruesome shit."

"Back up," Sloane says. "Did you trace Sayers's path to the scene?"

"I tried. Lost it outside Hotel Sofitel. Sayers's boss said she left the office Friday evening on her way to a client meeting. Her iPhone calendar confirmed: Friday, 6:00 P.M., Hotel

Sofitel, 20 East Chestnut. And guess what? The client was Alan Van der Meer."

"No shit. Have you talked to him?"

"He was on my list. I spoke to the cocktail waitress at Sofitel, Keiko Matsumoto—look in the file, her info is right there—page two. Matsumoto remembered Sayers and Van der Meer. She said she figured they were a couple, because they sat next to each other instead of across, and they argued the entire time. Matsumoto says Sayers left first, and Van der Meer stayed for another beer. We've got the credit card receipt—a copy's on the next page in the file—and it confirms that Van der Meer paid for a peach margarita and two Heinekens just after seven-thirty."

"That's as far as you followed her?"

"I checked with all the cab companies—none had record of a fare from the hotel to Hoyne around that time. I was waiting on the CTA to call back with information on Friday night's #70 and #56 routes—drivers, cameras, timing."

"What about the EI?"

"No good way to get to her place from the train."

"So the last person to see her alive, that we know of, was Alan Van der Meer."

"You want his address?"

"I've already got it."

Sloane sees Guzman come back out of his office and knows she's out of time. She gets up, says, "Thanks, Marchetti. I'll be in touch."

Sloane's got her bag and she's headed for the stairs when Guzman intercepts her at the DMZ and asks, "Pearson, what business do you have with Detective Marchetti?"

"None, sir."

"I don't like the talk around here."

"That makes exactly one of you, sir."

"Why do you have to get them started?"

"Why do I . . . ?" Sloane's voice trails off, feels sanity following. "I've been accused of a lot of things, sir," she says, as she walks across the room to where Swoop is bent over the desk, admiring Stag's wager board, and Stag is still hanging around, counting cash.

"Pearson," Guzman warns, and when Stag realizes she's there, he takes a nice swat at her ponytail.

"I get them started, sir," she says, "It's me."

Then she takes the scissors from Stag's desk, and the room shuts up.

She pulls her ponytail taut and cuts through it—chops the damn thing right off. Then she takes the money out of Stag's hands and says, "I think I win this bet, because you should all get fucked."

She drops her sheared ponytail in Mumford's lap and doesn't look back.

28

THE 26TH WARD OFFICE is in a storefront on Division, the west
side of Humboldt Park. The street is near-empty otherwise;
a couple of unoccupied new buildings, a couple of old abandoned ones. Sloane parks in a stream of water that runs
from the blocked drain on the corner of Spaulding all the
way to the open grate in front of the alderman's place. She
trudges through the water to the sidewalk, soaking her boots
and not really giving a shit, since she's already obviously
something of a mess.

The chime on the door makes the white-haired woman
inside at the front desk put her *AARP* magazine aside and
stand up. "Can I help you?" she says to Sloane's star.

"I'm Detective Pearson. I'd like to speak to the alderman."

"Just a moment," she says, and disappears through a cheap wood door.

Sloane takes a seat on the sun-bleached couch and watches dust float on bands of sunlight. The room smells like an old folks' home—that combination of spray air-freshener and all the ancient, dusty stuff the freshener is supposed to cover up. On the side table, a short stack of flyers for the neighborhood community center look like they've been recycled, the pages uneven, corners turned. Next to the flyers, a bowl full of Brach's candy has been picked over, only jelly nougats left, melted in their warped plastic wrappers.

On the wall adjacent to the front desk, a portrait of a man, presumably the alderman, is on gold-framed display: He's balding on top and filling out in the middle, and his expression looks like the photographer told him to say, *You betcha!*

"Detective," a man's voice booms from the cheap wood doorway, the *AARP* lady peeking at Sloane from around the sleeve of his expensive suit. Take away the *you betcha* and another inch of hair, and he's the same man in the portrait.

Sloane stands up. "Mr. Van der Meer?"

"Indeed," he says and moves around the desk to shake her hand. "How can I help you?" He's really trying for a smile.

"I'm here about Rachel Sayers."

He quits trying. "Please. My office."

The *AARP* lady looks up at the alderman, then down at the shame of it all.

Van der Meer leads Sloane into the back room where the furniture is significantly higher-end and it smells mostly like leather and fresh air from the back window. He invites Sloane to sit on the microsuede sofa next to his award-adorned mahogany desk, and she's a little surprised when he sits down with her, both of them facing the bookcase full of leather-bound, gold-titled books on the opposite wall.

"Rachel Sayers was an amazing young woman, and this community won't be the same without her." He unfolds his hands, looks at his palms.

Sloane can't tell whether his grief is a client's, a politician's, a lover's, or a fighter's, so she decides to shake him out. She says, "You were the last person to see her alive. I need you to tell me what happened Friday night."

"I met with her at Hotel Sofitel to discuss a meeting we were both supposed to attend today. She stayed for one drink and then told me she planned to go home to draw up papers for the meeting."

"I'm told you and Sayers had a fight."

"We did," he says, folding his hands again. "She is—she was . . . advising me on a development deal I'm trying to come to terms with here in the community."

"With Zimmerman and Company."

"Yes," he says, and Sloane can tell he's surprised she knows. "They have a bid on a TIF plan for the Pulaski Corridor—well—I'm sure you know that as well."

"Yes," she says, "but what I don't know is why you and Sayers were fighting."

"Rachel thinks—thought . . . she thought that there was no legal way to stop them. She thought I should concede, and focus on running for state's attorney. She said she wanted me to get the position so I'd be the one to indict the men involved in this deal."

"Are you talking about someone specifically?"

"I'm talking about a lot of someones, specifically. Alderman Watt for one. And your commander, Peter Wojciechowski, for another. Are you sure you still want to talk to me, Detective? Or would you rather just arrest me?"

Sloane sits back, says, "Keep talking."

Van der Meer turns to her, a knee sideways on the couch. "Gangs are going to ruin this community, and Alderman Watt and Mo Reyes are making sure of it."

"Why?"

"Watt is the one pushing for Zimmerman and Company to get the city's TIF money. If they get the development deal, he'll get cash for his state's attorney campaign."

"How do you know that?"

"Because Reyes did the same thing for me a few years back, when he worked for Englewood and I ran for alderman."

"You took city money to get the alderman's seat?"

"No, Detective. Reyes supported my campaign in exchange for getting his brother-in-law's company a few private construction jobs. Reyes threw me the fundraiser that changed everything. That night, I got more than enough financing to get elected. I also met Reyes's wife."

Sloane sits back on the couch, looks at all the volumes

of Van der Meer's law books. "It always comes back to Reyes."

"I thought Soledad would leave him, and after a few nights with her, I didn't care if she did or didn't. I didn't care about being an alderman or anything else; I was in the clouds. I was upside down in the clouds. Then she started asking me to do some favors for her brother."

"Lonzo Barreto?"

"Lonzo Barreto."

"What kind of favors?"

"Private jobs. Getting his company work. It was no big deal until I became alderman, and I realized I had to back off. The construction they were doing wasn't up to code, and they just kept demanding development money. When I tried to make a clean break from Panther, Soledad told everyone about our affair." Van der Meer looks at his hands again, ring-free. "I'm losing everything," he says. "But the worst part of it? It's losing all the progress I made here. If Watt becomes state's attorney, you can kiss progress good-bye. This ward is blighted, all right, and you wait to see what it's like when Reyes and Barreto get in here with city money and illegal workers and Imperial Gangsters. I have truly lost everything I worked for."

"Why would Watt support any of this?"

"They're fooling him, just like they fooled me. Last Sunday, after church, I saw Watt help my pastor arbitrate a neighborhood feud by forcing a gang member to pay cash to the mother of a dead child. I saw the whole thing from the alley behind the church and even though I understand it, I still can't believe it. Things have fallen so far from okay."

"Your situation was different," Sloane says.

"Not that much different," Van der Meer says. "I wanted the queen, and Watt wants to be king."

"Have you had contact with Lonzo Barreto since you split from Panther and Reyes's wife?"

"Only once. He came to me—to my house—about the Pulaski Corridor project. He said Reyes's company was taking over Panther's financing, and that I was the only one standing in the way. I guess I wasn't the only one. I guess Rachel was, too." He checks his watch, says, "I have to cut this short, Detective. I have funeral arrangements to make. Rachel's family isn't here yet, or her fiancé. They're going to have enough to deal with, don't you think?"

"Do you know who killed Miss Sayers?" Sloane asks.

"That question insults me, Detective. I've told you my mistakes. Now find yours."

29

SLOANE DRIVES NORTH TO Panther Construction and finds the place is a flat, block-long warehouse on Armitage Avenue, a street over from the proposed Pulaski Corridor project.

She parks on a side street where a metal fence protects a gravel lot, a set of Bobcats parked there, muddy and wet, like most everything else in the thaw.

Sloane returns to the main entrance on Armitage, a PAN-THER sign beside the door, the cat's green eyes watching Sloane go inside. One set of doors opens to another and then she is standing in a large, open space where a table of six Latino men play cards and another six stand around the hood of a car, its engine sitting on the concrete floor, sterile-clean and waiting like a transplant.

A *Tejano* song plays too loud to be background music, the button accordion's melody familiar and much cheerier than the general disposition of the place. Most of the men have noticed her, then decided to act like they didn't.

"Hello," Sloane says, no star, deciding it won't make her presence any more welcome. "Excuse me," she says; still no acknowledgement. Sloane figures she looks enough like a cop for them to play the *No hablo Ingles* game, so she stands tall, her .38 backup concealed, and says the one name she knows they'll understand. "Lonzo Baretto."

A man wearing a blue-striped work shirt buttoned at the collar folds his cards and gets up from the table. He stops a few feet shy of introducing himself, but his name patch says he's Santos.

Sloane says, "I'm looking for Lonzo Barreto."

Santos runs a hand around his shaved head, slow over a long, white, once-stitched scar. Then he stands square to Sloane, hands at his belt, the handle of a good-sized revolver jutting from his waist, and says, "Get the fuck out of here." Then he turns and goes back to the table, sits down, waits for one of the others to deal a new hand.

"Excuse me," Sloane says, opening her coat to show she's carrying too, and her star, making it legal.

This time Santos throws his cards on the table and all the men stand up, shoulder to shoulder, gun-hands ready; the men by the car come over, too, and join the line, all of them packing, and with the same single target: Sloane.

Twelve men, Sloane. Nobody says a word and the accordion plays on in the background, a bad soundtrack.

Some standoff, Sloane thinks, since there's no way she can back down, walk away from a firing line. No chance she can talk her way out of this, either. All she can do is stand there, look each man in the eye. One by one, she studies their faces—for a tell, a show of uncertainty, a sign of fear.

Halfway down the line, Sloane is sure she's on to the man next to Santos, his shoulders tensing, mouth drawn, like he's holding his breath.

Then a man just behind her says, "What's your plan here, bitch?"

Sloane darts back but she doesn't draw her gun: whoever is standing next to her is her saving grace because he's in the firing line, too.

Her saving grace is Nigeria.

He sticks his hands in his low-slung jeans pockets, says, "Hello, 'tective."

"What the hell are you doing here?"

"Please," he says like she should know, "I'm the foundation of this here motherfucker." He smiles, a new gold grill over his teeth.

"You? What about Lonzo Barreto?"

"We decided on a merger. You know how business run these days: cooperate, consolidate, conquer."

"You don't run a business, you run a gang."

"'Scuse me, 'tective. Panther is a business."

"You call sitting around with no work a business? Panther is an IG mascot and this place is a hangout."

"Don't test me now, 'tective. I could walk away, right now, and you could disappear."

"Is that a threat?"

"That's an option."

"Give me another."

"You could walk away. I'm the one running this here neighborhood now. I know you know better than to get up in my business."

"I don't give a shit about you, Nigeria, unless you know the man who is raping and killing young women. *That* is my business."

"I don't know nothing about that."

"Of course you don't," Sloane says, backing away, toward the entrance, "but now I know something about you."

A couple of the Latinos move up, hands on their guns, but Nigeria waves them off. "She going," he says, "or she gone."

"I'm going," she says, "but you tell Barreto I'm not gone."

30

"I NEED HIS LAST known address."

"One moment," the dispatcher says and then she says, "Barreto. Alonzo. Fifteen forty-eight Kilpatrick, Glencoe."

"Glencoe?" Sloane asks. "Too high a tax bracket for a guy like this. Will you reverse search?"

One moment later, the dispatcher says, "Property's owned by a guy named Maurice Reyes."

Sloane heads east and takes Lake Shore Drive toward the Loop, 50 E. Monroe. Forget Stephen's wishes not to speak to Reyes about Lonzo Barreto, according to dispatch, they're roommates.

As she waits for the left turn at Clark to approach the Drive, she digs out Reyes's business card from her bag and dials his cell. She dreads going up to the Zimmerman office; whatever bridge she'd had with Stephen was set ablaze and is still smoldering, she's sure.

"This is Mo," Reyes says when he answers.

"Mr. Reyes, this is Detective Pearson."

"I knew you'd call. Never send a boy."

"Can you talk?"

"I'm just finishing a meeting," Mo says. "Have you had lunch?"

"No, sir, but this won't take long—"

"I'm at the Aon Center. Meet me upstairs, the Mid-America Club? Tell security you're with me."

"I'm on my way."

THE AON CENTER IS a terribly impersonal building: tall and slim, cold and white. Sloane parks underground and winds up going in a few circles before she gets back to street level, finds the security desk.

She shows the guy behind the desk her star and her gun and when he looks like he's about to put her through hoops she says, "I'm running late, sir. Either let me through or call your boss."

"Just sign in," the guy says. He uses his metal detector wand to courteously direct her to an escalator.

She takes the escalator to another, and that one to an elevator, which launches up to the eightieth floor, her stomach feeling like it gets there before her head.

When the elevator door opens, Sloane steps into another

era: the entrance is done in dark green, burgundy, and gold—all the furniture delicate wood and busy patterns, making the room feel warm and elegantly cluttered. A few older ladies in various bright-colored dresses and hats wait on velvet-pillowed chairs, one of them trying to use the house phone to find the missing member of their luncheon group. A black-tailed waiter pushes a gold-plated dessert cart by, lace doilies underneath baked Alaska and chocolate cake and cherry pie.

Sloane figures the waiter is pushing his cart toward the dining room, which is at the other end of the hall, and that Reyes is probably in there waiting. When she takes off her coat, though, the ladies in waiting turn into a bunch of whispering critics, so Sloane ducks into the corner bathroom to find out why.

There are a number of whys: her big wet boots. The indelicate outfit. Bad haircut.

But it's probably her gun.

Sloane sits on a chaise lounge and uses a hand towel to dry off her boots. She decides the bathroom is the reason they used to call them restrooms: besides the toilets, there are couches and lockers, bottled water and tea, soaps and lotions and perfumes. The walls are painted warm pink with ornate, French white moldings; the mirrors are old, tinged yellow.

Sloane puts her coat in one of the lockers. She takes the ammo out of her .38, takes off her holster, and tucks the weapon underneath her coat. She locks the locker and drops the ammo and the locker's key into her pants pocket; then she washes her hands, messes with her hair. It doesn't look too bad: it's shorter in the back, and angled along her jaw line. She thinks it looks severe. She thinks it fits.

She picks the prettiest bottle of perfume and squirts a little here, a little there. Under her arms. Then she straightens her collar, readying herself for Reyes.

The dining room is near-empty, save for a couple of suits and the ladies who were in the hall, and there's no sign of Reyes. The waiter greets Sloane like he expected her and seats her at a white-clothed table for four.

"Sparkling water or still water?"

"Tap," she says, hoping that answers the rest of the expensive questions.

Windows wrap the room, floor to ceiling, and Sloane decides the view is the only thing keeping the place up to date. Burgundy walls, again, and more French white molding. The waiter brings the table of suits their entrees and both white-china plates have some kind of meat, potato, and overcooked vegetable.

The waiter leaves, momentarily returning with a silver water pitcher, pouring Sloane a glass of Lake Michigan's finest. "Thank you," she says.

"Mr. Reyes is running behind, but he has ordered for you. Is okay?"

She hasn't seen any of the diners look at a menu so she says, "Okay."

After that it's Crab Louie salad and Vichyssoise and a

bottle of Spanish Verdejo in an ice bucket. Sloane feels strange, being served two of everything and eating all alone. She picks at her food and watches Reyes's plates come and go with hers. She doesn't taste the wine.

She's sitting with two untouched entrees of broiled cod, au-gratin potatoes, and broccoli, looking out the window over all the tops of Loop buildings when her cell buzzes. She would send the call to voicemail, but the display says ZIMMERMAN AND COMPANY, and she figures this is Reyes's brush-off.

"Pearson," she says, sinking into her seat when a blue-haired, blue-capped luncheon lady shoots a disapproving glance over her shrimp cocktail.

"Sloane? It's Stephen."

"Oh," Sloane says. She realizes she's been saying that a lot lately.

"Mo asked me to call. He got held up at a meeting."

"Stephen," she says, "I'm sorry. I didn't want to bring you into this."

"You had to," he says. "Your job is your life, remember?"

"I'm tired of this life," she says, her gaze out the window and down, eighty stories. "I need someone to shake me out of it."

"You're the only one who can do that, Sloane."

The waiter comes by to retrieve the uneaten entrees, and behind him, Sloane sees Reyes enter the room.

"He's here, Stephen."

"Do me a favor? Try *not* to get me fired?"

"Your name will not cross my lips."

"You're a good person, Sloane. Shake yourself out of thinking otherwise. Good-bye."

His good-bye sounds so final Sloane can't bring herself to say it back so she cuts the call and stands up to greet Mo.

He says, "Please, don't get up. Please. My apologies for being late." He doesn't shake her hand and he doesn't look happy, either.

"Mr. Reyes," said the waiter, who's still got the cold plates of fish in his hands, "you like I heat up the lunch?"

Reyes takes the Verdejo from the bucket and says, "Just bring dessert. I've got a tight afternoon."

The waiter nods, presents the suits their lunch bill.

"So," Mo says, pouring himself a full glass of wine, "what are we doing here?"

"I need to talk to you about your brother-in-law, Lonzo Baretto."

"Really," he says.

"I'm still investigating the series of attacks and his name keeps coming up. His last known address is the same as yours. Do you know where he is?"

"You want Lonzo?" he says, unable to contain a too-loud laugh.

"I don't know why that's funny, sir."

"It's perfect"—he gulps his wine, hardly able to swallow through laughter—"this is perfect."

"I understand your company is—or was—financing Panther Construction."

"You want Lonzo," he says, like he still can't believe it. He puts down his wineglass, wipes his eyes to sober from the laugh. "You want him? Go ahead. Take him."

"I just want to talk to him, actually."

The waiter brings the dessert cart and Mo takes the chocolate cake from the top.

"That's the display, sir—" the waiter starts.

"It's edible, isn't it? Give her one, too."

The waiter nods, rolls the cart away.

Mo cuts into his cake, takes a huge bite. "Let me tell you a little bit about myself, Detective. I am a businessman. And I don't like to be fucked with. You can't trust anybody—clients, investors, friends—especially not relatives. You've got to show up, and they've got to know you're there. That's why I travel so often. That's why I was in Dallas this weekend. So my clients would know I was there, and that I mean business." He toasts his glass to himself, says, "It's impossible, though, to be more than one place at once. And sometimes, important people start to feel neglected. My wife, for example. So she depends on other people—her brother Lonzo, for one. In return, she'd do just about anything for him. Screw other men, screw me."

Sloane anticipated he'd bring up the affair with Van der Meer so she says, "If your brother-in-law is hurting women, your wife can't protect him."

"You don't know Soledad." He takes another bite of cake. "You fascinate me, Detective. The way you're told no and you just keep going, after Mercado, then Flores, and now Lonzo."

"I don't understand."

"Do you know I could make your job disappear with a single phone call?"

The waiter brings Sloane's chocolate cake and she says, "Thank you," and picks up her fork, to keep her cool. "I don't know why you'd want to do that, Mr. Reyes."

"Sure you do. I think we understand each other, Detective. You're just like me, looking for a fight."

Sloane grips her fork. "What did you say?"

"You heard me. Anyway it doesn't matter what I tell you about Lonzo. I could say he framed that kid Mercado. And that he must have been the one who stole old work shirts from my building. Does the name Jorge ring a bell, Detective? Flores outgrew those shirts working out all the time in jail, that madman. You know what? I'll bet if you follow up on the vehicles, the Hummer and the—what was it—the Taurus? Lonzo is the one who rented those."

Sloane puts down the fork. "It was you. You attacked those girls."

"Come on now, Detective. I was out of town. On business. Espeban can confirm that. Anyway, I have a clean record. I'm an important figure in the Hispanic community. And as far as I know, you don't have anything on me. No DNA, no willing victims, no motive. I was in Dallas when Van der Meer's attorney was . . . well, I'm sure you're heard."

"You motherfucker."

"Hey, you sound like my wife. Give me some credit: I have feelings, here."

"You think I can't catch you?"

"I know you can't. Your case is all but gone, Detective, and pretty soon it will be forgotten. You can try for Lonzo, but I'll bet he's on his way to Mexico. You can keep fighting, but it's only going to get you hurt."

"You set Barreto up and got him out of here."

"Please, I wouldn't do that to Lonzo. He's family. Just this morning, Soleded told me he left because he had a disagreement with a business associate. Someone who had a more thoughtful proposal for the allocation of tax increment funds. Someone who had a more thoughtful proposal for the allocation of tax increment funds. I understand. Mergers can be tough."

"Nigeria."

"It's the way things go. The smartest men are always left to run things." Reyes smiles, finishes his wine.

Sloane says, "You're wrong about me, Reyes. I'm not looking for a fight." She stands up. "But if it's all I have left?"

Sloane steps up on the chair between them and, though she feels completely rational, dives off, straight for Reyes, tackling him in his chair and tumbling to the carpet. His fall breaks the chair and he hits his head on the floor and he's stunned, but he still manages to push her away. Sloane's got strike two, though: she curls her fingers and scratches him in the face and as soon as he raises his hands to protect himself, her knee is swift and hard at his groin. The hit renders him fetal, but she doesn't give him time to recover: she climbs on top and squeezes her hands to fists and hits him, hard as she can—his head, his face, his arms—all the while saying, "Fight me. Fucking fight *me*."

When Reyes regains his composure and starts to fight back, effectively blocking her strikes, Sloane gets to her feet. *Finally*, she thinks, *these fucking boots*. She kicks him in the ribs, knocking him out of breath; she gets another good shot to his lower back.

Then he reaches back and grabs her foot and in a split-second twist, it's over: Sloane's falls to the floor, hitting her head when she gets there.

WHEN SLOANE COMES TO she can hear the suits above her, their voices cautionary; and the luncheon group, all gasps and whispers. There are other voices, too—security, maybe? But no Reyes. Nothing from Reyes.

She rolls to her side, her foot feeling like it didn't follow, and cries out. Her ankle is broken, or her leg. She's afraid to look.

Then she looks up, sees Reyes: He's being held back—or held up—by one of the suits and a security guard, his nose bloody, his lip fat, his face scratched.

Reyes spits blood, asks, "Was it good for you?"

Sloane says, "You didn't let me finish."

YOU SIT IN AN uncomfortable chair, or maybe it's you—you're uncomfortable. Time is healing your wounds, just like it's supposed to, but you still hurt, and not a day goes by when you don't think about what happened.

You have your iPod buds in your ears but you're not playing anything; you're listening to the commotion here, the phones and the orders and the conversation the two men next to you are having about a stolen car.

You wonder how long you'll have to wait here; you were supposed to be at work an hour ago, and you hope they'll understand. You hope they'll still respect you.

You were on your way to work, before; you were enjoying

the sun and the warmer wind and you were glad the snow
melted just as quickly as it fell. On your way to the coffee-
house, you noticed girls in shorter skirts and lighter coats.
You wondered how much longer you'd have to cover up.

Then right there, while you waited for your once-a-week
cortado, you saw the stack of newspapers, and the headline
on the front page of the *Sun-Times:*

Female Cop Takes on Top Exec

You bought a copy with your *cortado,* went out to the street,
and read.

Female Cop Takes on Top Exec

by Kurt Lutz

klutz@suntimes.com

It was a normal lunch hour at the Aon Center's private Mid-America Club: a few businessman talking
about the stock market over steaks, a group of long-
time friends having an annual get-together invited
by member Helen Richardson. It was normal, says
Richardson, until, "A woman walked in with a gun."

That woman was Sloane Pearson, an Area Five
detective who was there to meet Maurice Reyes,
the president of real estate development group
Zimmerman and Company. Richardson says she
noticed Pearson's gun when Pearson arrived and
removed her coat; a call to security put Richardson's worries to rest as she found out Pearson

carried a police badge as well.

Waiter Fernando Gonzales said, "Mr. Reyes is a regular customer. We appreciate his generosity very much, and we were shocked at what occurred."

What occurred, according to Richardson: "They were sharing what looked like an intimate dessert when all of a sudden, the woman jumped up from the table and attacked the man."

The article ran onto the next page, and there were pictures above it: Detective Pearson's official police photo and Maurice Reyes in a suit and tie.

But you knew him as Jorge.

The article finished:

A second call brought security upstairs, but the fight was already over. An unnamed onlooker said, "She was really beating the **** out of him. We were all amazed. It was over quickly, and security escorted them both out."

Ironically, Pearson is a sex crimes detective who has been working a serial assault case. Pearson said, "No**** comment."

Mr. Reyes also declined to comment.

Pearson suffered a broken ankle and has been placed on clerical duty while she recovers from her injury.

You tucked the paper under your arm and caught the first empty cab west on Randolph. You got in and said, "Area Five Headquarters."

Now, waiting here, you think of the burned black school-boy on the train that night. You remember thinking that whatever happened to him will never seem too far away. You remember thinking he'd have to have been a brave boy, to go through life with those scars. Now, you know the feeling. And you think you should be brave, too.

You look at the *Sun-Times*'s photo of Reyes again and also the sketch of the suspect that's tacked to the WANTED cork-board behind you. They do look alike, except that you can see the seething anger underneath Reyes's put-on smile in the newspaper photograph.

After a while a uniformed woman comes down a set of stairs to your right on crutches, and you know it must be the detective. She's much thinner than she looks in her picture, and her hair is short and more stylish than the ponytail in the photo.

She looks tired, and you can read the indifference in her expression, but maybe that's because, so far, she's been los-ing this fight.

You stand up and you have the newspaper in your hand and your voice cracks when you say, "I was raped," but then the detective's eyes flash, *yes*.

She wants to keep fighting.